Vegas Bites
Three Of A Kind

In Walks Trouble
By
Seressia Glass

Royal Pursuit
by
Monique Lamont

The Wolf That Wasn't
By
Natalie Dunbar

The Nature of the Beast
By
J.M. Jeffries

ISIS is an imprint of Parker Publishing LLC.

Copyright © 2008 by Natalie Dunbar, Seressia Glass,
Lawan Williams, Miriam Pace and Jacqueline Hamilton
Published by Parker Publishing LLC
12523 Limonite Avenue, Suite #440-438
Mira Loma, California 91752
www.parker-publishing.com

This book is a work of fiction. Characters, names, locations, events
and incidents (in either a contemporary and/or historical setting)
are products of the author's imagination and are being used in
an imaginative manner as a part of this work of fiction. Any
resemblance to actual events, locations, settings, or persons, living or
dead, is entirely coincidental.

ISBN: 978-1-60043-040-4
First Edition

Printed in the United States of America by Bang Printing
Cover Design by JaxadoraDesigns.com
Distributed by BookMasters, Inc. 1-800-537-6727

Parker Publishing, llc

www.Parker-Publishing.com

In Walks Trouble

By

Seressia Glass

About the Author

Seressia Glass is an award-winning author of paranormal and contemporary romance. A resident of Atlanta, Seressia works full time as an instructional designer for an international home improvement company. She is hard at work finishing up her next writing project.

Available Books

What White Boyz Want
What White Boyz Ride (coming soon)
Vegas Bites Back
Vegas Bites
Dream of Shadows
Through the Fire
Three Wishes
No Apologies
No Commitment Required

Dedication

To those who dare to do the opposite of what society expects of them.

Chapter One

"Sir, I think we have a situation."

Marcus looked up from a sheath of papers, eyes narrowing at the beta female standing eyes downcast just inside his office. She was one of the newer security geeks brought onboard after the last shakeup had gotten rid of a fair number of humans and low-ranking Weres. Family members being kidnapped or poisoned with silver dust in their own hotel hadn't gone over well with the elder Temples, and heads had to roll.

"Anything I have to interrupt Malcolm's honeymoon for?"

"No sir." The female fidgeted. Marcus remembered that she was a pup, turned against her will after going home with the wrong guy at a party, then let go by the human casino she'd worked for previously after her vaccination had failed. Marcus thought the human world's loss was the French Quarter's gain, but she had a lot to learn about being part of a pack.

"What is it, Sheila?" he prompted, making his tone as non-threatening as he could, something that hadn't been easy lately.

"We had someone attempting to shoplift at the jewelry store."

"And you're bringing this to me?" Marcus felt his eyebrows lift. "Should I rethink my decision to hire you, Sheila? Because if you can't handle a shoplifter—"

"She claims to know you, sir," Sheila interrupted, looking as if she wanted to be anywhere other than where she was. "Rather intimately, I might add."

"Does she now?" Marcus left his desk, crossing the wide marble expanse to enter the surveillance room. Several people, humans and non-humans alike, monitored banks of computers and displays that served as the "eye in the sky" for the French Quarter Hotel and Casino, viewing every nook and cranny of the sprawling casino complex. Recently, they'd decided to add cameras to the hallways and service routes of the family floors, though not without protest. Marcus ameliorated most of the complaints by making sure that only Weres he'd personally vetted monitored those floors and recordings were put on discs and locked in his personal safe. He'd also upgraded access to the family floors from passkeys to biometric scans, and high-clearance non-Were personnel couldn't even access the service elevators during Full Moon.

Lately he'd been the lone Were monitoring during Full Moon, but thinking of the reasons why only soured his mood further.

Sheila leaned over one of the human techs. "Cue up room four to monitor one," she murmured.

Marcus peered at one of the larger monitors as the security specialist keyed in the command to display the live feed for Interview Room Four, the one reserved for their more unusual offenders.

A woman sat at the faux wood table, flanked by two security guards. Even though her hair was cropped close, and her clothes more suited to a careless teen than an ad executive, her identity was unmistakable.

A growl seeped from his throat, causing everyone in the surveillance room to step back.

Sheila stirred first, tapping the tech on the shoulder. "Run facial recognition program."

Marcus found his voice. "That's not necessary."

As if she'd heard him, the woman lifted her face towards the camera hidden in the ceiling. The high-resolution camera picked up the rich chocolate of her skin, the fathomless black of her eyes. Even the fact that she'd lost weight she couldn't afford to lose. "Marcus? Marcus, are you there? I really need to talk to you."

He bunched his hands into fists, fighting the sudden lengthening of his canines. "I'll handle this one, Sheila."

Surprise rounded his assistant's eyes. "Do you know her, sir?"

"I thought I did. Then I married her."

Chapter Two

Devon Archer refrained from tapping her fingers on the table. Being nervous was one thing, showing it to the Were guards was another.

She couldn't help being nervous, though. Marcus was coming. She knew it in her bones. Finally, she'd get the chance to see him again, to get everything out in the open.

She hadn't been truthful with Marcus, even after he'd asked her to marry him. Leaving in the middle of their honeymoon had been unavoidable, but she doubted he'd see it that way—especially when he discovered why she'd left and why she'd returned.

She'd been in stickier situations. Just none that mattered as much.

The door swung open, and Devon got the first look at her husband in nearly a year.

He looked…different. Leaner, meaner. The kindness that she'd seen in his eyes the first time they'd met had vanished. He dismissed the security guard with a nod, then closed the door firmly.

With her heart hammering like a pair of 808s, she crossed to him, buried her face against the unyielding wall of his chest and wrapped her arms tightly around his waist. "Marcus," she murmured, allowing herself to feel, for just a moment, like a woman who'd missed her husband.

Closing her eyes, she breathed in his warm spicy scent, and her world settled just a little. "I missed you so much."

He'd frozen as soon as her arms went around him. Then he sniffed her. His hands settled on her shoulders, but he didn't pull her close as she'd hoped. Cautious, she risked a glance up at his expression.

He didn't look happy to see her. Actually he didn't look like he was trying all that hard to rein in his wolf, either. His eyes glinted gold instead of the dark chocolate she knew them to be. For a moment she thought she saw a spark of the man she'd married, then he blinked and the predator returned.

When he spoke, it wasn't to her. "Sheila."

"Yes, sir?" a disembodied voice immediately responded.

"Cut all monitoring of this room, including biometric."

Silence. "Sir, may I remind you that order is in violation of the Nevada Gaming Commission's regulations and the Preternatural Authority's civil rights provisions?"

Golden eyes didn't waver. "Consider me reminded. Now, I'd like a private moment with my wife. End all surveillance immediately."

Another pause, then, "You heard the Security Director. End monitoring of Interview Room Four in three, two, one."

Silence descended, thick and total. Marcus pulled his hands from her shoulders and stepped back, but his eyes retained their amber glow as he regarded her.

Devon licked her lips. She'd done some hairy things over the last few years, but this reunion with her estranged husband had her shoulders bunching with tension. "You're Security Director now?"

"Surveillance, not floor security. I switched shortly after our aborted honeymoon. Apparently my temper was no longer suited to public relations."

His eyes flicked over her, then away. "Speaking of temper, you may want to sit down and slow your breathing. Listening to your heart pound like a scared rabbit ain't helping any."

Understanding the roughness in his voice, Devon immediately returned to her chair. Marcus paced the perimeter of the room, a restless animal far from tame.

God, he looked good. The tailored navy suit fit his rangy six-four build perfectly, the kente pattern of his tie highlighting the Were-yellow of his eyes. His hair was still cropped close, his skin the smoothness of rich premium coffee and making a heat-inducing contrast to the pearl of his smile. More than one hundred fifty years old, he appeared to be a man at a prime thirty. He also looked furious.

"Where have you been?"

"Arizona."

His nostrils flared. "Doing what?"

"My job."

"Sure you didn't hit your head and lose some of your common sense?" he wondered. "Because I gotta tell ya—I'd have believed an amnesia story a lot faster than this bull."

"It's the truth, Marcus. I was working."

His eyes went amber again. "Working. One state over, for a whole fucking year, and you didn't think to tell me?"

"I couldn't tell you, Marcus. Believe me, if I could have told you, I would have."

His lips peeled back from his teeth. "And now you're back, attempting to hit the French Quarter's jewelry store. If you wanted jewelry or needed money, you should have just kept your wedding rings instead of leaving them behind."

Yeah, he was definitely angry. Devon took a deep breath. "I went into the jewelry store hoping to get your attention."

"There are easier ways to get in touch with me, Devon. Hallmark still makes cards. Email works fine."

She lifted her chin. "What I have to say couldn't be put in an email, and I couldn't be sure you'd speak to me if I called."

"Good point." He leaned against a wall, arms folded, deceptively relaxed. "Now, say whatever you want to say before we hand you over to the police."

She climbed slowly to her feet. "You can't turn me over to the police, Marcus."

"Really? You're an attempted shoplifter. Give me one good reason why the hotel shouldn't press charges."

"Because," she replied, bracing herself. "You'll put me in danger and blow my cover."

"Cover." The word came out as a growl as he dropped his hands to his sides. He looked as if he was preparing to pounce.

"Being an ad executive is my cover profession," she said, slowly reaching for her back pocket. "I'm actually an agent with the Department of Domestic Affairs."

Marcus looked at the identification card in the ubiquitous leather wallet for a long, tension-filled moment. "What the hell is the Department of Domestic Affairs?"

"It's an intelligence agency charged with homeland security," she began.

"Kinda redundant don't you think, considering that there's an FBI, the Department of Homeland Security, and the Preternatural

Authority?"

"The DDA predates all of them," Devon explained. "If you want the history lesson, I'll give it to you."

"Please do."

"The DDA began when the young federal government realized that super-humans were more than a handful of genetic aberrations. One of the reasons for the Indian Wars of the nineteenth century was the DDA's attempt to stop the proliferation of the Gift of the Wolf and coyote magic that many tribes gave to escaped and freed slaves. Two groups of dispossessed people with supernatural powers were too much of a threat. The government moved quickly to prevent open rebellion and loss of land."

"So let me get this straight," Marcus said, his voice like sandpaper. "There's a secret agency free to operate on American soil that no one's ever heard of. It has a history of fighting against the preternatural population, and my wife works for them?"

"That's what Domestic Affairs used to do," Devon clarified, suppressing a shiver at the way he said *my wife*. "As times changed, so did the DDA's focus. Now the DDA strictly monitors the preternatural community and human supremacist groups, taking steps to neutralize any threats to the sovereignty of the United States before they occur. We're the Black Ops version of Homeland Security."

"Neutralize threats?" he echoed. "The government thinks we're a threat?"

"I didn't say that."

"You didn't have to," he snapped. "They wouldn't have sent you here otherwise."

He paused, shock arcing across his features. Anger quickly replaced surprise. "Did they order you to fuck your way into my family?"

"Marcus—"

He rounded on her, advancing until he'd backed her against the wall. "Did they order you to fuck your way into my family?"

Devon knew he held on to his control by one thin thread; her next words would push him over. "I was ordered to infiltrate the Temple family," she said clearly, holding his gaze. "My superiors believed a human woman would be better accepted than a male. My first target was Malcolm, but he doesn't do humans. Then I saw you."

For a moment he just stared at her. As if in slow motion, a snarl sliced across his features. Before she could blink, he planted his fist into the wall beside her.

There was a knock on the door, then two security guards entered, hands on firearms. "Everything all right, sir?"

Devon took a deep breath, but Marcus brought his six-four frame closer, his breath hot on her neck. To the guards, even trained Were guards, it probably looked like an intimate moment between spouses. But Devon knew Marcus had his incisors mere centimeters from her throat.

Not that the guards would do much. She knew they weren't there to stop Marcus from attacking her, but to stop him from leaving the room and attacking the guests.

Forcing a throaty laugh, she stretched up to curve her arms around his neck, hopefully furthering the illusion of a passionate reunion. "Baby, I know it's been a minute for both of us, but can't we go upstairs first?"

Their eyes swept over her, over Marcus's rigid back. "Sir?"

With a growl he flattened his body against hers, clearly staking his territory. He didn't glance back at them when he spoke. "Thank you for doing your jobs. Now get the hell out."

The security guards left as quickly as they'd entered. Devon didn't breathe as Marcus scraped his teeth along her throat. "Do you realize that you've just admitted to betraying the pack? Do you even realize what they could do to both of us?"

"Yes," she whispered, her breath hitching with a damning combination of fear and excitement. Under Packlaw, Marcus was well within his rights to execute her. The pack could then execute him—or worse, exile him. No other pack would dare take him in. Just like natural wolves, Weres without a pack didn't last long.

She moistened her lips. "I know what could happen, Marcus. But I've got a plan, and I'm hoping you'll hear me out."

He finally eased away from her, and she could breathe again. She watched his features settle back to human as he held his fist against his chest. The knuckles were scraped and bloody. The wall wasn't much better. She wondered if either needed repair.

"I'm listening," he finally said.

"You knew who I worked for all along," she explained, knowing she didn't have long to convince him. "You went along with the DDA's plan because it provided the best cover for my assignment."

"Assignment." His lips curled in a snarl. "What's your game, Devon?"

"I'm not playing a game," she said, keeping her voice even, controlled.

"I risked my life coming here."

"Well now, I think that's the most truthful you've been since I walked through the door," Marcus drawled. "Because you most definitely risked your life coming back here. The question is, why?"

"Because you and your family are in danger."

"That's nothing new. Every time I turn around it seems like we're facing some new threat. It's part of being top dawg in Vegas."

"Dammit, Marcus, this is serious!" She reached out, wrapped her fingers around his bicep. The muscle tensed, but he otherwise remained still. "When I left here, it was to go undercover in a group called Humans First."

His upper lip peeled back. "I've heard of them. Some sort of neo-religious militia group. They hate anything that isn't human."

"That pretty much sums it up. The leader, Jack Cavanaugh, really has it in for your family. Pretending to run away from here because I feared for my life gave me an in with the group. When I found out what was really going on, I knew I had to escape to warn you."

"Warn me of what?"

"Humans First is going to try to blow up the French Quarter. And my boss wants to help them."

Chapter Three

"How's the reunion going?" Malcolm asked by way of greeting.

Marcus kept one hand around Devon's bicep as he guided her through the service corridor. "News travels fast."

"Not all of the news, considering you cut monitoring to the interview room," Malcolm pointed out. "A lot of bets were placed on whether you'd tear the place apart or wait until you got back to your room, then a side bet on how long it would take you to make it to the family level."

"Hope you didn't have money on me making a beeline across the casino floor," Marcus said dryly. "I called because I've got more news for you. Big."

"Assemble the family big?"

"Yeah." He stopped at the elevator bank, then juggled the cell phone to press his thumb to the biometric scanner.

"You can let me go," Devon complained. "I'm not going anywhere."

"Not tonight, you're not," he retorted, then returned his cell phone to his ear. "Malcolm, we're talking multiple levels of fucked-uppery big. I asked Sheila to ramp up surveillance to Level Two inside and out before going to meet Devon. We're on the way to your office now, but I can man the deck tonight if you want."

"Take your wife upstairs," Malcolm told him, his voice losing none of its air of unruffled command despite the nebulous threat facing them. Marcus was grateful his Alpha trusted him enough that if the latter thought there was imminent danger to the family, they'd evacuate first and ask questions later. "We'll meet in my office, eight A.M. Do I need Dexter to do some research beforehand?"

"Department of Domestic Affairs," Marcus replied. Devon started to protest, but clamped her full lips together instead. The elevator silently opened and he ushered her inside then released her. "He'll need a delicate touch seeing as it's the feds and Packlaw may apply."

"Damn." Malcolm whistled.

"That's what I said, along with a few other words," Marcus agreed, feeling his wife's eyes on him as he used his passkey to access his floor of the family levels. "This ain't gonna be pretty."

"Are you kidding? This is gonna be good. But we'll worry about that in the morning. For now, the only thing I want you to think about is enjoying your reunion."

"Yeah right."

"Don't even try to play me, bro," Malcolm laughed into the phone. "Everyone knows you made it from your office to the interview room in record time, even for a Were. I know just how long and how tough it's been for you. Use the other head for a change and let your wolf get wild. Even if Packlaw applies, you deserve time with your mate."

"All right." Marcus forced his grip to loosen some on the phone. "Thanks, man, see you in the morning."

He disconnected, then pocketed the phone. There was a reason why so many alpha males chose to be betas under Malcolm. He had that same combination of command, assurance, and care that his father Julian had. The same presence that had reassured frightened kids escaping from a slave plantation in Louisiana that everything would be all right. And it had been.

Devon finally broke the silence. "Why didn't you tell him the cover story?"

"I'm not lying to my Alpha, Devon. You might not have any loyalty to my family, but I do."

"I have loyalty to you, Marcus. It's why I came back."

"Bullshit." The doors silently opened. He took her arm again, guided her along the corridor. "You expect me to believe that after everything you've just told me?"

"Yes, I do." Her chin lifted. "I'm your wife—"

"Sure that's not part of the lie?" He dragged her to a halt in front of one of several identical doors, then used his passkey to open it, letting her enter before him. "After all, I wasn't your original target,

15

was I?"

"Every female that walked up in here, human or not, wanted Malcolm." She settled her hands on her hips. "But that doesn't matter. What does matter is that our marriage is real."

He stalked past her to the bar, brought out a rocks glass and a decanter of bourbon. Yanking the stopper from the decanter, he splashed a healthy serving into his glass. "Yeah, so real you left your rings behind and disappeared for a year without bothering to tell me you're a spy. I don't know who in their right mind would call this a real marriage."

Forgoing ice, he downed the drink, then grimaced. "We checked you out, a thorough background check before I proposed. You came back clean except for a couple of parking tickets in college."

She approached him slowly, as wary as a jackrabbit sensing danger. Smart girl. "All I had on my record were parking tickets. Nothing in my background is fake—I just left out the part about being recruited by the DDA while serving in the Peace Corps the summer after I graduated."

"Just left it out, huh?" He poured another splash of cognac. "Anything else you left out of this action-movie farce that you neglected to share?"

"No."

He whuffed. "I suppose I should be grateful."

She looked around the living room, taking in the Zen-like mix of glass, pewter and pale blue. "The place hasn't changed much."

"Considering that the first few months after your disappearance were spent scouring the planet for you, you'll have to forgive me for not giving a damn about the décor. I did eventually have all your photos packed away."

Her lips thinned as if she wanted to argue. He certainly wanted her to. God help them both if she did.

Instead she sighed. "I'm going to take a shower. Do I need your permission for that?"

He gestured towards the master bedroom. "Be my guest."

She moved past him, then paused. "It's real good to see you again," she said softly, then entered the master suite.

Marcus stripped off his jacket, tossing it over the bar before pouring himself another drink, larger this time. Hell, he should probably just turn up the decanter and be done with it. Thanks to his Were metabolism, it would take downing the entire bottle in fifteen minutes to give him any sort of buzz. He went through the motions anyway, needing the act of drinking more than the drink itself to ease him.

God he was angry. Angry and guilty. And more than a little pleased. Angry that he'd been used by Devon. Guilty that he'd given up looking for her while she'd been alive and in the next state all this time. Pleased that she was back, that she'd come back to warn him.

Still, it galled him that she'd fooled him so completely. Obviously his cock had overridden every bit of common sense he'd ever had.

Loosening his tie with a vicious tug, he crossed to one of the leather chairs, settled into it, then took a fortifying sip of his drink. God, he needed a run. Everything in him called for releasing his wolf, running out into the desert until he tired, chasing down a couple of coyotes or a rabbit. He would have headed out to the ranch to stalk one of the buffalo, but he was way the hell too pissed off to think clearly enough to outwit the mean-ass beasts.

He suppressed a growl. Fuck the buffalo, his wolf wanted to hunt its mate. The wolf didn't care what her story was. The wolf had claimed her as its own, and the wolf refused to be denied what was rightfully theirs. From the moment he'd scented her, he'd been hard for her. Discovering that she'd lied to him about damn near everything hadn't changed that.

Pressing against her soft curves in the interview room had brought back every searing memory. The way her hands stroked his back, the way her mouth took his cock. The way her nipples puckered, the left more than the right. How she tilted her ass in the air, inviting him to take her, how her breasts bounced as she rode him to orgasm. How she moaned and juiced and came for him.

How she'd used all of that to betray him.

Snarling, he threw the rocks glass against the slate fireplace surround, rewarded as the cut crystal shattered. Goddamn, he hated Devon Archer.

Problem was, he needed her too.

"Something wrong?"

He turned towards the bedroom. Devon stood in the doorway, wearing nothing but water, a gold belly ring, and one of his oversized bathsheets. Damn, she looked…delicious.

"Of course something's wrong, and you know it," he said, climbing to his feet. "You're nothing but trouble. I knew you were trouble, and I let you in anyway."

"So I've been a bad girl," she purred, dropping the towel. "Do you

17

want to spank me?"

Marcus grit his teeth as he took in the curvy, chocolate expanse of her skin. Yeah, she'd thinned out some in the time she'd been gone, but it was all too easy to remember how those long legs wrapped around his body, how she tasted as good as she looked.

"Don't start something you can't finish, Devon," he warned her.

"Oh, I intend to finish, several times in fact," she assured him, hands stroking down her throat, breasts, belly. "You play your cards right, you will too."

She sauntered across the floor, the sway of her hips deliberately inviting. He could scent her arousal filling the space between them, beckoning him. His mouth watered.

"One final warning, Dee."

She stopped, settling her hands on her hips. The movement thrusts her breasts up at him. "What, is the big, bad wolf going to blow my house down? Or maybe I should blow yours?"

He lunged at her, dipping low to throw her over his shoulder. With quick strides, he stalked to the bedroom, tossing her onto the king-sized bed without ceremony. He immediately covered her, draping himself over her naked form.

She wrapped legs and arms around him. Her scent, barely eclipsed by the mild soap all the Weres used, slammed into him, making him shudder. He ground his hips against hers, not really caring if she dampened his thousand-dollar trousers or not.

Her eyes closed to slits as she moaned. "Marcus, I need you, Marcus."

He closed his eyes. It was probably a lie, but he didn't care. His wolf sure as shit didn't. He remembered what it was like sliding into her, thrusting into her hot slickness, being milked by her eager sheath. He remembered it, and he wanted it.

By the time he was done with her, she'd really want it too.

Her legs flexed around his waist, trying to draw him down. Since he was fully clothed, there wasn't much of him that she could get. He brushed against her again, teasing them both. Her heat and groan were enough to make him want to shove down his pants and fuck her blind, but he'd waited too long to pop off so fast.

Instead, he captured her mouth with his own, kissing her thoroughly. Her body softened beneath his, flowing against him in heated need. Her fingers then ripped at his shirt and he allowed it, eager to feel her hands on his skin.

He groaned against her lips as her fingers flicked over his nipples. Her lips curved against his. Oh, not even. She wouldn't win that easily.

Pinning her hands to the bed, he traced down the column of her neck with slow, meandering strokes of his tongue. Her breath caught in her throat, and it was his turn to curve his lips in a smile.

He conquered her body lick by lick, stroke by stroke, unmistakably laying claim to her. Anticipation and want coiled feverishly inside her, setting her whole being trembling. By the time he reached the juncture of her thighs, he'd reduced her to a trembling mess of nerve endings.

He waited a heartbeat, then another, his mouth hovering an inch above her skin, his breath warm against her. Then he dipped his head. All it took was one long stroke of his tongue, just one, and she shattered.

Devon fought for breath as Marcus stripped his clothes away. It angered her that she'd come so quickly and easily for him, but she couldn't deny the power of that decadent mouth of his. Besides, it had been so long…

Her thoughts scattered as she stared at the magnificence of his dick and imagined all the delicious pleasure something that proud and thick could give her.

She reached out to cup him, to guide him to her mouth, but he backed away. "Later," he said, turning her over. "This is what I want now."

Eagerly drawing up on her knees and elbows, Devon waited breathlessly for him to fill her. She'd missed him, missed his scent and his heat and his cock. The night she'd left, they'd made love every way they could think of, teasing and touching and tasting and taking until they were both happily exhausted. Marcus had thought she was being adventurous. Devon had been saying goodbye, storing up sexual memories to sustain her for the long months without him.

The hot length of his cock sliding between her thighs brought her back to the present. She lowered her head and arched her back, needing him to fill her. He drew back, clamped his large hands to her waist, then slowly pushed inside her.

She sucked in air between her lips as her body attempted to reacquaint itself with the reality of her husband's size. The deliciously slow penetration had waves of bliss rippling over her. It felt good, so good tears pricked her eyes. She wanted to cry, to sing, to fucking tap dance out how good he felt filling her.

Marcus' grip on her waist eased as she felt his groin finally press against her buttocks. "Damn, you feel good," he muttered. "Better than a dream."

Then he began to move, long drawn-out strokes, as if he savored every second it took to fill her. Devon moaned her appreciation and her frustration, trying to rock back against him. "More, baby, I need more."

Oh so slowly, insanely slowly, he increased the pace, thrusting deep each time, making her gasp each time. It was as if he wanted to make sure she understood what she'd been missing.

She understood all right.

Points of pleasure danced along her spine, firing her synapses, leaving her aware of nothing but Marcus' cock driving harder and faster into her. She tried to match him by rhythmically clenching and unclenching her inner muscles, wanting him as crazy as he was making her. He responded by draping himself onto her back, his hands curving around her shoulders to lock them together.

Devon sank her fingers into the bedcovers, holding on for dear life as the bed rattled and bucked beneath them. No one had ever made love to her like this, so fiercely passionate. No one had ever demonstrated how just how much satisfaction she gave him while making sure she was satisfied in return. Only Marcus had.

She could feel her orgasm approaching like a freight train, powerful and unstoppable. A keening cry tore from her as the force of her pleasure pummeled her, her entire body buffeted. Marcus' last violent thrust knocked her flat, and his howl filled the room as he came.

For the longest time, she was aware of nothing but the staccato pounding of her pulse. Then Marcus pulled free of her body, rolling away from her. She turned her head to see him lying beside her, his forearm thrown over his eyes. She watched his chest rise and fall, trying to figure out if he was angry or overcome.

It made her remember that this wasn't real, wasn't a true reunion with her husband. Made her remember that he wasn't as completely thrilled to see her as she'd been to see him.

"Marcus?"

"I think we've convinced our neighbors that the reunion was a happy one. When this is over, you might want to think about heading to Hollywood."

Damn, that stung. Her afterglow evaporated. "I forgot that pillow talk was never your strong suit, which is ironic considering your previous stint in public relations."

He rolled out of bed. "No need to keep up the charade when no one's around. I'll take the couch."

Devon sat up. "Don't take it out on me."

"Excuse me?"

Her hands settled on her hips. "You enjoyed yourself. Don't even try to deny it. You enjoyed yourself, and it pisses you off."

His eyes swept over her. "You always were a fine piece of ass," he said. "What's not to enjoy?"

Faster than she would have thought possible, she leapt off the bed, crossed the room, then slapped him. The stinging report of flesh on flesh gave her a vibrant flash of satisfaction. Dammit, she was scared and horny and totally in love with him and he was too wrapped up in his anger to notice.

She landed a second blow and began a third until he caught her wrists easily—so easily that she knew he'd let her hit him. Growling in outrage, she tried for a head-butt but he held her away. She then tried to aim a kick at his nuts.

Her agency training proved ineffectual against a werewolf. Breath swooshed out of her lungs as he quickly and efficiently tossed her to the floor, his body trapping hers against the thick carpet, his cock hard and insistent between them. More adrenaline flooded her system, causing her nipples to pebble against his chest. He smiled that smug, knowing, and altogether male smile.

It pissed her off. She reached up, clamping his bottom lip between her teeth. He distracted her the only way he could, exactly the way she wanted, by thrusting his cock deep into her passion-slicked tunnel.

She hissed at the sensual intrusion, even as her legs wrapped high around his waist. Her fingernails sank into his back as she kissed him in raw brutal need. It was as if she'd thrown a switch. Growling in response, Marcus crushed her against the carpet, hips slamming against hers in wild fury.

Yes! Devon's body sang in ferocious pleasure. Goddamn, angry makeup sex was good!

Soon, too soon, she could feel her climax approaching, coiling tightly inside her. She reached for it selfishly, wanting it, needing it. Thrusting a hand between their colliding bodies, she fought for that pleasure.

The orgasm sucker-punched her, quick and vicious and overwhelming. She gave a guttural cry as her muscles spasmed, tightening around him, her hot sheath milking his cock. He thudded against her once, twice, then stiffened, a groan grating out of him as he came.

Slowly his muscles relaxed. He let her feet slide to the floor then collapsed against her, propping himself on his elbows to keep from crushing her, their foreheads touching. For a long moment, nothing but the sound of harsh breathing interrupted the silence.

Finally he pulled away from her, concern darkening his eyes. "Are you all right?"

She had to swallow before she could speak. "I've got carpet burn, but I think I'll survive."

With a casual flick of his wrist, he flipped her over onto her belly. She began to protest—she couldn't possibly go another round—until she felt the first sweep of his tongue over one particularly stinging abrasion.

She froze in surprise. After the overwhelming intensity of their second round of lovemaking, she hadn't expected this gentle reaction and didn't have any idea how to defend herself against it. Finally she decided not to.

Her vision misted over as she sighed. Closing her eyes, she let the defensiveness leave her body. She was back with Marcus now. He wouldn't hurt her. At the height of his anger, he'd hurt himself instead of her. Even if his family decided to kill her tomorrow, she didn't want to be anywhere else. Here and now, she was the safest she'd ever been since becoming an agent.

He took his time tending to every scrape, soothing her body and easing her toward sleep. She felt him lift her, carry her, deposit her beneath the covers. Afraid that he'd leave, she sleepily held her arms out to him. "Com'ere."

After a moment he did, slipping into bed behind her and draping an arm around her waist. She pressed back against his chest, gathered his hand against her heart. "Thank you," she whispered, then dropped off into a deep and dreamless sleep.

Chapter Four

This was not going to go well.

Devon and Marcus sat in guest chairs in front of a massive desk. Malcolm sat in the executive chair behind it, his expression as smooth as the handcrafted Italian suit he wore. His wife Ali sat on the edge of the desk, slim and pretty despite her orange and purple hair. Somehow it suited her, though Devon thought she hardly seemed like Malcolm's type.

Four other people completed the gathering: Malcolm's sister, Simone, and the house magician, Kadim. He seemed an odd choice until Marcus introduced him as Simone's mate. She also recognized Guy Temple, and noted that he'd gained a mate named Lelia. Both were dressed in pseudo paramilitary gear. Maybe they were her execution squad.

"A lot's changed since I've been gone," she said after the introductions. "Congratulations on your marriages, and your installation as Temple Alpha, Malcolm."

"Thank you." Malcolm leaned forward, his smile dropping. "Seeing as we haven't seen you since your wedding ceremony, there's a lot for us to catch up on. The way you left disrupted the pack and could have cost us a valuable member."

Devon stole at glance at her husband. His jaw tightened but he kept his gaze on Malcolm's desk. What the hell did Malcolm mean?

"Right now I have to determine whether this situation is just a family matter or a pack matter," Malcolm continued. "You're human, but you're not stupid. I don't think I have to tell you how important it is that you be straight with us. We take the pack's safety very seriously. If you lie, we'll know."

"You're going to hook me up to a lie detector or dose me with sodium pentothal?"

Ali snorted. "Like a special agent isn't trained to thwart those. We have different ways of making you talk."

As Devon watched, the woman's hair turned bright blood red. Her nails grew another two inches and sprouted flames.

Devon swallowed, turned to Marcus. "Looks like we've got some pretty powerful allies on our side."

His answering smile offered little reassurance. "You have no idea, sweetheart."

She looked at each person in the room with fresh perspective. Guy and his mate were Weres, but obviously the badass, take 'em down hard members of the pack. The magician grinned at her, and there was something neither human nor lupine in the baring of teeth. What the hell was he? What the hell was Malcolm's wife?

She inhaled deeply. "Okay, so I'm the only human in the room. I realize that my marriage and my life are at stake here. Believe me, I know. You guys will kill me for coming back. My boss will kill me for leaving empty-handed."

Malcolm opened a file folder. "And your boss is James Porter, former colonel with the Marine Corps, retired with honors."

"How...how do you know that?"

"Information is easy to find once you know what you're looking for," the alpha replied. "The Department of Domestic Affairs sure has taken advantage of the Patriot Act, haven't they?"

Devon bristled. "If you know that much, then you also know just how many threats we've neutralized."

"Neutralized." Malcolm's gaze bored into her. "That's one way to put it."

Marcus clamped his fingers around her wrist. She rethought what she'd been about to say, choosing explanation instead.

"I joined the DDA because I believe the preternatural community has every inalienable right that human citizens have. And I have a problem with people who hate others because of what they are instead of what they've done. My team's focus has always been human hate groups."

"What changed?" Simone asked.

"Porter changed. I don't know if something specific happened, or if it was just cumulative. I was placed here to report back any threats against the preternatural community. I made several anonymous tips to the Preternatural Authorities for the small stuff, and reported the larger stuff to my superiors back in Washington."

She turned her wrist to capture Marcus' fingers. "Porter ordered me to come in during my honeymoon. Told me that our focus had changed, that my goal was to infiltrate Humans First. My cover story was that I was so freaked out by my marriage to a Were that I ran for my life."

His hand tightened on hers. She looked at him, at the anger in his eyes, and silently apologized. "Cavanaugh, the head of Humans First, ate it up. He wanted a reason to take on Weres. Thanks to Porter sending me in, he had one."

Human or no, she could feel the tension mounting in the room. Marcus tightened his grip on her hand. She managed not to whimper in pain.

"Obviously they bought your story, because you were able to stay," her husband said. "Good job."

She didn't know if he said it for her or for his packmates, but she still warmed in response as he released her. "Thanks."

"You've been there for most of the past year," Malcolm observed. "You've gained their trust. How did you manage to get away from them?"

"Their plans to take you on kept getting thwarted. Apparently you had a lot of demon activity going around during Malcolm's installation," she said. "I said I'd get back into the pack's good graces by saying I'd been kidnapped and brainwashed. Then once I was in good again, I'd steal the French Quarter's blueprints and security layouts and pass them on."

Guy unfolded his arms. "I've heard enough."

Marcus rose as Guy stepped forward, but Guy's mate, put a hand out to stop him. "But that's not the story you gave Marcus," Leila said. "Why?"

Devon wrapped both arms around Marcus' forearm. She'd awakened to find him ordering breakfast and clothing for her, not a big thing, but it touched her anyway. He'd even joined her in the shower, but as they toweled dry, need had returned. Instead of having breakfast, she'd loved him with lips and teeth and tongue, drinking down his pleasure even as he fed from hers. They hadn't spoken at all, but they didn't need to.

"I never had any intention of turning that information over to Porter." Devon dropped her gaze. "It was easy when I knew who the bad guys were. I thought I was making a difference, protecting people. I respected my boss, but he's changed. Now I think Porter needs help, or to be stopped."

Tears surprised her as she raised her gaze to Marcus again. "I stayed because thought I could help him. I thought I could change his mind. When I realized that I couldn't, I started gathering evidence against him. And when I knew that they were serious and determined to attack you, I knew I had to come home."

Simone stepped forward. "The problem is, you're bringing trouble with you. I suppose you want us to handle that?"

Devon sighed. "It's my problem. I'll take care of it. But I'm hoping you have some trusted contacts inside the Preternatural Authority that could leverage. Is Garen Roy still there?"

Marcus' fingers tightened on hers.

"Actually, it is our problem," Malcolm said, settling back in his chair. "You got evidence against Porter and Humans First?"

"I've got documentation and a few recordings that I managed to conceal from Porter and Cavanaugh," she admitted. "I'm hoping someone from PA can contact higher-ups at the DDA. I don't know if I'm flagged in any way, so I'm cautious about trying to make direct contact."

The alpha nodded. "I'll make some phone calls. In the meantime, you should stay on the family floor."

She didn't expect that. "You're confining me to our apartment?"

Marcus answered. "Your safety is important. Our surveillance is good, but we can't keep you as safe as we can if you stay away from the public."

Well damn. She knew enough not to argue with Marcus in front of his alpha, but she didn't appreciate them making decisions like that without at least asking for her opinion.

Marcus raised an eyebrow as if he knew exactly what she was thinking and dared her to say it out loud. She swallowed her comment down and dropped her head. Like she hadn't made a butt-load of decisions over the past year without Marcus.

"Don't worry, Marcus," Ali said then. "We'll take care of her. I think I can speak for the ladies when I say we'd like a chance to get to know our pack sister."

Crap. Her husband had just thrown her to the she wolves—literally.

Chapter Five

Two days later, Devon began to wonder if she should have stayed out in the Arizona desert.

The women of the Temple pack intimidated her, not that she'd ever admit it. Esther Temple, the matriarch of the family, had set the bar high. The children she and her husband had brought from slavery had all learned from her example. They were tough, they were survivors, and they were close—pack brothers and sisters who protected their own. The women of the pack were a force to be reckoned with, even more so than the men.

Just as the day before, she sat in Simone's office, flipping through design swatches and clothing catalogs. She knew Simone from before, and even though Leila was a recently converted Were, Devon found the born Were to be more relatable. Ali, well…Malcolm's wife made her want to keep looking over her shoulder.

Devon silently flipped through yet another catalog, waiting for Simone to acknowledge her presence.

A throaty laugh wafted across the expanse of the office. "Eyes up, Dee. You don't have to be all submissive around me."

"Oh, thank God," Devon raised her chin. "I hate doing it."

"Why are you doing it? Your mate's part of the original family and head of Surveillance. Besides you didn't do it when we were planning your wedding."

"Things are different now. I figured that's what you'd want me to do," Devon answered, "and seeing as how I like my head just where it is, I figured it would behoove me to play it safe."

"Play it safe?" Simone laughed again. "Girl, you haven't played it safe since you first walked into this casino. A human giving the female Weres a run for their money. There were quite a few people who didn't shed a tear when you left."

"I bet. And Marcus led the pack."

Simone cocked her head. "You think so?"

Devon looked down at her hands. "I actually think he hates me," she confessed in a misery-filled voice. "At first I thought we were just having angry make-up sex, but now... I really think he's going to ask me for a divorce."

Simone didn't respond. When Devon dared at look, she found the older woman staring at her in a mix of amazement and pity. "You may be a great special agent, Devon Archer, but you know jack shit about relationships. Marcus doesn't hate you. If he did, he wouldn't be so pissed."

Somehow Devon managed to lift her jaw off the floor, pushing past her surprise at hearing the crude words coming from such a cultured mouth. "Do you really think so?"

"The opposite of love isn't hate," Simone said gently. "Both are too strong and vibrant. The opposite of an feeling like that is a complete lack of emotion, total apathy."

Simone closed the magazine before her. "Lord knows you've given Marcus plenty of reason to hate you and completely shut off from you but he can't. He needs you too much, much more than you need him."

"Needs me? Marcus doesn't need me. He's done fine without me—I'd even say he's done better."

Simone settled a hand on her hip. "Didn't they teach you anything about Weres before sticking you in the wolf's den?"

"I learned what I could, but I'm sure there's plenty that I don't know." Devon pushed a hand through her hair. "And I certainly don't get what you're talking about Marcus needing me."

"You're his mate, Devon. That means something to a Were. Marcus chose you above all others. You're the only one for him."

"The only one?" Devon repeated. "You mean, even though I'm human, it's like he chose a female Were? We're mated for life?"

When Simone nodded, Devon sank into her chair, flummoxed. Yeah, she'd sworn to be with him until death do they part, but she hadn't really thought about what that meant for Marcus.

Two days of doing nothing but waiting was starting to grind on her. She needed to something, anything other pacing her apartment or working out in the family gym. Sure she had sex with Marcus whenever he wasn't at work and it was wonderful, but each day that she didn't do something to move them—all of them—forward was a day she lived in fear and uncertainty. She was tired, so very tired of that.

She jumped to her feet. "I need to go."

"Where?"

"To Marcus. I need this to be done," she declared, clenching her hands. "One way or another, I need this to end. This holding pattern is driving me crazy!"

"The government moves at its own speed—surely you know that, Ms. Federal Employee?" Simone smiled. "Or are you talking about your reconciliation?"

"Both, I suppose." Devon ran a hand through her scraggly hair again. Once this was over, she'd grow it out, think about spending some of her money on designer duds and spa treatments the way Simone did. "You're sure Marcus won't ask me for a divorce?"

"The only ones who can be sure of that are you and Marcus," Simone answered. "Talk to him. Really talk to him. It's the only way you'll know for sure."

An hour later, Devon paced the living room, waiting for Marcus to return. She'd thought about ordering up his favorite meal, then decided against it. She didn't really know if he still preferred leg of lamb, and she had a feeling that he'd react suspiciously if she made the gesture.

Nah, she'd always been blunt, even deep in cover, and "wait and see" had hardly been in her vocabulary.

The door clicked as a passkey activated the lock. She spun for the door, heart suddenly pounding as Marcus entered. Her throat went dry as she looked at him, so gorgeous and miraculous and hers.

At least, she still hoped so.

"Is it true?" she asked him.

"Is what true?"

"That when you married me, it meant that you wouldn't be able to have another woman if we divorce."

He gave her a baleful stare as he moved deeper into the living room. "Who told you that?"

"Simone."

He sighed. "Sometimes that woman is too pack-mama for her own good."

"Is it true?"

Ice clinked in the rocks glass. "What does it matter?"

"Just tell me. Please."

His hand tightened on the brandy decanter. "Fine. When I married you, I claimed you as my mate. Female Weres are no longer on the menu, even during Full Moon, even when we divorce."

Damn, she'd really screwed him over.

He gave her a frighteningly pleasant smile. "Congratulations, my dear wife. You basically neutered me when you left. Only death breaks that sort of bond."

He tossed back the drink, immediately poured another. "Don't know about human women though. Might be worth investigating."

The idea of another woman with Marcus made her want to shoot something. She turned away, unwilling to let him see just how deep a hit he'd scored.

He noticed anyway, damn him. The crystal decanter hit the glass bartop with a sharp crack. "It's a little late to be jealous, don't you think?"

"Why did you marry me?"

"What?"

"You heard me." She lifted her chin. "All these powerful supernatural women running around. You can't tell me none of them were interested."

"Most of them want alphas, and I'm happy being a beta. I fought enough over the years surviving slavery, Indian wars, and Jim Crow. I didn't want to fight my pack brothers. Once the dominant females realized I wasn't trying to leave to start a pack or move further up in this one, they left me alone."

She swallowed down the hurt. Tried to, anyway. "So in a way, little ole human Devon was your second choice too."

"If that's what you think, then you really don't know me." He stalked toward her. "I chose you for all the reasons a man chooses a woman. You're smart, sexy, and funny. I noticed you because you were good at your job. I fell for you because I was a fool. I fell in love with you, and love didn't care that you're human. So I took you as my mate and ended up damning myself in the process."

Her back stiffened. "Damning yourself? Was being with me that bad?"

"No. Being without you was that bad."

31

He captured and held her gaze. "At first, I let people think you'd been kidnapped. Then came the worry that you might have been killed, but since I didn't display the typical grief of mate-loss, everyone came to the rightful conclusion that you'd left me, especially since I'd gone along with you staying human. Then I became a target."

"What do you mean, target?"

"A wolf who can't keep his mate is no wolf at all. I'm part of the original family, the firsts of the pack, yet I became a pariah. Your running out on me forced me to defend my place and my existence in the pack."

"Marcus." Tears welled in her eyes. The fact that he wasn't a testosterone-laden alpha had been one of the things that had appealed to her. She hadn't imagined that her disappearance would have consequences for him.

"Of course, I had plenty of new-found aggression to work out," he continued, his words as fierce as his expression. "After I sent the third male to the hospital, people got the hint. Just because I choose to be a beta doesn't mean that I can't represent like an alpha. Bottom line, I defeated all my challengers, got moved to Surveillance, and made sure people pretty much leave me the fuck alone. Then you came back."

"Are you saying that me coming back messed up your life?"

"I don't know what I'm saying." He ran a hand over his dark waves. "I settled into it for the most part. I had work, I had runs out at the ranch. My wounds scabbed over soon enough. But I'll never forgot that you didn't trust me or the family with the truth. We could have helped. I would have done anything for you. But you ran instead."

She spun back. "Would you like to know why I had to leave the way I did?"

"Do you think telling me why you left will somehow mitigate the fact that you did in fact leave?" he demanded. "You lied, you ran, end of story."

"My boss was going to kill you!"

She sank onto the bed. "I was going to tell you everything," she confessed. "About my job, my mission—everything. Porter called me in, gave me the Humans First assignment. I reminded him that I was on marital leave but he didn't care about the honeymoon. He told me to come in or he'd take you out."

"And you believed him?"

She just looked at him. "Porter is black ops in a domestic agency that doesn't exist on paper. Of course I believed him."

"Why did you leave your rings behind?"

"I couldn't leave a note. I thought if I left the rings you'd know I wasn't in danger. I didn't think I'd be gone as long as I was, but I always planned to come back. I always dreamed of being with you for the rest of my life. I love you, Marcus. You're my home."

For a long moment he just stared at her, his face and posture carefully neutral. "You smell like you're telling the truth," he finally said, "but we both know that you've fooled my nose before. How can I believe you?"

"I don't know," she said, her shoulders slumping. If he didn't believe her now, after everything she'd said and done, she didn't know how she could convince him. "What do you want me to do, Marcus?"

"I don't know." His echo of her words sounded the same, bleak and completely empty of emotion.

She took a deep breath. "You could change me."

His smile was sad. "No."

"No? Why not?"

"You're acting as if it's a death sentence, instead of the gift it is. You don't want it. You've never wanted it. It's why you put it in the pre-nup, remember?"

"Because I wanted to still be me! You Temples are so overwhelming, I felt lost. I thought my identity would be lost. And maybe even my humanity. I couldn't do it then, Marcus—I was too scared. I can do it now. We can be together, the way you want us to be."

"But not the way you want us to be."

She drew back, mortified. "That's not what I meant—"

"It's okay, Dee. It doesn't...it'll be okay."

Ice filled her veins. She remembered Simone's words, how the opposite of love wasn't hate, but apathy. Everything about Marcus— his words, his voice, his posture—said he no longer cared one way or another whether she stayed or not.

He turned and headed for the door without saying another word. "Where are you going?"

"To one of the bars." He kept walking. "I need a drink."

She stared at the full glass sitting on the counter. "Should I wait up for you?"

He paused, but didn't turn around. "No, I'll probably head out to the desert for a run. I won't be back. Not until late anyway."

Don't go. She tried to say the words, tried to speak past the panic that seized her chest. Please stay.

Her lips moved, but the words didn't come. The only sound that filled the room was the opening and shutting of the outer door.

Devon sat in stunned silence, struggling to understand what had just happened.

Marcus had left her.

Her husband had walked out on her. Now she knew what it felt like to be the one left behind, wondering if the other would come back.

Somehow she didn't think he would.

He didn't believe her. She'd laid everything out on the line, bared heart and soul, and he still hadn't believed her. Worse still, he'd rather be alone than be with her.

A whimper escaped her throat. She covered her mouth with a fist to keep the grief in. Never once had she considered the idea that Marcus wouldn't want her. She'd known he'd be angry, that he'd maybe even hate her. But she'd carried the memories and emotions of their courtship and honeymoon like a beacon, lighting her way back to him.

She'd fucked up. Big time. She didn't have anything left to lose. Might as well go double or nothing.

After scrubbing the back of her hand across her face, she pulled out her prepaid cell phone, dialed a number. "Let's do this."

Chapter Six

In the casino's weapon room, Devon geared up.

"You can still change your mind."

Devon strapped on her leg holster, pulled her jeans down. "There's no one else who can do this. Besides, it's my job."

She straightened, took a deep breath. "I don't suppose anyone's heard from Marcus?"

Simone shook her head. "Guy's searching the ranch, but it's a lot of ground to cover. We sent more pack members out to help."

Her eyes softened in sympathy. "Do you want me to tell him anything?"

Devon's jaw tightened. What more was there to say? She'd thrown her heart on the line and he'd walked out anyway. There were no more words left.

"Fair's fair. I did it to him. He's got a right to do it to me."

"Devon…"

She threw her chin up. She wasn't weak. She wouldn't be weak—not to these wolves, not to the humans who wanted them obliterated, not to the husband who'd rejected her.

Detective Gunderson held out a small Kevlar vest. "We'd prefer you wear this, Agent Archer."

She shook her head. "My boss isn't stupid. They'll check me for wires and weapons. I can make them ignore the low-level transmitter in my belly ring but if they see that vest, I'm toast."

Gunderson frowned, then gave a curt nod. "All right." She handed Devon a long metal cylinder. "The blueprints have a tracking spell on them. We'll follow at the maximum range of your transmitter for recording purposes, but we'll always know where you are."

"Don't worry," Malcolm assured her, "you won't be alone."

The PA agent frowned again. "Mr. Temple, you know we can't have any of your wolves on the scene."

Malcolm gave her a look. "I've already said that none of my wolves will interfere with your operation, Detective Gunderson. Surely Detective Roy told you that you'd have no reason to distrust the Temple Alpha?"

Gunderson blinked. "No, sir. I mean, yes sir."

The detective's discomfiture gave Devon her first real smile in hours.

Simone stepped closer to her, settling her hands on Devon's shoulders. "You may be human, but you're still our pack sister," the female Were said. "We protect our own."

For a moment her vision wavered. She wasn't their own. Marcus had made that perfectly clear.

She cleared her throat. "Well, in a couple of hours this will all be over anyway. Let do this thing."

Marcus lay in wolf form beneath the unmarked car watching the warehouse's open bay doors. Tension filled his body. He'd returned to the casino to talk to Devon just in time to see her pull out in one of his cars. A laughing group of people had piled into a stretch Humvee after her, but he'd immediately tagged them as PA agents.

It was going down. Devon was facing two men who surely wanted her dead, and he'd walked out on her.

A shadow coalesced beside him. His lips pulled back in a silent snarl and remained that way even after he recognized Kadim.

"Ease, wolf." The magician's voice was barely a whisper. "Ali is here as well."

Another shadow coalesced. Even in the darkness, Marcus could see that Ali had dressed for the occasion, looking like a character out of a monster-slaying video game. "Did someone say my name? You know what they say about speaking of the devil."

It was suddenly very crowded beneath the old car. "I don't need jokes right now. I'm going to get my wife."

The hellhound nudged his shoulder. "No you're not."

"You think a hellhound's going to keep me from my woman?"

"No, but your Alpha will."

Marcus lifted his head. He neither saw nor smelled Malcolm, but clearly heard his voice. "Where the hell are you?"

"In the main bar, where everyone can see me," his alpha replied. "Ali's projecting my thoughts to you. And look, a wolf who looks a lot like you just joined me for a drink. All I need you—the real you—to do is keep your tail out of sight."

"No."

"No? You want to go barging in there and put Devon's life in danger? This is her job, Marcus. You yourself said she was good at it. Let her do it."

Marcus snarled.

"Bro." Malcolm's power filled the space beneath the car. "If you want a fight, I'll be more than happy to give you one. But you sure as shit better bring it. Otherwise, stand the fuck down."

"That's my woman out there, man." Marcus bit back his temper, his fear. Devon was in danger. He thought of the way they'd left things—the way he'd left things—and felt sick. "That's my woman, and she doesn't—we didn't—"

"I know," his Alpha said then, his tone gentle. "Which is why Kadim and Ali are out there as back up, to make sure you get that chance."

Marcus sighed. "PA's not going to be happy about this."

Malcolm laughed. "What? You didn't really think I'd let my pack sister do this unprotected? I promised no Temple wolves. I said nothing about djinns or hellhounds. Now, let them do their jobs. But if Devon is threatened—"

"If Devon is threatened, someone's gonna die."

Devon made sure that she stood in the warehouse's bay doors so no one would lose sight of her.

"How do I know you're not wearing a wire?"

She unbuttoned her shirt, then unhooked the front clasp of her bra. "Do I look like I'm wearing a wire?" she asked, turning in a slow circle.

37

Cavanaugh stepped forward to frisk her, lingering a little too long. "You're three seconds from becoming a eunuch," she warned him. "Two…"

He stepped back. "You fuck dogs, you ain't got the right to be offended."

"Yeah, I'm a bitch. And so's your mother."

"That's enough," Porter barked when Cavanaugh stepped forward again. He turned his flat-eyed stare to Devon. "So you completed your mission?"

"Of course I completed my mission." She allowed her anger to poke through. Pulling her shirt back on, she kept her cool by imagining herself ripping Cavanaugh's tiny little dick off with her bare hand. Still, he'd been so fixated on her tits that he'd completely skipped the bellybutton ring with its microscopic transmitter.

Porter's eyes bored into her. "You got them?"

She nodded. Retrieving her bag from the floor, she started to open it, but Cavanaugh took it from her. "Blueprints to the French Quarter Hotel and Casino, and a family passcode, just like you asked."

Her boss looked suspicious, not that she could blame him. "And how did you manage that?"

Her lip curled. "How do you think? Cavanaugh hasn't stopped drooling since he felt me up. My husband became the Chief of Surveillance while I was gone. We had a heck of a reunion, and I went through his files and cloned his passkey. He may be a werewolf, but he's all man where it counts, unlike Cavanaugh here."

Cavanaugh started forward again, but Porter held him off. "And they just let you leave?"

Devon swallowed, looked away. "I guess you could say karma bit me on the ass. My husband made it clear that he doesn't want me anymore. He just wanted me to fall in love with him again so that he could get revenge for me leaving the first time. He's taken up with a female Were and they're going to mate as soon as a judge signs the divorce papers."

"Artic Archer sounds like she's actually broken up about it," Porter said, a slimy grin wreathing his face. "That's what you get for not sticking with humans. Lie down with dogs, you get fleas."

"Yeah well, no one makes a fool out of me and lives to tell about it," she declared, allowing her hatred for him and Cavanaugh to fill her voice. She was so going to enjoy killing them. Or imagining them playing butt-buddies at Gitmo. "You know how women are, Porter.

First we get mad, then we get even."

"Oh, you are a vengeful bitch, aren't you? Remind me never to piss you off."

Too late for that. "You gotta move fast," she told them, injecting a dash of fear into her voice. "And I want out of Vegas. Once they find out what I've done, I'm dead."

"You're dead anyway," Cavanaugh sneered.

"What the hell are you talking about?"

"I'm sorry, Devon," Porter said, pulling out a semi-automatic and pointing it her way. "You really were a good agent, but I don't think I can trust you and your loyalties anymore."

Oh, shit.

"This is bullshit," she challenged, taking a cautious step back and wishing she had a weapon of any kind. Surely the Preternatural Authority had enough info to move in now. Where the hell were they? "I've done everything you've asked me to do."

"And now I'm asking you to be a diversion. I think finding your bullet-ridden carcass on their doorstep will be distraction enough. Your country thanks you for your sacrifice."

Everything happened as she dodged. She heard a roar, but it didn't sound like a firearm discharging. Porter's first bullet ripped through her left bicep. The force of the impact spun her, and she saw a bunch of people, a wolf, and a flaming dog racing towards her. The second bullet hit her in the side as she dove, breaking a rib.

She hit the ground hard, rolling as more bullets flew, people shouted, and pain engulfed her. "Marcus," she gasped, then gritted her teeth as she dragged herself across the warehouse floor. She had to get to Marcus. Every instinct in her screamed out for him.

Mar-cus!

Suddenly he was there, his wolf changing to human form before dropping to the ground beside her. "You're here."

"Like I could be anywhere else." His hand brushed her bangs from her eyes. She hurt too much to feel it, and she really wanted to.

Black spots danced before her eyes. She sucked in dirt and blood and stink, fighting for every breath, fighting to say what needed to be said while she had the chance.

"I-I didn't want to leave you, Marcus," she bit out between teeth clenched against agonizing pain. "I love you. Always. I need you— God!—I need you to believe me."

"I do, baby, I do."

Tension left her body. "Thank you. Waited...so long for that. You'll be...you'll be okay now."

Someone else leaned over them. "We've got to get her out of here."

"She's human," a female voice said. "Her body won't survive a transport, magical or otherwise."

"...S'okay," she tried to tell him. She'd known when she left the hotel that she wasn't going to make it back.

Marcus dragged her across his thighs, gathered her shattered arm. It was probably a bad sign that she couldn't feel it anymore. It didn't matter. He believed her, finally. Nothing else mattered but that.

"I'm sorry, Devon."

"For what?"

"This." His face contorted into a hybrid of man and wolf a heartbeat before he sank his fangs deep into her injured arm.

She thought she'd felt pain before. Her mouth mimicked the widening of her eyes, but neither tears nor screams would come. Agony bowed her body, radiating outward from her arm.

Marcus released her. She inhaled in relief—then stiffened as his jaws stretched across her throat, teeth sinking into either side of her larynx. Her legs scrabbled on the ground as her body released its last reserves of adrenaline in a futile attempt to escape.

Black and red swirled until it filled her vision, blotting out Marcus, blotting out pain. It pulled her down, further down, and she let it.

Chapter Seven

She was alive.

How the hell had that happened?

Devon kept her eyes closed, trying to get a sense of where she was. Hard bed, harder sheets. Soft electronic noises. Hospital.

Hospital? Last thing she remembered was her husband killing her.

Grief welled, strong and acid-bitter. A sob surprised her but she quickly clamped her hands over her mouth, her gaze skittering around the room until she saw him.

Marcus lay curled in wolf form in front of the door, watching her with wary yellow eyes. He'd bit her, jaws clamping down on her throat, cutting off her air, finishing what Porter had started. So why wasn't she dead?

Because he'd changed her instead of killing her.

Why?

"Change," she whispered through a parched throat. "Change so I can talk to you."

He rose silently to his paws, padded closer. Just as silently he shifted, then pulled on the sweats waiting on the bedside chair.

"You're in the preternatural wing of the hospital," he said after giving her a careful sip of water. "It's been two days. Cavanaugh's dead and Porter's been whisked to Guantanamo. They're probably going to charge him as a terrorist and attempted murderer, among other things."

"I'll need to debrief my superiors," she said, though it wasn't what she wanted to say. "I have enough evidence on Humans First to make sure they're permanently disbanded."

"Someone from Washington's already here." His lips curved, but the smile was bitter. "Seems they want to charge me with a whole slew of crimes—assault on a federal agent, attempted murder, conversion without permission, and spousal abuse because I refused the anti-lycanthropy vaccine on your behalf. I'm not even supposed to be in here right now."

What the hell? Devon pressed the heels of her hands against her forehead, struggling to shake off her unconsciousness and make sense of his words. She started with the simplest. "You converted me."

"You were dying," he told her, chocolate brown eyes rimmed scarlet, "and there wasn't time for finesse. I had to make sure enough of the lycanthrope virus hit your system to combat your body's desire to give up."

Her body may have fought giving up, but her heart had capitulated long before she'd even left the hotel. When she'd thought Marcus wouldn't forgive her, when she'd believed that he'd abandoned her as she'd abandoned him, she'd believed their relationship was over. Words hadn't been enough. Wasn't that why she'd apologized to him?

"I thought you were executing me," she admitted, her voice wobbly. "You said only death could change things, so I thought you were making sure. I poured my heart out and you left. Y-you left that night, and you didn't come back."

She swallowed back tears. "Now I know a little of how you felt when I left. No wonder you hated me."

"I don't hate you."

"Y-you don't?"

"If I hated you, I would have let you die." He sat at the foot of her bed. Exhaustion pulled at his features. "I didn't want you to die."

That didn't make any sense. "But you would have been able to choose another mate, a female Were—"

"I already have a mate. And she just happens to be a Were now."

For a long moment, she just blinked at him. She wanted to believe him—she needed to believe him. But with everything she'd said and done and faced, she was too chicken-shit to ask.

"I suppose I'm out of a job. My cover's pretty much blown."

"You were out of a job the moment you came back," he told her. "You chose your duty to our family over your duty to your job."

"I owed you."

"Is that why you did it, out of some sense of evening the score?" His dark eyes swept her face as he moved closer to her. "I don't think so. But it doesn't matter anyway."

"Why not?"

"Because you're not going back."

"Marcus…"

"I'm not apologizing for converting you," he told her, holding her at arms length. "You're going to stay here, stay married to me, and you're going to like it."

"Yes, sir."

His mouth closed with an audible snap. He frowned at her. "You're not going to argue with me?"

She managed a smile. "Sometimes I do follow orders."

"So maybe you'll follow this one." He dug into his pocket, pulled out a ring box. "Marry me again. With everything out in the open, no more secrets, commit to us."

"You kept my rings." Tears filled her eyes. "You kept them."

"I kept a belief, a belief that I'd find you. A belief that we'd be together again, this time for good."

He slipped the platinum bands onto her finger. They still fit.

"I kept a belief that there was a good reason why you left," he told her, his expression solemn. "I'm glad you followed your conscience and your beliefs, no matter how much danger you had to face. I'm proud of you, proud to be your husband."

He'd given her the one thing she'd needed from him, the one thing she'd craved for more than a year. Her cheeks hurt from the force of her smile until her vision wavered. "Marcus." She hiccupped. "Marcus."

His arms encircled her, gently pulling her to his chest. "I love you, Devon," he whispered against her hair. "I've never been more afraid than when I saw that bastard shoot you. If you hadn't called for me, I would have killed him."

She burrowed deeper into the comfort of his arms. "As much as I wanted him dead, I'm glad you didn't kill him. You belong to me, not the feds. I'm not going to be without you again."

"That's good to know, since we've got another century or so together. Plenty of time for you to find new trouble to get into."

"The only trouble I want to get into now is sneaking out of here with you."

Marcus grinned. "Now that's trouble I can handle."

The End

Royal Pursuit

by

Monique Lamont

Dedication

To the man who makes me howl, my husband. My darling daughter who waited patiently to talk to me while I was on deadline. Thanks always to family and close friends. To the writing ladies at Starbuck's 7467, many thanks. AJ, for every time I said, "I need another pair of eyes" and never groaned as you assisted me. To my brother who always gets tickled each time I tell him about my paranormal romance, but sits for hours and listens. To Jackie and Miriam: last year was one hell of a ride, hugs to you both.

Thank God for the inspiration of the Song of Solomon.

Available Books
Fire and Desire
Passion's Blood (Vegas Bites Back)
Freedom's Quest (Merlicious 2)
Healing Hearts
Double Take
Merger for Life

Chapter One

Oliver Montague walked out of the French Quarter Casino and pulled the keys to his black and chrome Suzuki Boulevard M109R out of his pocket. He'd just left his pack brother and leader's office, letting Malcolm know that as of today he was taking an extended leave of absence. He was leaving Jimmy, his assistance manager, in charge of the pit bosses and dealers. Placing his Ray-Ban Ultra's over his eyes to block out the mid-day sun, he strolled to his motorcycle in the garage and straddled it. Revving the engine, he smiled. The sound of it's roaring sent adrenaline pumping into his veins as he pulled away from the casino. He wish he could say he felt relief or at ease, but he didn't.

He hadn't experienced those feeling in a long time. Too long.

Sighing, he allowed the road to lead him where ever it willed. He had no map or destination. Hell, he didn't even have direction for where his life was going.

Now that there was a shift in power in the Temple pack and his sister, Octavia was settling in comfortably with her mate, he was a ship without an anchor. Nothing to hold him down. Even his wolf was restless.

With the wind in his face, the open road before him and the city disappearing at his back, he prayed to the Great Spirit to guide him and his wolf.

"Your Highness, you must wake up."

Tashi heard the soft, anxious whispering of Danuwa, her personal assistant. A voice she was as familiar with hearing as her own. Danuwa had been serving her since they had taken their primary lessons. "What is it? It can not be morning. Why are you waking me?"

"Please, my princess, you must come with me quickly." Danuwa's speech became even more hushed and rapid.

It was not her assistant's rate of words that made her open her eyes and stared through the darkness, but Danuwa's hand that grasped her arm and shook her. Because of her status, she was rarely touched. Not per her own request, but their respect for her position. The fact that Danuwa was grabbing her set off warning bells.

Rolling onto her side toward Danuwa, Tashi listened intently. "What is wrong?"

Danuwa's face was barely illuminated in the moonlight coming through the bedroom window. Her eyes were glassy and her lips trembled as she spoke. "Leult Tashi you must come with me and see. I do not want to waste time explaining. Trust that I would not disturb your peace if not for the urgency."

Tashi trusted her people immensely. They were small in numbers and needed each other to survive. And Danuwa she considered a close friend and confidant. She nodded giving her agreement to follow.

Danuwa helped her sit up. They worked silently to gather her slippers and robe. Once she was covered, Danuwa moved toward the corridor.

Tashi's heart rate accelerated as her assistant pressed the code along a large portrait of Leul Ras Eze, her father, the old prince. Seeing his face in the glow of the moon weighed her shoulders with sadness, more than a year had passed and she still grieved. She missed both her parents. Their time had come too soon for her.

Watching the portrait split and open, revealing the royal corridor, Tashi began to worry. The corridors were only used in case of emergency. "Danuwa, are we under attack?"

"It is best we travel this way." Stepping back, Danuwa allowed her to enter first then moved quickly behind her and pressed the button on the other side that would seal the door.

Pausing only a moment to await the soft light to fill the room, Danuwa moved fast through the cool mountain caverns of the Eritrean Highlands. Her people had built the tunnels in early 1800 in order to save some of the cattle from the Italian invader and plague.

Curiosity nipped at Tashi's mind. *If we are not under attack, what is going on? Why the secrecy and rush?*

They finally paused. Tashi knew where they were, she had played in these hidden passages as a child in order to be familiar with every twist and turn. "Why are we in the labs, Dan--"

Danuwa's fingers gently touched her lips, silencing her. Tashi raised an eyebrow at her assistant. Clearly letting Danuwa know that whatever was going on, she would only permit such disrespect.

Tashi knew her friend comprehended her message when she witnessed Danuwa's teeth seize her bottom lip and lower her eyes in apology. Just as quickly, Danuwa's eyes rose and she tapped her ears. Entering the tunnel's viewing control room with mini televisions showcasing various rooms around the palace, Danuwa directed her toward the one filming the lab. The small screen only allowed part of the room to be seen. Switching on the small speaker to the room, Tashi stared inside. Yerodin, the clan's doctor and lead scientist, spoke with her first cousin, Kumi Bomani Shayera. Her cousin was the chief of her guards, a strong warrior who she could count on. Two other members of the guard team were with him, Paki and Azikiwe.

Her eyes roamed along each male frame to see if perhaps one of them were wounded, but no site of blood or injury could be seen.

"So, what is the hold up? You had her here this morning, why did you not draw her blood?" Kumi Bomani stood like a fortress, his thick arms crossed over his chest.

Yerodin eyes shifted around to each of the men around him. *Surrounding him?* Tashi's own eyes shifted at them men. *What is going on?* She wanted to ask, but instinct told her to remain quiet.

"I-I-I did. But the analysis shows as I suspected. The DNA shift is only temporary." Kumi Bomani took a step toward him. "Now... is not the time?" Yerodin was nervous and it was very evident in the hesitance in his voice.

"What is the hold up? I have been waiting for months." Kumi Bomani stepped closer. "If you are stalling..." his words died off, but his growl became pronounced.

Yerodin ran his fingers through his hair making his normal unkempt strands appear more wolf-like.

Tashi's body stiffened. *Something's not right. Yerodin was always odd, but never nervous, especially not in his own lab.*

"I'm not stalling. There is nothing that can be done. I told you that the blood needed for the serum has to be taken in wolf form. When it is purest. However, there are other options."

"Causing her to attack and bite me would bring division among the people." Kumi Bomani's words were menacing, barely audible. "We have tried everyone? No one else will work?" he growled and began pacing.

Yerodin shook his wild mane. "Until she conceives, she is the only pure royal line left."

Stopping, Kumi Bomani gazed at the doctor and the other man around. "Mine should have been enough."

Yerodin stepped out of Kumi Bomani's path. "Because your mother was human and never became--"

Kumi Bomani stopped. "I know of my mother!" He howled, barked and shift into a horrific lycan-like beast, sending beakers and tubes full of liquid into a shattering mess on the floor.

Tashi's breath locked in her throat as the room captured in the screen fell silent. She'd never seen anything so horrific in her life. Her cousin had not shifted into his wolfen form as their pack had done for centuries. No. He'd become some massive hind-leg nine foot monster. His ears lay flat as his head pressed against the ceiling.

Paki and Azikiwe observed the monstrosity with their eyes spread wide and filled with envy.

Her friend began to whimper beside her at the sight. She grabbed Danuwa wrist sending the message for her to keep silent. Even though the secret passages were sound proof, the last thing Tashi needed was Danuwa's fear surrounding her. She watched as Danuwa placed her palm over her mouth, quelling her whimpers. Danuwa was a beta female, who on occasion still acted as a new cub.

Trembling, Tashi could feel her wolf demanding to be released to fight and protect her people as she faced the lab once again.

Now having shrank and returned back to human form, Kumi Bomani leaned naked and weak against a table, his clothes that had split upon his rapid change, lay in tatters on the floor surrounding his feet.

Yerodin mumbled as he stooped to the floor collecting the shards of glass. "I told you the shift will not last long. Only with pure blood can it be made permanent."

"W-we are running out of time, sir." Paki interrupted. "Soon, Leult Tashi will go into heat and she is sequestered, no one but Danuwa and the other women are allowed around her."

"This would not be a problem if you could convince her to take you as her mate. Then we could have the blood of the child for our army," Azikiwe her cousin's second in command, commented.

Tashi shook her head in silence. She would never take her cousin as her mate. Before her feelings did not lean her toward him. And now… She could not conceive of it.

"I am tired of waiting. Her repeated refusal aggravates me." Her cousin resumed his full height and took a deep breath, appearing calmer and renewed in strength. "At the Hunter's Moon, she will feed heavy because of her coming time of confinement. Then I will take what is mine."

"The blood only, right?" Yerodin asked.

The sinister smile curved Kumi Bomani's mouth. Apprehension slid down her spine and her claws came forth. Her wolf wanted to launch at him and rip out his heart. Tashi could not believe what she was hearing from the people who were closest to her. She thought she could trust them with her life and they were plotting against her. Her cousin's voice drew her attention once again.

"Yerodin, do not concern yourself with matters that are none of your business. You will have her wolfen blood to concoct a more permanent serum. I will use it to inject Were's and human's who will pledge allegiance to me.

"It can't be used on humans. It will be too strong--"

"Unlike Tashi I will give everyone the gift who desires it. Then I will lead the most powerful army." Kumi Bomani's chest swelled. "The most powerful Were's and everything will be mine for the taking. Ethiopia. Africa. Europe… I will have what was supposed to belong to me all along. I have played second long enough. My father was a fool. He should have snatched what was his right." His arm sliced through the air. "No more waiting. Now my time has come. No Were, man or royal bitch, will be able to stop me." Laughter erupted from him like vengeful lava spewing from a volcano's center.

Unable to take anymore, Tashi switched off the volume. Her knees weakened and she collapsed to the floor. "This can not be happening," she mumbled.

"Leult…" Danuwa kneeled in front of her.

"How did you discover this?"

Looking shame faced, Danuwa turned her head away. "Azikiwe."

Tashi knew that her assistant and Azikiwe had been lovers off and on, but was her friend even plotting against her? "So, you planned this--" Pushing away from the wall, Tashi moved back up the cave passages until she reached her quarters in the palace.

"No, Leult Tashi, no." Danuwa whispered, jogging to keep up with her strides. Once they crossed into the room, Danuwa fell to her knees grabbing the hem of her robe and pressing it to her forehead. "I would never conceive at betraying you in anyway. I pretended that I would keep Azikiwe's secret but quickly I come to you." She began to weep. "Please believe me, Leult Tashi."

Glancing down at the bowed head of her assistant and friend, Tashi placed her hands on Danuwa's hair. "No worries, I believe you. Now, you must help me."

"Anything." Danuwa released her clothing and rose. "You want me to call the guards. Awake everyone in the palace and tell them of the mutiny against you?"

Crossing the room, Tashi rushed into her closet. "No. I can not risk it. Kumi Bomani was correct, division of the pack can not be put at risk, jeopardized. This country has seen enough war and destruction." From her closet she removed a rucksack and began to fill it. "I must go. Draw them out. Away from the pack."

Pacing at the doorway of the closet, Danuwa feet came to a halt. "Go? That is a great idea." She nodded. "I will get my things."

Tashi grabbed her friend as she turned to rush toward the door. "No. Danuwa, you must stay."

Perplexity obscured Danuwa's features. "Who will go with you?"

Shoving the last few article's in the bag, Tashi changed into slacks and boots. "No one. I do not know how far my cousin's toxic deception has spread." She pulled the bag onto her back. Staring at her friend, she continued, "I do not know who I can trust."

"Leult Tashi, you always have my faithfulness." Danuwa drop to the floor once again. "What do you require of me?"

Even though earlier she had questioned her friend, she no longer had doubts. Their were people who would give their life for her. It was her job as princess of the pack to protect them. "In a few days Kumi Bomani and his guards will come to take me to feed. He will discover I am not about. When he questions you, Danuwa, do not cover. Tell him I have traveled away."

With anxiety filled eyes, Danuwa said, "But he will come for you. You know he will not stop until he has what he wants. Your blood. Your Power. With the tracking chip he can find you."

"Exactly. But I will deal with him on my terms. I want him off of my land and away from my pack." The sour taste of bile rose up the back of her throat at the thought of her cousin's trickery. Her wolf clawed inside of her. With Kumi Bomani after her blood it was too dangerous for her to shift, she quelled her wolf. This was not the time.

Taking Danuwa's hand in her own, she squeezed them and looked at her friend. "Once he leaves, go to Tegene. Tegene protected my father. He is older, but a wise Alpha wolf." Picking up a piece of paper, she wrote a note, then scribbled her signature. "Give this to him. It is my word that he is in charge of the pack until I return."

"But--"

"I will return." She silenced her friend.

Danuwa nodded. "Where will you go? You are strong, but can not fight them alone."

Strutting towards the door, she said, "I do not plan to fight alone. There is a pack that is mighty and strong. One who has stood against many attacks and their stories were told to me by my father."

"Yes." Excitement laced her words. "Who are they? Where are they, Kenya, Botswana, Cairo?"

"The Temple pack is in America."

Oliver's breath remained steady, as if he were at rest. He'd lost count of the days he'd been lying on the mat covered floor in the Shaman's chukka. His eyes were dry from the smoke created by the incense filling the small room, fanned by Silver Foot the old wolf shaman. Through the haze of his mind and gaze every thing around him was out of focus, except her. Even now, as he came out of the trance and the mumbles and rhythmic singing of the man who'd watched over him, called him out of the spirit world, he could still see her.

Her skin, the color of midnight, reminded him of his favorite treat. And just like black licorice her skin held a proud radiant shine with no apologizes, silky smooth. "I am black, because the sun has looked upon me," an old scripture verse whispered in his mind as he gazed upon her image. Unable to see her face, he had no idea of who she was, but he wanted to touch her. But just as he had done many times before he reached out to her. His hand once again attempted to stroke the image that was trapped in his mind. It called to him as if it had been pulled from the soul of his wolf. He wanted her. He craved her.

She is mine. His wolf cried inside of him.

Oliver, the man, allowed his arm to fall heavy with a thud back upon the mat. Exhaustion rested in his pores mingling with the smoke that scented his skin. He had come here to bond deeper with his wolf. Come here to find peace and direction. However, coming here had been a mistake. Now not only was he without his pack brothers and sisters, but now he was haunted by a mysterious woman.

"I need to get out of here," he croaked using vocal cords neglected during his time in the medicine man's chukka. Rolling to his side he struggled on weak trembling arms to push himself up to a sitting position.

"Yes. It is time. You have seen your promise. Destiny. You and your wolf now go on to your future." Silver Foot babbled his gravely wisdom, as if sure of his words.

Shaking his head, Oliver eyed the Choctaw Indian. "I have seen nothing, old man. Confusion still rests before me like fog. There is no destiny. No promise of my path." Turning his back on the old man's knowing gaze. Oliver breathed deep attempting to right his world, before standing. "I can't take anymore old man."

"Man has been known to do amazing things when they least expect it."

"No more riddles and games." Even as he said it, he was amazed how much his wolf wanted him to change and travel all over the world looking for this woman. His mate. That was not going to happen. He'd come here for direction, but that was not the one he was going to take. He would be no better than his brother Malcolm being lead by the piece of flesh between his legs. Discouraged, he stood and asked, "Silver Foot, can't you just call a blessing upon me that will give me guidance?"

Glancing back at the silent wise man, he noticed the Shaman had shifted to a white wolf, with fur the color of cotton except for one front paw, a soft silver hue. The Shaman's intense eyes, appeared as two hematite stones surround by snow assessing him. Then turning, Silvered Foot headed toward the exit of the small structure.

Taking this as the shaman's confirmation that it was time for him to go, Oliver grabbed his meager belongings and dressed. Sighing, he followed the wolf out the door.

Chapter Two

After hours on his bike from the reservation, Oliver stopped his Suzuki in front of his cabin. This was his home. With its' over grown vegetation and all, it was his. He didn't get to visit it as much as he liked. He barely made a trip out every few months. Most of the time he stayed at the Temple ranch, because it was closer to the casino. However, his pack brother Malcolm was currently residing there on a honeymoon with his new hell hound wife.

A tremor inside let him know his wolf was not happy, but he pushed it aside. He wasn't here to reconcile himself with his brother's decision. Malcolm was a grown wolf and could choose his own mate. For a moment, the thought of his pack sister Iva crossed his mind. He sent a prayer up to the Great Spirit for his protection of her. As an Alpha female, she could hold her own, but she was extremely hurt and angry with Malcolm's decision and he couldn't help but worry about her.

Even for her, he couldn't allow his thoughts to waver. No, he was here for himself. His wolf.

Gazing back down the dirt path he stared at the wood structure. Unlike the ranch an hour outside of Vegas, his cabin sat on five acres of land just off Interstate 15. He was as close to the California state line as he could get without crossing over, almost a no mans land after Clark County. Even tree hugging tourists didn't venture this far once they got into the heart of the mountain area.

He could see the stretch of interstate from his porch, but that wasn't the view he wanted. It was what he got from his back porch, the southwest end of the Potosi Mountains. The unyielding rugged terrain beckoned him.

Getting off his Suzuki, he walked it up the driveway and into the port on the side to protect his ride from the strong Nevada sun. Entering the house from the side door, he stopped. Something was off. His wolf went on alert.

Slowly, he pushed the door closed behind him and glanced around his living room. Nothing appeared out of place. The sheets over the furniture were undisturbed, but he could feel the hairs on the back of his neck become stiff. Someone had been here. That wasn't an unusual occurrence, hikers traveling around the mountains frequently stopped by his place.

He took a step toward the hall and froze. Someone was still in his home. The subtle and foreign scent played with his olfactory sense. Following the smell he crept down the hall toward the single bedroom.

As he progressed the aroma became stronger, overpowering as he prepared to move past his bathroom, halting him midstride. Catching the sight of someone in his peripheral view he shifted his stance, preparing for an attack. A woman, his mind registered, before he found himself seized by instant desire as he'd never known before.

His knees went weak as his wolf clawed and whined inside of him wanting to get out as the fragrant blend of tuberose and calla lily tantalized him. Beads of sweat popped out along his forehead and the scent of his own sweat mingled with hers, making an erotic cornucopia of images flutter before his eyes. His skin tightened with lust, causing his fingers to tingle and his shaft to become erect.

"Damn."

Oliver pressed his back against the cool wall and stared. The woman lay on the tile floor, her face away from him as blood leaked down her skin from long slashes along her back. Claw marks and gashes covered her shoulder blades and the small of her back. She was nude accept for the towel wrapped around her hips.

Full hips, made perfect for a man hands. His hands.

Three things that he noticed instantly, she needed his help, she was a Were and she was in heat.

More importantly, there was no doubt, she was the woman from his vision.

Her unmarred skin was dark as ebony. "Rise up, my love, my fair one, and come away." Once again his mind was inundated with the lover's scripture as he moved toward her and knelt down. He didn't touch her. Instead he attempted to see if she was hurt anywhere else. Not noticing anything, except the blood on her fingers that let him know she had made the obscure marks herself.

Why?

He'd heard of wolves gnawing off their own paws to free themselves from a hunters trap. However, the scratches on the she-wolf's back didn't make sence. Sniffing around her, he assured himself that she hadn't consumed any poisonous plant from the mountains that may have caused her to hallucinate and attack herself. Nothing peculiar was detected, just more of her scent.

He had been holding off touching her, almost afraid. If his body was stirring out of control from her scent he could only imagine what would happen when their skin touched.

"Well, it's got to be done." He spoke out loud to himself.

The woman remained still, unmoving.

Slipping his arms gingerly beneath her shoulder and legs he rolled her to him. He did his best not to hurt her or place too much pressure on her back, but it was practically impossible once he had her cradled in his arms. Staring down into her face he was awestruck.

To say she was beautiful was an understatement. Her braids were high and tight, forming a bun on the crown of her head leaving her features revealed. Her oval shaped face was graced with high cheekbones, eyes that were slightly tilted up in the corners, a proud nose and lips full enough to kiss for hours. He wanted her to open her eyes so he could see their color. Were they brown, black or the color of moss that grew deep in the forest?

Continuing his perusal he noticed the slender column of her neck. Her smooth skin beckoned him further. His observations took him passed the curve of her shoulders and on to her full, bare breasts. Breast that sat high and round, the size of mango's and nipples as dark as raisins. It would have taken little effort to lift her to his waiting mouth for a sample of such delectable treats. Holding her so close allowed the complexity of her exotic scent to envelope him.

He took mental hold of his raging hormones and his wolf. Mother Esther Temple would have chided him on his manners toward a wounded woman. Turning, he headed toward his bedroom.

"Ay tänäka," she moaned and attempted to push against his chest.

Pausing only briefly in stride, Oliver heard her words, but had no clue what she was saying. He easily deciphered her accent as being African from his travels, but other than that he had no clue of which country in the Mother Land.

"Try and stay with me. I need to check your wounds." He spoke to her, even though as quickly as she'd spoken, she returned to her previous state of unconsciousness.

He assumed it was due to the amount of blood she had lost. Kicking his door open, he crossed the room and placed her on her stomach in the center of the bed.

Why hasn't she shifted? He pondered. The cuts on her back were deep, but not to bad that her wolf would not have been able to heal her. Maybe she'd passed out, before she had a chance.

"That's okay, beautiful, I'm going to take care of you, then your wolf can do the rest."

Sounds came from her parted lips again, but they could barely be heard. Oliver readjusted her towel over her hips, refusing to give his wolf the opportunity of looking at the treasure covered underneath.

Leaving the room, he returned to the bathroom. Pulling a towel from underneath the sink he tossed it over the small pool of blood on the floor. He'd clean it up after he saw to the woman from his vision.

Grabbing a washcloth and his first aid kit from the medicine cabinet, Oliver went to the kitchen for a bowl of water and returned to the room. Sitting on the bed beside her he looked at her again.

How did she get here? Why is she here? Why did she harm herself?

As the questions volleyed around in his head, he cleaned her back with the water so he could better see the wounds.

His vision sighed once, then settled back into the bed. When he began applying the medicine to her cuts she cringed away from him once then remained unmoving.

Opening a wide bandage he spread it over her abrasions and gashes. He could already see small signs of her healing. But, it would be a slow process if she didn't shift.

Now that her skin was cleared of blood, he rolled her to one side than the other as he removed the dust cloth from his bed and slipped her underneath the blankets.

She needed rest and he needed to straighten up the bathroom and fix some food. He was starving. Fasting was part of his spiritual journey while he had been in the chukka and he couldn't recall when he'd eaten before that.

Before he left, he couldn't resist touching her. Reaching his hand out, he slid a finger along the side of her face. Her skin was like warm satin, soft and inviting. Moving across the curve of her shoulder and down the length of her arm until he reached her fingers splayed on top of his pillow.

Not stopping to consider what he was doing or why he did it, Oliver laced his fingers with the she-wolf's slender ones. Holding her hand, he stroked his thumb over the backside of hers.

Mine.

His wolf called out. The force, determination and possessiveness of the single word shook him to his core. Releasing her hand, he rose abruptly.

Exiting the room, he closed the door silently behind him. Entering the bathroom, he stared into the mirror, into the onyx pools of his own eyes.

"She is not mine. Can not be mine. She is not even from this country."

The wolf reminded him of his vision.

"It was only because she needed help. She's hurt. That's all."

Shaking his head, Oliver refused to listen to his wolf. This was just more proof that he and his wolf were not in sync.

Gathering the bloody towel from the floor he placed it in the small waste basket by the toilet and began spraying cleaners on the tile. Putting more effort than was needed into the scrubbing he ignored his wolf's whinnying about the woman being his mate.

After the bathroom was in order, he took out the trash and opened some cans of soup for dinner. He would have preferred a large steak from the casino restaurant or even better a fresh caught rabbit, but with his visitor unwell he needed to be close to home. While the soup heated, he prepared his home for his stay.

He didn't know how long he would be there, but removing the dust covers kept him busy while he awaited his food to get hot.

Later that night, Oliver sat in the dark in a chair beside his window staring at his houseguest. He'd spooned a few drops of broth into her mouth, hoping to arouse her enough to eat so she could regain some of her strength and shift. But she refused all of his beseeching words to change into her wolfen form.

From where he sat, he could easily see the beads of sweat rising on her forehead and the side of her neck. She was becoming feverish from her wounds.

She needed to shift. He had no idea how long she had laid on his floor bleeding. Her human body was not strong enough to fight off fever or an infection without strong medicine.

Even with the mountain ranger station down the road within fifteen miles, he didn't want to have to use that option. He lived undisturbed out here and he wanted to keep it that way. As night fell, she became more restless. He watched the waxing moon's beams shower her skin with a seductive glow. Earlier he'd bathed and changed into a t-shirt and sweat pants. Now with his growing erection he was grateful for the comfortable attire.

Mate or not, the pungent sophisticated floral scent of her heat called out to him. The purity of her smell made him acutely aware that no other mate had claimed her. She was within his reach and his for the taking.

There was no way he'd make a move on an injured female wolf. That was crass and low, a way he didn't bend to. However, if she shifted and sprinted into the mountains, he wouldn't hesitate to give chase.

The woman began tussling with the covers, in a feverish fit. Moving across the room, he rested a calming hand on her shoulder. Her skin was hot to the touch as he mopped her brow with a cool wet cloth.

She settled some, but not completely.

"Shift, sweetheart." He swiped the towel across her forehead. "I need you to shift." He whispered in her ear, calling to her inner spirit.

"Ay…ay," she muttered over and over again, as she squirmed on the sheets. "Ay."

Somewhere deep in her mind, she was refusing to change. Oliver didn't understand why, but neither did he have time to discuss it with her. If he didn't get her body healed soon, she wouldn't make it through the night. Short of picking her up and dragging her bodily through the Nevada plains until she became angry enough to shift and attack him, there was only one other thing he could do. Help her heal.

Fisting his shirt with one hand, he pulled it over his head, then removed the blanket from her body. Crawling on the bed beside her, he called on the aid of his wolf. He didn't allow himself to change but he needed its healing properties in his salvia. Peeling the remainder of the blanket off her body, he stared transfixed for a moment. The towel that had been around her waist earlier was long gone among the tangled bedding, now she lay on top with only the thin sheen of sweat over her body.

Oliver felt the growl rumble in his chest and move into his throat, he stifled it. Resisting the temptation to howl at the moon in thanksgiving, he reached out and removed the sticky bandage from her back. Tossing it to the floor to be discarded later, he inhaled deeply then began. Straddling her hips, he started at her neck and executed a series of slow, long licks across her skin.

The first taste of her flesh was metallic from the multiple wounds covering most of her back, but still pure nirvana to his senses. He felt outside of himself. As if the heady flavor of her body filled his soul and took him to a place of ecstasy he'd never known before.

Surely, this was an illusion. A trick of the mind played on him by the night and the coming Hunter's Moon. The lunar tide had captured his senses and made him delusional.

Whatever the cause, both man and wolf were enjoying the moment.

His tongue swirled and flicked across her skin, drink deeply of her essence. The feel of her skin drawing tighter as her wounds began to pull together, filled him with relief.

Her body trembled against his tongue and her sighs tickled his ears. These tremors were slightly different than the shivers that rocked her body when he first began.

The scent of her arousal kicked up another notch, letting him know that even in her sickness she was not immune to the desire between them.

He licked down her side, feeling the cushiony pillows of her breast against his mouth. If he but slipped his tongue down an inch he would easily be able to swirl the tip around her nipple. Instead, he back tracked and gave the same treatment to the other side. His canines elongated and he wanted to nip her skin, mark her as his, but he restrained himself. Instead he continued licking down her spine and around the sides of her waist.

She began to calm and her body stilled.

Aware that his services were no longer needed, Oliver couldn't deny his wolf the treat of laving the round globes of her bottom. He allowed his tongue to glide down the crease that split the two glorious halves. The scent of calla lilies became stronger, cloaking him like a blanket and filling his mind with lustful images.

"Hmm," she moaned and arched toward him. The sound of a woman's enjoyment was the same in any language.

Forcefully, he pulled himself away. He'd barely kept himself from tasting the delectable treat he truly wanted to savor, the sweet nectar at the crest of her thighs. The place on her body he desired to mark as his and his alone. Placing even more distance between them, he leaned back on his haunches.

She returned to a quiet rest, as he collapsed beside her and stared at the ceiling.

"This is going to be a long night." He considered the possibility of going to the couch, but he didn't fool himself. There was a need inside him to be near her.

So, he didn't argue, he just pulled the blanket up over both of them and stayed.

Chapter Three

Tashi snuggled deeper into the warmth of the covers and curved her body around a pillow in the predawn hours. The feeling of security and relaxation enveloped her. Anything was better than the pain and fever of the night before. She had felt hopeless, desperate and alone. And saw no way to get to or contact the help she would need for her people. The fear of Kumi Bomani catching up with her had pushed her toward creating her wounds. It had been a mistake. It had been pure misery not to allow her wolf to take its form and heal her body. But, she couldn't risk it. It was the safest choice while her cousin was hunting for her. And she knew they were tracking her. Her cousin wanted ultimate power and considering his words, she was the only one who could give it to him. Today she would find a way to locate the Temple pack.

Pushing aside the thought of her cousin, she allowed herself a few more moments of peace. Her peace gave way to her arousal. Last night she had been so feverish, she'd become delirious with erotic thoughts.

Her body pulsed with desire. Ached for fulfillment. Even now, her mind conjured up the smell of a male wolf, piquant and robust like coffee. Not any male, but an Alpha. Strong and powerful enough to give her what she needed.

The swelling and throbbing of her sex became unbearable as she hugged the firm pillow tight and pressed it between her legs to quell the longing. Being a princess had its disadvantages. She had to suffer her time of heat alone until she chose a mate.

Blocking out her yearnings, she focused on the sounds around her. The early morning birds called to her. They sounded foreign to her ears. It wasn't the haa-haa-haa-haa sound of the Wattled Ibis, but something else. More of a rhythm and a beat. Like ceremonial drums surrounding her. Not avoiding the seductive thumping her body moved on its on natural course as her hips gyrated and rotated in concert with the sound. The beat of her heart matched its pace.

Unable to hold back the moan of satisfaction, she allowed it pass her lips, "Mmm--"

"If you continue to move like that sweetheart, you're going to make me break my promise."

A rumbling through the pillow and under her ear interrupted her utterance and brought her movements to a halt. *Has Kumi Bomani discovered me?*

Launching herself to a seated position, Tashi stared into the intense dark eyes of a man. No, a Werewolf.

"Tadiyas." She clutched the blankets to her body. Evidently she had not been lying on a pillow.

The man's face scrunched into a frown as he continued to observe her.

Used to speaking in Amharic, Tashi realized that he most likely did not understand what she had said. "What is going on? Why have you touched me?"

"I wasn't the one crawling and rubbing against your thigh, beautiful." His voice, it rolled like thunder before a storm, low and pronounced.

Her face became hot with anger. "Do not mock me."

"Never that." The man rolled to his side and propped his head on his hand. With her fierce hold she had on the blanket it left him without. He was bare to the waist. His chest was sculpted like fine art covered with warm caramel. He was golden. The sight made her mouth water.

"I don't mind you looking, but I'm going to expect a turn."

Returning her gaze back to his face, she eyed him through squinted lids. "What's going on? Why are you in this bed with me?"

"It's my bed." One side of his mouth lifted in a half smile.

Shaking her head firmly, Tashi said, "The house was barren, neglected. What is your proof? Who are you?"

"I'm Oliver. Oliver Montague." He sat up then rose from the bed.

"This is my house and it's just the way I like it, believe me."

Confident and self assured, were the words that came to mind as Tashi watched Oliver get out of the bed. He might be telling the truth about the house being his, but that did not mean that she could trust him. "If this place is yours then return my clothing and I will go."

"No." Standing at the foot of the bed he stared at her.

"Ay?" Trepidation caused her to slip back into her native tongue and grip the covering tighter to her nude form. "Do not tell me, you mean to hold me a prisoner."

Leaning forward, he placed his hands on the footboard. "When I hold you, it will be what we both want."

Tashi's heartbeat accelerated at his words. "Then let me go. It is not safe for me to stay here."

Oliver shook his head. "It's not safe for you to travel still injured."

The tightness and slight soreness, reminded her of her back. What she'd done. What she'd attempted to do. What she failed at doing. "Minor scratches." Tired of this male wolf looking down at her, a position she was not use to, she rose and wrapped the sheet sarong style around her body. The secure material made her feel more confident and in control as she lifted her chin with pride. "I am not your concern."

"Wrong, princess." He resumed his full height, towering above her by a foot even with her tall frame.

Aiming a finger at his chest, she questioned vehemently, "Who has told you about me?"

Oliver folded his arms over his broad chest. "I don't know anything about you, except you're a woman with a lot of questions and very few answers."

She ran her hand over the thick braids surrounding her head. She was confused and weary. *Maybe he does not know who I am. However, when he had called her princess it made her think that her cousin may have contacts in the states and had sent someone to find her.* By now, Kumi Bomani would surely have discovered her absence and would be even now headed to America. She was running out of time. She needed to contact Danuwa.

"If I may have my wardrobe than I can be gone." She mimicked his stance by folding her arms under her breast.

"What you need is to eat, regain your strength and shift so your body can heal fully. In whatever order you chose."

"My body is not your concern."

It wasn't only the growl emitting from him that put her on alert, but his quick movement as well placing him in front of her. "Let me be the judge of that."

Her normal reaction to another wolf challenging her word would have been to pounce and take them down, letting them know she was in charge, a strong force to be reckoned with. She was the ruler of her people not only by birth right, but more importantly by strength. Dominance.

With this wolf, Oliver, she felt apprehension for the first time. Not because she feared he would do her harm. No, it was not malice that she witnessed in his eyes, but hunger. Pure unadulterated animal lust.

That look made her take a step back. She had seen that same desire in the eyes of her cousin many times. But her cousin's gaze never made her feel what she was experiencing now standing before this great wolf.

Within a blink all of her senses became hypersensitive. Her skin became ticklish as if she could feel each hair on her body swaying in the electric current surrounding them. Sweat rolled down her spine coating her tender back. Her nipples tightened and pressed against the sheet and her thighs became slick. Even more powerful she could smell him. As if it were the first time she had smelled a male wolf on this level. His scent was earthy and spicy, reminding her of teff grass. The strong wheat lovegrass of her homeland.

She saw his nose twitch and knew this man was aware of the changes in her body. Of her heat. Use to being alone during her time, she felt lost in the unfamiliar territory.

"You know my name, what is yours?"

Still not sure if she could trust him, she answered vaguely, "Tashi."

Oliver lifted a single eyebrow and she knew that it hadn't escaped him that she'd only given her first name. He moved closer, closing the distance between them and placed his mouth beside her ear. "Why don't you shift, Tashi? For both our sake."

Initially, when she had begun her journey she'd been afraid of shifting and giving her cousin the advantage of taking her blood. But, now she resisted allowing her wolf out, because she knew within moments she would be mounted by this male. Her wolf would give herself quickly and willingly. With animal instinct as her guide, her wolf would seek to ease the ache.

What scared her was that for the first time in her life she wanted to be taken, dominated, by a force stronger than her. Oliver was definitely that.

Pushing away from him, she took a deep breath to clear her head. Not stopping her feet until she was at the door, she said, "You were correct, Oliver. I should eat and regain my strength. Then I must go."

She exited the room, and walked up the hall to the kitchen. There was no need for her to turn her head and see if he was behind her. She knew with ever fiber of her being, he was following. Closely.

Oliver took several bites of food as he watched Tashi in silence. There was something about this mystery woman. Something other than her heated scent driving his hormones crazy, she was an enigma. Sitting at the kitchen table with her back stiff as a pole, she ate out of her bowl of canned beef stew and rice in a delicate manner.

The nonperishable fare wasn't the best breakfast, but he didn't stock his shelves for company. A few miles down the road was a small gas station store that sold basic supplies for hikers, similar to what he already had. However, Tashi consumed her food as if she was sitting in a fine dining restaurant.

His ear perked up as he heard the coffee pot switch to warmer as it ceased percolating. Getting up, he poured them both a cup. It was the only thing he had in the house to drink until he went to the gas station store down the road. Grabbing a small can of evaporated milk from the cabinet and a glass jar full of sugar from the counter, he put them on the table. Returning, he took his seat and placed the hot brew before her.

He sipped his own, preferring it without sugar or cream.

Lifting her cup she smelled it. Maybe she was one of those 'don't talk to me before I've had my morning coffee' people. Small creases wrinkled her smooth brow, before she took a taste.

Quickly, she spit it back in the cup with a look of disgust on her face as she shoved it toward the center of the table to join the condiments. "That must be what evil tastes like."

Taking offense, he said, "Hey, that is one of the best brands available and I pride myself on making a fine pot of coffee."

"Maybe you should take pride in something more promising," she declared with earnest.

Laughter erupted from him, shocking them both. "Maybe the cream and sugar will cut it to your palates satisfaction."

Observing him cautiously, she said, "I doubt anything could make that transform into what I am accustomed to drinking."

"I'll have to take your word for that and I'll concede."

A hush fell over the room once more as they resumed eating.

Breaking the silence again, he asked, "So, you care to tell me now why you're running?" He took another bite of food.

Not making eye contact with him, she kept her gaze downcast and paused only a moment in eating. "Who says I'm running?"

He was disappointed that she wouldn't look up. He wanted to see her eyes again. She had the most magnificent forest green eyes that he desired to lose himself in. Consuming the last bite of food, Oliver pushed the bowl away. "Of course not, sweetheart. You're just out for a nature hike."

Taking one last bite she set her spoon down and finally looked at him. "Why is any of this your concern? I already said I would leave your house."

Oliver didn't know the answer to her question. He'd been silently asking himself the same thing. Why was he so concerned with this she-wolf? Hadn't he come here to align himself with his wolf, having Tashi around would just get in the way of that. Or would it?

"Humor me."

Rising from the table she grabbed her dishes. Moving to the trash can, she scrapped the remainder of her food out of the bowl then crossed the small area to the sink. "I think not, Oliver."

He watched her turn on the water, admiring the sheet still hanging securely around her body. "Why did you come to my house, Tashi?"

"If I had known someone lived here, I would have continued moving."

"This is not the type of area that people come to by chance. Everyone who comes here are coming for the mountains or on their way further up I-15 to Vegas." He picked up his own dish. "I didn't see a car out front which means you didn't drive in."

Tashi glanced at him over her shoulder, and he noted the shadows of uncertainty filling the emerald pools.

They were strangers; she had no reason to trust him. But he wanted her to.

She resumed washing the dishes without responding.

Standing, he walked up behind her, placed his bowl in the warm sudsy water she had made and felt the slick heat of her hand. She didn't pull away immediately as she'd done earlier. Putting his mouth beside her ear, he asked, "Are you in trouble, Tashi?"

He knew when she took a deep breath as her shoulder rose and sank, causing her back to brush against his chest.

Kindness told him to step back and give her space. At that moment he wanted to be a lot of things but kind wasn't one of them.

"Please, Oliver, just let me go on my way."

Seizing her arms, he swung her around to face him. "Look, Tashi, no more riddles and games. I know you're in trouble."

"You know nothing!" Pressing her hands against his chest, she attempted to push him away.

He held his ground and disregarded her denial. "With your clipped speech and accent, I'll say you're from Africa. How long have you been here? Who are you with?"

Oliver pulled her body closer to his as he bit out each word. Something was coming over him. He'd never experienced the compelling emotions running rampant inside of him now.

"Let me go. My life is not your concern. You, a lone wolf, can not help me," she screamed, anxiety filling her eyes. She shoved hard, fighting her way from him.

The foreboding look in her eyes caught him off guard and allowed her the advantage she needed to break away.

She headed for the door, but he gained on her quick. They tussled around until they fell to the floor and she was pinned under his body, her hands locked above her head by his.

When she arched up from the pain in her back, he rolled them to the side but kept his hold on her. Breathing hard he stared at her. "Never before have I felt so consumed by someone. I want to protect you and I don't know why." He allowed his words to sink in. "Tashi, I need you to tell me what's going on. Or may the Great Spirit help us both, because I promise I will make love to you right here and not stop until you agree to tell me the truth."

Astonishment filled her gaze as she accessed him, searching as if checking the validity of his words. She must have seen the seriousness of his words because she nodded.

"Please let me rise."

"No more running," he commanded.

Her body relaxed against him and her fingers interlaced with his and squeezed. "No more running," she declared.

Easing his body off hers, he stood then helped her rise. Removing her hand from his, she crossed to the window and stared out at the mountains.

Leaning against the front door, he waited.

Tashi looked at the ridged mountain range in the distance and longed for home and the Eritrean Highlands. However she knew there was no way for her to return until the situation with her cousin had ended. Maybe this wolf--Oliver, he could be the help she needed to get to the Temples. She would confess to him enough that will ease his questions and get her to Las Vegas.

"Let's start with Tashi. Is that truly your name?"

His voice drew her out of her thoughts. Looking at him, she said, "Awon. I am Leult Tashi Shayera."

His brow furrowed. "Leult? Is that part of your first name?"

She smiled. "You could say that." Not translating the truth, she turned back to the window for a moment she took a deep breath. "As you have guessed, I am not from America. I have only recently arrived. I am from Africa."

Hearing his footsteps, she glanced at him. Watching him, she observed his confident stride as he sauntered across the room and claimed a seat on the couch. "Where on the continent?"

"Ethiopia is my home."

"So, Leult, what brings you all the way here? Alone." Onyx eyes filled with inquiry as a single eyebrow arched high.

It didn't sound right hearing him call her princess. A title that was reserved for those under her command. This wolf would be domineered by no one. "Please call me Tashi." Moving to the middle of the room, she stood before him. "I came by myself by choice."

"Why, Tashi?" Leaning back against the cushion of the sofa, he continued, "What would drive a beautiful woman from her home land?"

"Safety. Protection. Adventure," she interjected.

The other brow joined the first. "Are those your reasons?"

His gaze was so intense and searching she had glanced down at her bare feet against the floor. "Awon na Ay. Yes and no." Choosing the seat across form him, she sat on the single chair. "You were correct. I have fled my home country."

She recognized the gesture he made for her to continue. He was not going to interrupt her, but expected to hear what she had to say. With her back erect, she looked directly into his gaze and confessed. "One night I discovered that some people were after my blood."

The bold statement was deliberate, she could have easily given him a little information at a time, but she needed to know if he was scout for Kumi Bomani and sent to guard her until he arrived.

When his brow scrunched tightly and he leaned forward resting his upper weight on his forearms she could see the deep curiosity in his gaze which let her know he didn't know anything about it. However the knowledge eased the tension in her spine. Or he was an excellent deceiver.

"Who?"

"My cousin and his men." Purposely she kept her voice void of emotion.

"Some family you have there."

She wanted to be angry at his mocking words, but could not. Oliver had not spoken, what she had not already thought herself. Kumi Bomani was not operating in the fashion of betäsäb, but that of greed. His own selfish goal.

"What's so significant about your blood?"

"I'm a pure blood."

Nodding, Oliver said, "Your mother and father had the gift of wolf before you were conceived and born."

"Awon," she answered affirmatively.

"So, what does your cousin plan to do with it once he has it?"

Staring at him from her seat, she hesitated for a moment. Once she told him what was going on, there was no turning back. Did she truly want to reveal all to this man? Would he help her if she did, or would he run scared with the possibility of what was to come? Allowing her gaze to search Oliver's onyx eyes a peace came over her for the first time since she'd discovered her cousin's hideous secret. *What is it about you Oliver that makes me want to trust you?* She silently asked.

"To my understanding, there is an injection of a steroid serum mixture." She inhaled, then exhaled slowly, then said, "My father hired doctors and scientist many years ago after the rinderpest brought to our country by the Italians had killed off so many käbt herds. The medical people helped blend our Sheko breed of cattle with Kenya's Boran and Sanga cattle from Botswana. Now through coercion, threats or greed my cousin has them working in more sinister fields." Tashi rubbed her arms attempting to stave off the chill in the warm air rushing along her skin. To have been deceived and plotted against behind her back made her angry to think about, however she held onto that anger to assist her in dealing with her cousin when the time came. "They plan to use my blood to create a race of Were's that are massive, vicious and destructive. A race that will allow them to take over Africa and beyond. They would be unstoppable. "

Oliver's eyes tightened at the corners and appeared obsidian as he sat quiet for a moment. "What kind of madness is this?" He shook his head in denial of her words or the possibility, she didn't know which. "How could this happen from your blood?"

Glancing down at her hands fidgeting with the sheet, she said, "I would not have believed it myself if I had not witnessed with my own eyes. I am not sure of exactly what takes place, but with anger or high emotion he can transform. What I gathered was that the effect is temporary without using pure blood. Even more, my blood is strongest while I am in wolf form." She gave him a direct on wavering look, before she continued. "I have not shifted since I learned of his plan. I can not risk it."

"I take it to mean that your cousin's blood will not work?"

Tucking her feet beneath her hip, she said, "Ay. His father was Were, but his mother was human and even though she loved my uncle Wendimu, she refused the gift. Because of this, my cousins blood is that of a Were who was changed after birth."

"As is true with most of my pack." He exhaled a strong and audible breath. "So you escaped. Are you looking for a place to hide? Is that why you are at my home?"

Lifting her chin she stared down her nose at him. She wasn't use to people questioning her courage. "It is not my intention to hide. There are too many that count on my succeeding in my journey."

Not appearing fazed by her look, he continued, "Yet, I found you here and bleeding."

"I needed to use a phone to call my pack." Becoming agitated she unfolded herself and she rose once again. "The clerk said the pay phone at the station had been broken for years, but he never saw a need to have it repaired. I saw your house and thought maybe."

A single shoulder rose and fell as he commented, "I don't have one here. I purposely don't want to be found when I'm here. I even left my cell in my apartment in Vegas."

"So, I discovered." She curled her hand around her neck and rubbed the back of it, an attempt to relieve tension. "My cell did not work out here and I have not gotten through since my lay over in Germany. At that time my absence had not been discovered. So, I will try again in Las Vegas."

"Why didn't you rent a car and drive? Better yet, you could have flown directly to Vegas when you arrived on the east coast."

"I did not know how much time I would have to get there before I was found. The first flight out was to Los Angeles, so I took it." She shrugged. "I met a group of hikers on the last leg of my flight, headed to the mountain and offered me a ride in this direction, so I took it. I did not realize that the area would be so barren. I was considering hitch hiking when I saw your cabin."

"An easy mistake made by a foreigner." He gave her a small smile. "Why Vegas? Why not San Diego, Los Angeles or even Mira Loma? Hell, you could have stayed on the east coast and went to New York."

This she would not tell him. Once she got into the city it would be the end of her and Oliver. If the Temple pack was anything like her father had described, they would help her extricate her cousin forever. "My father once told me of a friend he had in Las Vegas. He said that if I ever needed help to get to him."

His gaze was intense, but he remained silent, allowing her, a bit of privacy. Oliver dragged his hands through his short hair. "Well, you're safe now. You left and they can't find you here, Tashi."

He sounded so confident she almost laughed, but Oliver did not appear to be the type to appreciate the humor at his expense, so she quelled it. "I am not safe. I am never safe. They can find me." She resumed her stance at the window viewing the mountains.

The furniture creaked as it released Oliver weight. She did not turn.

"How?"

Turning, she faced him. "I have a tracking device in my body."

Chapter Four

"What in the hell!" His own voice sounded like an explosion to his ears. Oliver eyed the woman before him from head to her small toes peeking out below the toga style sheet covering her body. Was she crazy? Some kind of alien or sci-fi android?

Even with the intense green eyes staring back at him, he could see the slight turn to the corners of her mouth. Was she laughing at him? Was this all some kind of joke? There was a lot of things he didn't like, being played with was at the top of his list. "You better not be pulling my leg."

Her gaze dropped for a moment to his sweats pants than back up to his face. "Trust me. I do not joke about this, Oliver."

Grabbing her arms, Oliver barked, "Where is it? Who put it there?" The last thing he wanted was some wild, demon morphed pack of wolves bearing down on him unaware. Having to deal with his brother's hell hound in-laws was bad enough. Now this.

She took a deep breath. "My father gave it to me."

"Gave it to you? Like some damn gift?" Searching her neck and arms for any lump that appeared out of place, he asked, "What ever happened to jewelry, Tashi? Chipping is what people do to their pets, not their family."

"Not a gift, but for safety. Everyone in our pack has one. There were times in Africa that we were hunted down for our powers the same way the Ethiopian wolf was hunted and killed or kept as pets. Over the years, famine and poverty have become so prevalent that people became desperate. My father wanted to be sure he could account for our whereabouts if we went missing. My family has always made it a point to protect as many people as we can and to help families with jobs, but we can not give all the gift. It can be easily used unwisely."

He understood what she meant. Since paranormal and human world had begun to co-exist more and more people desired a new adventure. Thrill seekers sought them out like a new tattoo or piercing. Being a Were, Vamp or Witch was the "in thing". The Preternatrural Authorities stayed busy.

"Tashi…" Observing her, he was prepared to question her about where the chip was located when he recalled how he'd found her bloody, torn and unconscious on his bathroom floor. "Turn around."

In his lower peripheral vision he noted the rise and fall of her chest. She remained still for a moment then slowly turned. Tashi didn't utter a word as she presented her back to him. The sheet shimmied around body as she stood before him, waiting. He extended his hand out and laid it on her skin.

Warmth greeted his palm. He slid his fingers over her shoulders and down her spine. Not stopping to consider that he would leave her without cover, without anything protecting her from his view, Oliver yanked the sheet.

A ripping sound and her gasp echoed in the room. His breathing became labored as he observed the now faint scars on her back and her naked form. He brushed his fingers across her delicate skin, tracing her spine until he reached the center of her back. "You tried to remove it on your own?"

"Awon," she whispered on a soft breath. "But it is impossible to reach alone without the proper instruments."

Between her shoulder blades, he could barely feel the slightly raised skin under the pad of his thumb. Some of her scratches had come close, but the skin securing the device was perfectly intact. "What would you like me to do?"

Deep green eyes met his as she glanced at him over her shoulder. "You must take it out."

Was she going to run and leave her pack forever? "Why, don't you want to confront them?"

"I will finish what I have started and meet them on my terms," determination laced her words.

She was right, there was a need to plan and do things right before meeting with her adversaries. "I can understand that. I'll help."

"Thank you, Oliver."

He lowered his hand to her waist, taking a step forward he closed the gap between them. Purposely, he allowed her to feel the harden length of his manhood against her backside, restrained beneath his sweat pants. Pressing his lips to her ear, he said, "After I remove it, Tashi, you will need to shift so that you can not be tracked by your wounds."

"I know," she responded in a breathy whisper.

The trembling of her body and rising scent let him know that she understood the message his body was communicating. Tonight she would shift and become his. Everything else they would deal with afterward.

Sitting in the bathroom on the edge of the tub, Tashi held onto the cold porcelain as her bottom was protected from the hard surface by a folded towel. Glancing over her shoulder she observed Oliver as he stood behind her burning the tip of a kitchen knife with a lighter. After the steel tip was blackened from flame, Oliver wiped it across a small cloth removing some of the soot. Then he poured alcohol over the blade and completed the laymen sterilization.

His gaze met her own across the small room. "You ready?"

"Awon. I am ready." She told him, her emotions all twisted inside of her. Fear of him removing the chip did not play a factor. However, one of the flutters in her stomach did stem from the fact she was sitting naked in a bathroom with a man that was not her mate. A stranger to her. Other feelings were doubts and concerns about whether or not she'd truly be able to stop her cousin and save her pack. The emotion that claimed most of the space was anxiety about her and Oliver, and what was destined to happen between them once the device was removed.

Placing a single hand on her shoulder he must have felt her tremors because he asked. "Are you sure you want me to do this?"

She rounded her back and pulled her shoulder forward, in this area she trusted him. Even though they both knew that a single cut too deep could hit her spine and render her paralyzed, she reassured him, "I am not afraid." When she looked over her shoulder again, her gaze met his and she saw that his eyes had darken with restrained passion that matched her own.

Take a moment to stroke his thumb along the side of her face he smiled at her, causing her heart to miss a beat. He then glanced away and began to concentrate on his job.

The first cut stung. She gritted her teeth, squeezed her eyes and held on tight to the hard porcelain. Oliver spoke to her in low, calming tones telling her what he was doing.

Blocking out the burning pain, she focused on the deep sound of his voice.

"I'm done, Tashi."

She did not know how long it had been since he'd begun, but when she opened her eyes she saw her blood coating his hand and the small thin silver square in the center of his palm. The device was barely a half inch in size.

Reaching out, she picked it up. Turning it to the side she noticed that it was barely as thick as a stick of chewing gum.

"What should I do with it?"

"Take it with us to Vegas and set a trap."

Raising her gaze from the tracker to Oliver, she repeated his word. "Us?"

He stroked her chin. "Yeah, us. I'm going to take you to Vegas."

Tashi admitted to herself that she was have sexual feelings toward this wolf, but other than that she was keep her emotions under tight reign. What ever was developing between the two of them would end in Vegas. This was not her country and she was headed home after this.

"When are we leaving?"

"First things first," he said noncommittally. "I will leave you to shower and wash the blood off. I can put a temporary bandage on you when you're done."

Needing to be alone, she did not argue.

Standing up, she turned on the shower, got inside and closed the curtain behind her. Closing Oliver out. Lifting her face to the warm stream of water, she attempted to close off her mind.

She did not want to think or feel. She just wanted to empty her mind and give herself over to the moment.

As afternoon turned to dusk and then to evening, Oliver gave Tashi her space and allowed the she-wolf to come to grips with the coming evening. They had both showered, cooked and ate lunch in a companionable atmosphere. The more things he learned about her, the more he was beginning to agree with his wolf. This woman was his mate. Now all he had to do was get rid of her cousin and convince her of the inevitable.

She would fit in with the Temple pack. Octavia and Tashi would get along well together. Malcolm most likely could give her a position as an international hostess or head of ballroom activities. The way she carried herself with regal airs, she'd add another level to casino atmosphere. Their high roller guests would love her.

Through out the afternoon he'd kept himself from touching her. Tashi was in full heat now and he'd been digging his nails in his palm over the last few hours not to seduce her. The closer the evening came and the moon dawning, the stronger her aroma fermented the air. Enticing him to seek her out. He'd lost count of how many times he caught himself moving toward her, frequently reminding himself that he wasn't a pup and could control his urges.

Once he'd almost slipped.

An hour ago they'd been in the kitchen washing the dinner dish and Tashi's hands had begun to shake causing her to drop a bowl. The dish shattered on the floor. He'd stooped down to pick up the pieces and found himself apprehended in the thick aroma cloud of her heat. A more fragrant perfume than the best colognes in Paris. The smell of calla lilies had beckoned him and he'd licked her thigh before he could stop himself. Tashi had whimpered, moaned and then ran to the bathroom and locked herself inside. He'd removed himself from the house until he could trust himself again.

A sable blanket cloaked the desert as night fell and welcomed their wolves to come out and play. This was the time of day Oliver loved the most, the time he'd waited on to take Tashi out. All the hikers were sitting by campfires now and preparing themselves for the night and planning their adventures for the next day's light. This time would allow them the solitude Tashi needed to feed and heal her body completely.

Standing on his back porch, he glanced at the person next to him. Tashi stood there staring off into the dark open space. "It is time." He told her as he removed his shirt.

His voice must have pulled her out of her thoughts, because she turned and looked at him. Noticing his bare chest, her green eyes

79

traveled along his chest then lowered. He noticed the rapid rise and fall of her breast beneath the t-shirt he had given her. Tall, and yet she was so petite in form that his shirt ended mid-thigh. Below it her legs were left bare.

"If you don't stop staring at me like that, we'll never make it off this porch."

Her gaze met his, she smiled and before he knew it, she'd removed the shirt in one sure snatch. "You will have to catch me first."

Before he could blink or respond, she had launched herself off his porch and shifted mid flight. It was the most amazing thing he'd ever seen. Even better than Malcolm, who was a pure breed as well. When she landed on all fours a few yards away a wolf with orange and brown pelt and emerald green eyes gazed back at him. An Ethiopian wolf.

She was smaller than most in his pack, but recalling the wrestling match they'd had earlier in the day and the strength she'd exhibited, he didn't doubt that she was a force to be reckoned with.

A small howlish bark got his attention.

"Are you coming?" She enquired telepathically.

"Nothing could stop me," he called back seconds before he shifted into an ebony colored wolf and joined her. Now that he was in wolf form her scent was even stronger, his tail began to wag in obvious excitement.

"You are a sight to behold. With your fur and eye color you become one with the night."

"I'd rather become one with you," he expressed.

She didn't respond as the moon erupted from behind a passing cluster of clouds. The Hunter's Moon bathed the area with an ethereal tangerine veneer.

Tashi the wolf leaned back on her hind legs and howled loudly at the moon. Oliver joined in and when she ran for the hills he followed, allowing her the lead for the moment. He admired how her powerful legs pressed her paws deep into the earth, kicking up dust in her wake. His wolf relaxed into the pace she set, enjoying the freedom of being out in the night air and mountain range. Before this night was over freedom would be had on many levels.

Invigorated, stuffed and restored to full health Tashi vaulted up on the cabin's back porch and resumed her human form. Oliver was right behind her as he'd been for the last hour. He'd allowed her to direct their path and feed first on the rabbit fare. Never pressureing her to give more than she desired.

However what she desired now was before her as an aroused and naked male. Sweat glistened on both of their bodies from the exertion. But it wasn't a turn off, just the opposite. The smell of his perspiration was an earthy scent like the woods after a heavy rain.

"Being alone with a male wolf. This is all new to me." She spoke barely above a whisper. "Thank you, Oliver for helping me and protecting me while we were out." She moved toward him, closing the gap between them.

"No, I'll always protect you. You are my--"

Sealing her lips to his, she silenced him. She didn't want to hear promises of tomorrow. No, she wanted to rejoice and live in the here and now. Wrapping her arms around his shoulders, she palmed the back of his head and slipped her tongue across his lips.

Needing no more encouragement, Oliver's arms surrounded her waist as he propelled them onto the cabin's wood siding. His tongue entered her mouth as his growl vibrated against her lips.

Lost in the feel of their bodies pressed tight to each other, she did not care that they were close to consummating the sexual act outside like animals. Her wolf instincts were guiding her and she had no urge to stop it.

Pulling away, Oliver trailed his kisses down the side of her neck causing a frisson of heat to follow in his wake. Everywhere his hands and lips touched set her on fire.

When he captured her breast in his palm then licked her nipple she began to tremble. Her head arched back as he captured her beaded peak in his mouth and suckled hard. She never experience the avalanche over emotion assault her body. These sensations were the reason her pack sisters pranced around the male wolves, bitches in heat once they encountered their first mating. No wonder this act had been forbidden to her, except with her single mate. She always thought it was to protect her from males, but apparently she'd been wrong. This made a person weak with need. Insanity was sure to come.

Later, she would evaluate the wisdom of her actions and willingness to succumb to Oliver. But, right now she didn't care about anything else but the man who was steadily licking a path down her belly to the swollen pulsing area at the apex of her thighs.

Pressing her hips against the wall, he held her secure, keeping her in place. She quickly became grateful for his hold once his tongue dipped into the dewy nectar between her legs and laved the full length of her sex. Her legs turned to pudding, causing her to rest her hands on his strong, broad shoulders for support.

Pushing her folds apart with his lips, he dove deep as he guided his agile tongue along her slit, flicking the sensitive bud of her desire with each pass. She cried out, begging and pleading with him for mysterious erotic things she did not know or fully comprehend. But, she knew Oliver was the only one who could appease her ache. Her longing. "My beloved is mine…and I am his…he feeds among the lilies." The passionate words of old burst forth from her mouth as if pulled from her soul by Oliver's salacious caresses.

The moment his thick tongue ventured inside of her, tasting the origin of her essence the moon and earth collided, her world shook and exploded. Still Oliver's devoted mouth drove her higher as he continued to lick her center and nip at her thighs.

The scream that burst from her lungs was half wolf howl, half woman cry. She did not know if she had shifted or remained the same, but moments had passed before she was aware that she was cradled in her lover's arms.

"Oliver," her mind felt muddled and alert at same time as she looked into his midnight gaze.

"In the house, now!" he barked, leaving no room to question his orders.

Launching to her feet, she strutted briskly through the house and down the hall to his room, without once considering her royal lineage as she responded to his command. By the time she crossed the threshold, he was hot on her tail.

Before she made it to the bed, she found herself seized in his arms. Oliver kissed her shoulder and the side of her neck. She clutched at his arms around her waist as he lowered his hand between her thighs.

Her hot juice coated his hand as the rich, heady taste of her sex still seasoned his pallet. The stiff, swollen flesh of her clitoris pressed against the pads of his fingers enticing him to circle it, heightening her arousal. Oliver needed to bury himself inside of her or die trying. There were positions that were optimal for a woman's first time, but his mind was fogged up by the demands of his wolf, who had been to long denied.

Crossing the few feet to the edge of the bed, he ordered, "On your knees."

With curious eyes, she gazed at him as she moved forward. Even if the woman was unclear, her wolf understood his demands. She sank into the mattress, not stopping until she was on all fours before him, palms down and knees bent.

Staring at him with passion filled eyes as she arched her hips high toward him, her hair now loose and falling in waves around her shoulders since her shift. Her glistening, cream coated sex called to him. He had to force himself not to taste her and feast on her nectar once more, but to begin the completion of what they had started on the porch.

"Do not make me wait, Oliver." The husky sound of her voice as she articulated her need was his undoing.

Stepping forth he grabbed her hip and guided his stiff member along her slick folds, moistening himself for the entry of a lifetime. Locking his gaze with her green one, he pushed inside her tight haven. Tashi's teeth bit into her bottom lip as he pressed against the thin barrier he wasn't surprised to find. Pulling out, he gave her a moment to fortify herself then plunged deeply into her, breaking through any resistance.

She cried out, but dipped her back low and surrendered herself to him. He was the captain of their ecstasy, guiding them through waves of pleasure.

One of his hands held her hips firmly in place, while his other caressed the satiny skin of her hips, back and thighs. Her sweat slick flesh was as warm and inviting as cashmere.

When he would have restrained himself, she cried out, "AA-moooon." The word he had come to realize through their conversations meant yes.

He translated her cries to mean yes she wanted this. Yes this felt as good to her as it did to him and she didn't want him to stop.

Following her request, Oliver began to show her the language of love.

The walls of her sex squeezed him tighter pushing him to the edge as his thrust deepened. Her hips bucked back against him, and her claws extended as she tore through the sheets and dug into the mattress. Tashi's cries and mannerism were feral and unrestrained, different from the proper etiquette she normally exhibited. He enjoyed watching her abandonment and felt pride in being the one to institute her transformation.

As he gave himself over to the sensual act, he found himself bewildered when every sensation felt like it was his first time. Every thing became new, like the smell of her skin, the squeezing of her sex around his shaft and the feel of her liquid heat painting his member as if she marked him with her essence.

Even greater than that, he realized he'd lost his soul in the heart of her body as he released himself into her.

Joy as she had never known before pulsed like electric current through her body as she climaxed once again. In an instant, she found herself flat on her back, Oliver parting her legs and fitting himself between them. Her body felt sore and ravaged but she wanted more. She wanted this. She wanted Oliver.

When he buried his long thick length inside of her once again, her energy reached it's pinnacle. She wrapped her legs around his hips as they thrust forward, capturing him, refusing to let this moment pass. His power kindled along with hers as his manhood extended and expanded touching her womb and stroking her soul. Through the haze of ecstasy she noticed his incisors elongate and his eyes turn dark glassy as two onyx jewel. It was not fear that touched her heart at the sight she beheld, but pleasure and excitement even though what was to come should have alarmed her.

Oliver's head bowed with intent and without preamble seized her flesh at the curve of her neck leading to her shoulder and sank his teeth deep into her muscle. Turning her head to the side she availed herself to his marking as her extended claws buried themselves in his back. He groaned in satisfaction as a cool pleasure showered over her.

Chapter Five

"Let him kiss me with the kisses of his mouth: for thy love is better than wine."

Oliver heard Tashi reciting the words from the passionate book of Solomon. He smiled as he pulled her sweat slick frame along his him, enjoying the feel of her curled against his side. Running his hand from her hip to the smooth, unblemished skin of her back, he welcomed the feeling of peace that surrounded him for the first time in months. Mating with Tashi, made his world right and he and his wolf align. Maybe because both man and wolf wanted her beyond reason or shame.

What was it about this woman? Was it a momentary height of pleasure that he was experiencing or was she truly his mate as his wolf claimed?

Glancing down at the top of her head and seeing her hair in wild disarray from her shift and their amorous lovemaking, he knew the answer. There was no doubt in his mind or soul. This woman was his. Whatever the reason the Great Spirit had seen fit to bring her to him.

Now what do I do?

Leaning down he kissed her forehead.

Smiling she looked up at him, and he was lost in the forest depths of her eyes. *I'll never let her go.* His wolf whined and the man agreed. How would he be able to convince her to stay here with him, once the threat against her people had been eliminated?

"What do you think about yäwäsib wädaj?"

His gaze searched her face. "yäwäsib wädaj?"

"My lover," her lips curled up in a small shy smile.

Bowing his head, he kissed her deeply, allowing his tongue to slip between her parted lips and claim her mouth as he'd branded her body as his. "I like that word," he whispered against her lips.

"Good, I have never used it before."

"I know." Fingering the soft cotton of hair surrounding her face, he said, "Tell me about your people. How did you all receive the gift?"

"Like my countries history, the lineage of the gift to my people is almost as long." Her touch was light as it caressed the curve of his shoulder and down his arm. "My people were guards and protector of Makeda or the Queen of Sheba as you may know her."

"Are you trying to tell me that you are related to the Queen of She-
-?"

Her fingers on his lips stop he question. "If you want to hear the story, you must remain quiet."

Oliver nodded, showing her he agreed.

"As I was saying." Tashi lowered her hand. "I am sure you are familiar with the fact that Makeda and King Solomon had a son, Menelik."

His nodded again, maintaining his vow of silence.

She smiled. "When Makeda's son grew older and was called to visit his father, Makeda agreed and selected members of her court to protect her son while he was away from her. One of his guards were from my family."

She settled against him. Oliver loved the sound of her lilt voice as she spoke with pride.

"After Menelik's sojourn and he returned home to his mother, protecting him became our main responsibility. Upon Makeda's deathbed, she spoke with her amakari mänfäsawi, spiritual advisors. After her passing they gave those protectors of her son the gift by her request and royal positions. Once Menelik passed, the men were free to live their own lives. One of those men was my ancestor. The others have left Africa and are scattered around the world. Where I do not know. My family is the only one who has remained in Ethiopia through the centuries. We own several plantations."

Hearing that word made Oliver tense. Even though Tashi's wolf and family lineage went back to times before Christian's Christ, his heritage began with slavery in America and certain words took him back to that time easily. He envied her knowledge of knowing her beginnings. Something that was stolen from him. Because he was black, he knew he had African roots, but from where he would never know without an expensive in-depth search. Breaking into her soliloquy about her family roots, Oliver told her about his life and the Choctaw Indians. "So, here I lay, a former slave. A wolf."

Bring her body above his, she looked down into his eyes. "Well, have no fear, Mr. Montague, our plantations are for cattle and growing 'black gold'."

Wrapping his arms around her, he held her firmly against him. "What is black gold?"

"Buna." She kissed his lips. "Coffee."

Laughing, Oliver lowered his hands and squeezed her hips, pressing her to him as he grew erect. They'd just made fierce love, but he wanted her again. Their time was running short, they would have to leave this place soon, before their blood thirsty visitors showed. "Now I know why you didn't like my delicious morning brew."

"Delicious br--"

Fisting her hair, he guided her mouth to his and kissed her, stealing her words. As much as he loved hearing her voice, he refused to waste anymore of their time talking.

Getting his amorous message loud and clear, Tashi began grinding her pelvic against him and spread her legs until her thighs sandwiched his hips. Without ending their kiss, he reached down and guided his steel like shaft to the opening of her wet heat and thrust inside of her.

At his entry, she gasped into his mouth and her nails, more Were than woman's bit into his side.

Understanding that this act was still new to her, regardless of their earlier adventures, he paused.

"Ay, yäwäsib wädaj do not stop," she moaned.

He loved her blend of both of their language, a verbal illustration of their mating. "Never," he promised as he grabbed her hips and showed her a new position of copulation. His energy over took him as his body hummed as his wolf increased its' power inside of him.

Tashi learned quickly as she rose above him, her breast bobbing in the full moonlight. She was beauty incarnate as her body glistened with sweat and her elongated canines showed as she howled her pleasure for the countless time that night.

Careening down Las Vegas Boulevard, on the back of Oliver's Suzuki motorcycle, the million lights on 'The Strip' blurred around her as her lover weaved in and out of traffic. Tashi clutched the waist of the man who had awakened her body and showed her the strength in her womanhood. She was unsure of where he was taking her in the city, besides his apartment. Unconcerned at the moment, she waited patiently to arrive at their destination where she would be able to call Danuwa for a status report as well as discover a way to locate the Temples.

Turning a corner Oliver guided the bike into a garage. Pulling into a parking space, he killed the motor. Placing his feet on the floor, he held the motorcycle steady as she got off then lowered the kickstand and swung his leg over the top of the bike.

Briskly, she rubbed her hands down her thighs in an attempt to stop the vibrations racing along her skin from being on the bike for more than an hour.

"You okay, sweetheart?" Oliver stepped toward her. "Riding a motorcycle takes some getting use to." The bass in his voice stroked her senses.

Heat radiated along her spine and centered on the bite on the side of her neck. "I am okay." She turned and moved away, she need to start putting distance between them. This was it. They were coming to the end of the line. "So, where are we?"

His arm circled her waist, pulling her against his side. Intense ebony eyes assessed her and searched her face for answers. She was grateful when he didn't question her further.

"This is my job. My apartment is here as well, as I promised."

"That is convenient," she responded with extra cheer in her voice.

"Hmm," the grunt was his only comment.

Taking her hand in his, he steered them down a walkway and passed a sign embossed with Convention Center and Shopping Mall, complete with directional arrows. If this had been another time she would have loved to tour the area, but she was on a mission. Apparently, Oliver was as well, because he barely said two words to her as they moved toward the casino. She told herself that she was okay with the silence. He was probably just as anxious to get rid of her as she was to leave him.

Liar. Her wolf accused, she ignored her.

Once inside, they arrived at a bank of elevators. Oliver reached out and pressed in a code for one of the two that were marked PRIVATE. People scurried pass them, entering and exiting through the automatic doors. In the distance she could hear the rings and chimes of the slot machines, as well as the loud murmur of voices. This atmosphere was a far cry from her palace and plantation. Field workers, her personal staff, attendants, as well as children taking their studies filled the place, but the noise level was nothing compared to this. She wondered how Oliver worked and lived in an environment where one could not hear themselves think.

The dinging of the elevator, signifying its arrival drew her attention.

The door slid open and a medium height white man exited with blue eyes and a wide smile on his face. "Oliver! Man, it's good to have you back."

"Jimmy, it's good to see you too."

Tashi watched the two men shake hands and exchange pleasantries. By Jimmy's cologne scent and the peppery smell of human sweat tickling her nose she knew Oliver's friend was not Were.

"Well, I can see why you've been gone for almost two weeks." Jimmy commented as he tilted his head toward her and their joined hands.

If Oliver's grip had not held hers so firmly, she may have pulled her hand from his. She did not want to give people the wrong impression. She also pondered Jimmy's words. Oliver had been away from work for a while. Was he in jeopardy of losing his job? Where had he been? Even though she been sick, she knew they had only been together for a couple of days.

"There were many reasons for my leave time, but I should be back for good now. But I knew my responsibilities were in capable hands." Turning to her, Oliver released her hand and placed his on the small of her back. "This is a friend of mine name Tashi. Tashi this is--"

"Jimmy." She extended her hand.

"Yes, you're correct." He graced her with one of his infectious smiles and she returned it. Holding her hand his piercing sapphire blue eyes appraised her. For a moment, she witnessed his penetrating gaze changing to a clear aquatic blue and then darkened once again. "A pleasure also to meet Oliver's mate."

Not just human, but a clairvoyant, as well. Well, he missed the mark on this one. Not knowing how to respond she stroked the side of her hair, reassuring herself that Oliver's mark was covered. She had wanted to shift before they left to heal the spot, but he had told her that there was not time. Just as urgent as he, she had gotten on the motorcycle and left.

Oliver's strong hand squeezed the small of her back, she ignored that too.

She pulled her hand away, not wanting this man to see anything else.

Turning back to Oliver, Jimmy said, "I just finished giving the weekly report upstairs, do you want me to brief you?"

A slight pressure on her back, propelled her forward with Oliver into waiting elevator.

"No need having to repeat yourself. I'll get the information from the boss man."

"Will do." Jimmy waved as Oliver pushed the button to the ninth floor.

"Your co-worker seems nice," she commented, as she stared at the changing red numbers.

"Perceptive."

"No one knows the whole of the future," she looked at him, attempting to communicate her feelings. It was difficult because Oliver made her feel feverish and weak in the knees. Her body and mind were at war, one wanted to obey him and follow his lead, the other declare her independence and sovereignty. She made the choices for her life and her people.

When his arm curved around her waist and brought her body flushed with his, her body won this round.

"I don't have to be seer to know what I want…what's mine." His head lowered and he fused his mouth to hers.

Her mind and thought process became vaporous particles in her head, intangible. She was unable to focus on anything but Oliver. He consumed her and made her feel strong at the same time. Burying her hand in his low cut hair she gave into the kiss. Promising herself this was the last time.

Something dinged in the distance and they parted, Oliver lead her out of the elevator and down the elegantly decorated hall. Led by his sense of smell, they arrived at a door with no numbers.

Unlocking the door with a key card from his wallet they entered. Instantly she was enveloped by the warmth of Oliver's heady scent, it denoted the apartment as his.

Anxious, she asked, "Where is the phone I may use for my calls."

He nodded toward the set of doors on the other end of the living room. "The one in my bedroom will get you a call to anywhere you wish."

"Thank you." She headed in that direction, then paused. "Is there a city directory book as well."

Moving into the kitchen, he opened up a bottom door and removed the thick yellow and white book and gave it to her. "I have a few calls to make so take your time."

Oliver watched Tashi's fluid gait take her into his bedroom and close the door. Her nervous agitation was as thick as cheese around her. He was more than aware that she was uneasy with the two of them as mates. But, in the last few months of his life he hadn't been clear on a lot of things, however there was no doubt about his feelings for Tashi. He'd give her time to come to terms with it. After they'd dealt with her conniving cousin, they'd address this issue.

Moving to his end table, he pulled his cell phone from the charger and dialed his sister first.

"Oliver Montague, I'm pissed at you," she vented into the phone when she answered.

"I love you too, Octavia." He smiled at hearing his twin's voice. He may not have known who his parents were, but he would forever be grateful to the Great Spirit for allowing him to have his sister with him.

"Save it, big brother."

He chuckled at her antics. Neither of them knew who came first, but it was what Octavia used when she wanted to get the message across to him that he wasn't being responsible. "You have someone to take care of you now little sister."

She was quiet, then said, "Antoine says to tell you hi." Even after a couple months of marriage, there was still a giddy sound to her voice when she talked about her mate. Antoine was a human who his sister had given the gift of the wolf. Antoine was a new mooner who loved his sister and strong enough to stand beside her, as well as be someone who would protect Octavia's six from danger when he couldn't be there with his sister.

"Tell my brother in-law what's up." Not to lengthen the phone conversation, he said, "Can you meet me at Malcolm's office in about fifteen minutes?"

"Yes, I can." She paused. "Are you okay? You still bent about Malcolm's mate choice?"

He'd spoke with his sister in length before he left regarding his feelings toward his pack leader and his decisions. But, since meeting Tashi, he understood Malcolm a lot more. Sometimes the choice was out of your hands, the Great Spirit had clearly exhibited that fact to him. "I'm fine. I'll need a favor from you when you get there."

"Anything, Oliver."

They ended the call and he dialed Malcolm's office line directly.

"Temple," the bass in his pack leader's voice came through the receiver.

"It's Oliver," he said, he speech brisk.

"I saw that on the I.D."

Oliver began pacing his thick carpet. The tension still between them was evident. They hadn't parted on the best of terms, but Malcolm was still his brother and he'd give his life for Oliver or any of the others without pause.

"Yea, well, I need your help."

"Trouble?" The tone in Malcolm's voice changed to concern, the agitation dropped like water off a cliff.

"In a big way, but it'll be much easer for me to explain in person."

"I'm here. See you shortly."

Oliver heard the door to his room open. Facing it, he saw Tashi exit. He was unable to discern the expression on her face. "Give me a few minutes and we'll be right there."

He hung up and crossed the distance. Standing before her he asked, "Did you get through to your home?"

Her forest green gaze met his. "Amon. I spoke with Danuwa and she had told me that my cousin and his men have been gone for almost as long as I have. She could not keep them from demanding to see me regardless of what she told them. When Kumi Bomani discovered my absence the next day after I left he was furious and gathered his men to search for me. She waited one more day and told them as I instructed that I'd come here, to America."

"Perfect. Then things have worked out just as you have planned."

She sighed. "Too well. Danuwa stated that they took the portable tracker with them as I predicted. When I asked her to access the mounted one in my rooms she told me that my signal and their's was hours apart."

He noticed the slight tremors in her hands. He didn't smell fear on her, so he chalked it up to everything coming to a head very soon. No Were ever wanted to have to bare their claws against a fellow pack member no matter what the cause. Oliver had no worries the device was in his back pocket. So, if they caught up with them, he'd be the one they would meet first.

"We will get through this. I promise." He stroked his thumb along the ebony silk of her cheek.

Reaching up she clutched his hand, "How? I was unable to reach my father's friend. I was told he was out of the state. Now what will I do. I can fight a single wolf at a time, maybe two and protect what is mine. But, my cousin if he shifts into that monstrosity..." she shook her head as her words faded.

Enough was said, Oliver understood. "You may not be able to handle the situation alone, but you have me and my pack. We'll stand by you through this."

"I hope they are strong," she murmured.

He kissed her forehead and said, "The strongest." They headed out the door. "We've had to guard our territory for many years and you wouldn't believe the forces we've had to reckon with."

Chapter Six

Tashi watched the two Alpha males embrace with firm pats to the back. Oliver did not have a chance to introduce her briefly before he was swallowed into a bear-style hug from the other man.

"It's good to have you home," the well dressed man in the suit told Oliver.

They broke apart and Oliver stepped back.

"It's good to be home. Your wife?" Oliver asked.

"At the amphitheater practicing for her first performance next week."

She saw one of Oliver's eyebrows arch. "You don't say. Came up with that one all by yourself to keep her off the poll and bar tops did you?" Tashi noticed the smile playing at the corners Oliver's mouth, evidently this was a private joke between them.

"Hell, yeah." The man laughed. "Simone helped with getting her into the acrobat show. Now I can keep my sanity."

"Sister's, what would we do without them," Oliver commented.

"You'd be nothing and no where." A stylish woman with thick curves entered the office accompanied by a dark skinned man with silver eyes.

"Octavia!" Oliver wrapped the woman in his arms and kissed her loudly on the cheek.

"A cell phone is meant to be carried not left charging in your room," she admonished as she stepped to the side, allowing Oliver to shake hands with the man with her.

"So, you went into my apartment?"

"Of course," her hand flitted in the air, waving the question away. "So are you going to introduce the pretty lady or make us wait?"

Tashi had been enjoying the sight of Oliver with his family. It made her heart ache to wonder when this all would end so she could go home. She crossed the room as Oliver waved her over.

"Leult Tashi Shayera. This is my sister Octavia and her husband Antoine Lancaster."

Octavia shook her hand and smiled warmly. "It's nice to meet you Leult."

"Tashi, please." She corrected as she turned to the woman's mate and shook his hand. For the second time that day a strange man's eyes assessed her. Lord, the last thing she needed right now was a clairvoyant wolf. But, his silver eyes didn't change color as he held her hand briefly and inclined his head toward her in a greeting.

Oliver's hand caressed her lower back and brought her before the suited man. "This is my brother, Malcolm Temple, the leader of our pack."

"It's a pleasure to meet my brother's mate."

She lifted her hand and covered the side of her neck, as her heart, lurched, plummeted then resumed beating. Not at his words, but at the knowledge of who he was. "You are the one I've been looking for," her excited words rushed out of her.

Everything went still and quiet in the room, with the exception of the low growl emitting from Oliver as his hand flexed on her back.

Pure lime green jealousy had seized his soul at the knowledge that Tashi had been seeking out Malcolm. Because of his position, women from packs all over the world sought Malcolm out. The instinct to claim and fight for what was his had consumed Oliver, to a degree that almost scared him. Would he fight Malcolm, his brother?

In an instant, his wolf declared.

"For me?" Malcolm's gaze shifted as he took a step back.

"You need to do some fast talking?" Octavia stepped closer to Tashi and folded her arms under her breast as her amber eyes darkened to an ancient gold.

He stifled the growl that even elevated toward his sister. Tashi was his mate, whether she believed it or not and his instinct to protect her knew no bound.

Appearing oblivious to the disturbance her words had caused, her gaze ping ponged around the room.

"Oliver, remember the pack leader my father told me about? His American friend. He is your brother."

Relief washed over him at her words. "I thought you said the man was out of the state."

She glanced at Malcolm. "When I called the number in the book the person who answered said you were gone. But, I did not know that in America they called you something other than Julius. Does it mean leader? Is Malcolm your middle name or perhaps your mother's family name?" Her forehead scrunched. "Why would your staff tell me you had left the state?"

Laughter rumbled around the room, as Tashi's mix up became clear.

"Julius is Malcolm's father. He was head of the pack until recently when Malcolm assumed command of the Temple clan. Julius is out of the state. In Alaska."

"Oh," was all she said, but looked crestfallen for a moment. Then her green gaze focused on him and she said, "So, all along, Oliver, you have been a part of the pack that I have needed to assist me."

Disregarding everyone else in the room he pulled her in his arms, pushing her wild curls back behind her ear, he said, "We were fated. The Great Spirit has ordered both of our steps."

"How am I to lead my pack, when I can not see what is clearly before me," her voice wavered with doubt.

He saw the water fill her eyes, before the tears fell.

"Don't cry, beautiful." He used both of his thumbs to brush both streams away. "Everything will work out, just like us. I promise." Leaning down he kissed her.

Malcolm cleared his throat. "Before things become anymore wolfy, why don't you tell us what's going on."

Without releasing Tashi, Oliver looked at his leader. "While Octavia tends to Tashi, I'll fill you and Antoine in. By the time they get back we should be ready to plan."

"What do you want me to do?" Octavia asked.

Stepping back, he said, "Take her to your clothing store and get her something to wear."

"Thank goodness. I thought you were trying to make a new fashion statement dragging her around in these hide-away sweat pants."

He rolled his eyes at his sister. She was right. His sweat pants were way too big for Tashi's petite frame, the extra length from the tight waist cord dangled below the hem of the oversize t-shirt. "She can shower and dress in my apartment. I'm sure you have a key."

Octavia gave him a huge smile. "Of course." Turning, Octavia faced Antoine and kissed him. Antoine whispered something in her ear then let her go.

After his mate and sister exited the room he looked at Malcolm and said, "We got a big problem headed our direction."

"How big?"

"Nine feet or greater."

"What is it, some kind of moving mountain?"

"A Were."

"One second." Octavia called out to the knock at Oliver's apartment door. When Octavia pulled the door wide Tashi saw a man in uniform standing in the doorway with a tray.

"Hi, Sam, I didn't order anything." Octavia informed him

"It's not for you, Mrs. Lancaster, but Ms. Shayera."

Staring at Oliver's sister and the room service attendant, she said, "I did not call for service either."

The man with the nametag SAM entered the room and moved toward her. "Mr. Montague asked us to bring you some coffee."

Tashi stifled a groan. The last time she had consumed American style coffee it had left a bad taste in her mouth. With Oliver's sister standing beside her with a knowing smile she figured it would be rude to turn the offer away.

Setting the tray on the table, the attendant filled a cup with the steaming dark mixture. "Mr. Montague asked me to tell you to have no fear, he didn't make it and he's sure you will enjoy this cup."

Hesitant and curious at the same time, Octavia accepted the saucer and cup taking a moment she lifted it and sniffed. The robust aroma of spicy, rich beans tickled her nose with its familiar scent. Not wanting to make assumptions, she took a tentative sip. The full-bodied flavor caressed her taste buds and its' smooth taste brought her pure satisfaction. "It is delicious. What is it?"

Smiling, he said, "Ethiopia Sidamo from the Voodoo Café's Starbuck's blends. I'll tell him you enjoyed it."

"That's okay, Sam. I'd rather tell him myself."

"Of course," he said with a knowing smile and left.

She wondered at Octavia's silence as she resumed the position behind her and continued styling her wet hair.

Tashi could feel the comb slide down her scalp sectioning her hair off, when Octavia finally spoke from behind her. "So, when do you plan to tell my brother you're an African princess?"

Now, showered and dressed in a pair of slacks and button down blouse and sitting before Octavia as she placed medium size braids across her head, she asked, "How did you know? Do speak Amharic?"

"No, my mate Antoine a very intelligent man. Before his change he worked at the university and many of his colleagues are from Africa, Leult Tashi."

Now she understood the look in Antoine's eyes when they had met. "Yes, I am a princess and leader of my pack in Ethiopia. But, that does not change this situation between Oliver and I. It was his wish to help me. As you already know, I was looking for someone else's assistance. I am grateful for Oliver's help."

Finished braiding, Octavia moved around the chair and stood before her. "Yes, but your missing one important fact." She pointed at the slow healing bruise on the side of her neck. "Oliver is doing it because he believes you're his mate."

Feeling accused of an injustice to a man who had showed her nothing but kindness and passion, Tashi lowered her gaze. "Nothing is ever a certainty."

"Love is."

When they arrived back at the office, she was introduced to Weres, a Djinn and a woman who pulled power from the moon, but Tashi was only looking for one person. She needed to get Oliver by himself before everything started to unfold with Kumi Bomani. The things Octavia had said to her made sense. She cared for Oliver and he had opened his home and heart to her and she could not let him go into this fight ignorant.

Seeing him in the corner talking to a male Were she had yet to meet, she approached him.

Facing her, Oliver's gaze travel the length of her body and caused heat to trail its path. Making a return trip he smiled. "You look great."

"I feel more like myself now." Stepping closer to him, she said, "Thank you for the coffee."

"Better?" He stroked her arm.

"It was much better."

"This is another one of my pack brothers Guy, and his mate Leila, the packs Enforcers."

Tashi was impressed. Maybe her father was right the Temple's were the pack to see when you needed help. She spook to them both, then faced Oliver. "May I speak with you for a moment, Oliver?"

"Anytime." Concern, filled his eyes. "Are you all right?"

Forcing a smile, she said, "Amon. I just need to talk to you."

Looking at Guy, he asked, "Guy, can you and your beautiful moonbeam," he winked at Leila. "Go outside the city and bury this deep in the Nevada soil." He pulled the small plastic bag out of his pocket with the chip in it and passed it to Guy.

"I think Leila and I can handle that." Guy circled his mate's waist.

"Great. Keep watch on the area and we'll meet you there."

Guy saluted him with two fingers, then left the office with Leila.

Taking hold of her hand, Oliver moved through the throng of Were's until he entered a conference room off the side of Malcolm's office. "What's up, sweetheart?"

Feeling nervous about what she needed to say, she removed her hand from his and stepped back. Rubbing her hand over the neat braids decorating her hair, she exhaled and began, "Oliver, I have not been completely honest with you."

"About what?" Frowning he placed his hands on his hips and stared at her.

Refusing to look away, she forged ahead. "About this situation. Who I am."

"Are you Leult Tashi Shayera?"

"Amon."

He walked towards her. "The she-wolf I just spent two days with in my cabin?"

"Amon."

And still he moved closer. "The woman who I made love to until the moon was high in the sky?"

Her breathing became labored at his words. "Amon."

"Do you trust me to protect you?" He now stood before her.

"Amon."

"Then that is all I need to know for now." Grasping both her hands, he rained kisses along her knuckles.

"Ay, Oliver, that is not all." She squeezed his hand, imploring him to listen. "The wolf who is after me, Kumi Bomani Shayera is not only my cousin, he is a wolf who is power hungry." She saw his shoulders roll back and stiffen. "He wants to be ruler of my people through me."

"By your blood, right?"

"By blood and by mate, so he can become Mekwanint."

"Mekwanint?"

"Appointed prince by the people because of his power and strength."

Squinting, he stared at her. "How can this be? You're a member of a pack of Were's that are cattle herders and coffee farmers."

It was her turn to roll her shoulders back and tilted her nose up with pride. "Ay, Oliver, I am Leult. Princess Tashi Shayera and my father and all those who came before him were princes, since they guarded Makeda's son. My mother was not only Were but a princess in her own right out of Kenya."

Oliver released her hands. "You wait till now to tell me this after I've enlisted the aid of my pack brother's and sisters, your highness?"

She knew he had a right to be angry. "I am sorry, Oliver. It was not my intention to mislead you. I only wanted to get this monster away from my people."

Growling, Oliver turned from her and ran his hand down his face. His voice rumbled. "Do you desire this man? Have you enticed him? Do you wish to be this man's mate?" he growled, "Have I involved my family in some lover's dispute?"

Gripping his arm, she pulled at it until his gaze locked with her own. "Amon. You know I have known no other lover but you."

Nodding, he said, "Let's go."

He didn't take her hand, but exited the room ahead of her.

She was a princess. Ethiopian royalty. There was no way he would be able to ask her to stay. Tashi had a greater responsibility than working in a casino in Las Vegas by his side. Kneeling low on the high cliff close to the flat desert floor below, Oliver watched three men using stealth steps toward the hard packed dirt as Tashi whispered translations to him of the interloper's words. It was the place where Guy and Leila had dropped the chip approximately four feet down into the dry earth. The observation point was up wind from the trio. The full moon shone down on the men like a spotlight. One Were held a small laptop-like portable device and punched in entries on the key pad.

Oliver heard one of the Were's with broad shoulders and a thick neck that he wanted to sink his teeth into and rip out, speak. "This is the place. Dig," he barked ferociously.

"Are you sure the directions co-ordinance were correct?" The shortest of the group asked.

"Leult Tashi can not be buried here." The thin one sounded unsure.

With lightening speed, the broad shouldered man reached out and grabbed the collar of the shortest of the team. "Do not question me."

"The one barking the orders is Kumi Bomani. The short one is Paki and the thin one is Azikiwe, Kumi Bomani's second in command."

Oliver listened to Tashi's continued translations and the identification of each man. Malcolm, Claire, Simone, Troy and Marcus were all crouched behind him, awaiting his signal. Guy and Leila were behind the men somewhere. Kadim, Simone's mate was off in the distance placing one of his wards around the area to keep the men contained.

"Dig!" Kumi Bomani threw the short man down to the hard packed surface.

The stench of their sweat was tainted with the acrid scent of their desperation. Paki shifted into a brown wolf with an orange tipped tail and followed orders. Grunting and digging, his paws clawed into the ground.

"Do you think she is dead?" Azikiwe squatted beside Paki staring into the hole as it deepened. "Perhaps killed in her travels for money?"

"Whatever the case, I do not care. We can still draw her blood."

Oliver felt Tashi shiver beside him as her voice waivered with the last translated sentence. Reaching out he stroked her back, neither of them taking their eyes off the group.

Thick dust clouds and sand fluttered in the air, obscuring the view of Tashi's pack brothers.

"Wait!" Kumi Bomani voice barked.

As the desert dust settled, they saw her cousin had moved with the tracker to the pile of loose soil Paki had kicked back. His face twisted in a frown, Kumi Bomani dropped to his knees and clutched handfuls of the dirt sifting through it frantically. Pulling up the small plastic bag he stared at it perplexed.

At that moment, Oliver stood high and proud. "Have you lost something?" He spoke down to them from the cliff.

Glancing upwards, Kumi Bomani asked in English, "Who are you? What concern is this to you?" He got to his own feet and his two side kicks followed, sniffing the air as they moved toward Oliver.

As he progressed forward to meet them, Tashi rose and walked beside him, staring her cousin down.

"Tashi?"

"Leult Tashi," Paki, oblivious to the nudity of his human form, and Azikiwe scrambled forward out of training dropped to one knee and bowed their heads as the groveled in both Amharic and English.

Oliver almost laughed at the humor of the situation. How could men who tracked across continents to find their princess and steal from her, still find it within themselves to exhibit honor to her.

Tashi gazed at the bowed heads of men who were supposed to be devoted to her and protect her. The cruel irony was that she had ended up needing protection from them. She was tired of the fox and hare game. "Get up! Get up!" She stalked towards them. When they stood, she slapped Paki, her nails scraping across his skin, then without pause she backhanded Azikiwe. "I want no respect from you conspirators."

Kumi Bomani pulled the men back and took precise steps to her. "What is the meaning of this, princess?" His dark brown eyes traveled along her face, lowered to her neck and his nostrils flared at the sight of Oliver's mark. "Why have you allowed this African-American mutt to manipulate your mind and keep you privately?" he said, his English precise, clipped and distinct.

She felt and heard Oliver's growl as he came up beside her understand the insult. She placed a quelling hand on his chest. "You are no longer keeper of my affairs, Kumi Bomani." She lifted her chin and looked at him with disgust. "I know why you are here. I know what you have done. What you attempt to do."

"Tashi, show me the traitor who has deceived you and I shall cut out his tongue." His eyes darted toward Oliver.

"Then you will be removing your own, my cousin."

Kumi Bomani looked back at her. "You speak things of no sense. It is time for you to come home." He lowered his tone mockingly, "You're pack needs you."

"Yes, they do. Because I am Leult Tashi Shayera, leader of the Shayera Pack because of my blood. You are nothing! You are finished, Kumi Bomani!"

Everything happened in a flash as her cousin began to snarl his displeasure, taking this as a sign to attack, Paki and Azikiwe shifted. Clouds hid the moon and all hell broke loss. The brown and tan wolf barked and advanced on her and Oliver, until they noticed the Temple pack vaulting down the uneven terrain of the cliff, speeding toward them. When the two wolves skid to a halt it was almost ludicrous to witness as they attempted to backpedal. By the time they turned and took a few steps, Guy and Leila came upon them.

It was a massacre to watch, but she had her own problems to deal with. Kumi Bomani took off across the dirt and around a bend. On foot and in human form he may have been able to beat her, but she shifted quickly, refusing to allow him to get away. She pushed along the earth easily tracking his fetid scent in the dim light. As she turned the corner, she was knocked across the ground as something hard struck her shoulder. Dazed she attempted to get her bearing when she felt the sharp prick in the side of her neck.

She struggled against his full weight pressing down on her. The moon came into full view, its radiant light revealing. She could see the greedy determination in her cousin's gaze, as well as her blood flowing rapidly filling a tube. Realizing her mistake in shifting, she increased her thrash against his hold and managed to swipe one of her back paws across his thigh, her claws sinking deep.

Kumi Bomani yelled and raised his arm to strike her. That arm became a chew toy for the midnight colored wolf who latched onto her cousin's bicep and pulled him off of her, the needle still clutched in his other hand went with them.

As man and wolf fought, there came a roar of pure evil that caused her heart to race with trepidation of what was to come. Now, on four paws she took in the sight before her. A chocolate furred Lycan-like beast, half man, half wolf that was once her cousin hovered over her and Oliver. He was a hideous display of fury as he barred his canines and claws at them. This is the army Kumi Bomani is desperate to create, something drawn from a wolfen nightmare. It can not be.

No Betas, she and Oliver moved around him gauging the right mode of attack. Oliver's onyx gaze held hers, and she understood that he was there for her. Moving beside him, she would not allow him to do this alone. They would stand together.

Tashi lunged for the beast's throat, sinking her teeth deep and tasting the tinny flavor of his blood. Oliver bit into the fiend's side, removing a pound of flesh causing the Lycan-like beast to waiver in his stance.

Sharp pain burned along her ribs as the mutated wolf dug his claws into her, prying her off and tossing her like a ragdoll. She hit the ground hard.

Oliver growled and launched at the beast's offending hand, gnawing it to the bone. Rising, she went after the creature again as he slammed repeated blows into Oliver's side with his other hand. On her hind legs, she dug her front paws deep into Kumi Bomani's to side tear away flesh from bone. His roar became a whine as he staggered backward, away from them and dropped to his knees as he began to decrease in size rapidly, before her and Oliver. The torturous cries of a wounded man echoed through the night. Kumi Bomani's unwounded hand clutched as the open gasp at his side as blood ran down and dripped into the dirt.

"Finish him." She heard Oliver's voice in her head.

Staring at the injured shell of her cousin she could not to it. She could not bring her self to give the final blow of his demise. She no longer looked upon him as family, nor could she take his life. Shaking her head, she looked away from Kumi Bomani. "He is dead to me already." Nudging Oliver, she turned away from her cousin in disgust of the man he had become.

As their wolves took steps to leave, she heard the beasty roar once again and out of the corner of her eyes she saw her cousin attempting to shift once again. However, before Tashi could respond she heard someone yell, "Down!"

She did not have time to turn her head and see who it was, before Oliver's wolf turned with lightening speed, knocked her to the side and rolled his body on top of hers. Then all of a sudden she'd thought that heaven had come to earth as a luminous light shined out of Leila and into Kumi Bomani, rupturing his flesh in an explosion.

It was not until all was dark and quiet once again, that Tashi became aware that she and Oliver had shift back into human form. His warm sweat slick body lay covering hers.

"It's a good thing Leila has learned to channel her energy in a more precise fashion or we'd all be charred vulture snack." Oliver called over his shoulder.

"We'll take that as a thank you, from your naked ass." Guy said, as he looked down on them dropping a pile of clothes beside them, then turning and walking away.

"The Temple pack is quite the blended family," she said, still stunned.

"You have only seen a fraction of what we can do." Leaning down, he kissed her. "Would you like to be a part of us?"

She understood what he was asking her, without hesitation she said, "Yes, most definitely." She didn't know how she and Oliver would work this relationship out, they would. She loved the wolf and refused to live her life without him.

"I don't know which I want to do more, howl at the moon or make love to you."

"Well, since your family is waiting for us, the howling might be the best choice at the moment."

Moving off her, he helped her up. While she dressed in another pair of sweatpants and a t-shirt, Oliver's black wolf howled at the vanishing pale moon as dawn began to break into the horizon behind them.

Oliver watched his brother hang up the phone. "What did they say?"

"That was Garen at the Preternatural Police Department, he wanted us to know that their counterparts over in Ethiopia already have Yerodin, the scientist in custody." He sat on the corner of his desk. "They also confiscated all his reports on the DNA reconfiguration serum."

"He was as much a pawn in Kumi Bomani's vicious game as I." Tashi commented. Her head bowed, she stared at the vial of blood in her hand.

She hadn't let it out of her sight since he'd located it in the dirt and given it to her. Oliver wrapped his arm around her shoulder.

"Yeah, but he didn't report it either," Malcolm said.

Glancing up, she sighed. "I am glad it is over and my people and country are safe."

"Our country," he corrected her.

"Are you sure this is what you want to do?" Malcolm asked, observing them.

"Very sure."

"You have always been as much a leader as I am." He pretended to wipe sweat his brow. "Now, I don't have to worry about you wanting to fight me for head of this pack."

Oliver laughed. "The thought never even crossed my mind."

Rising off the desk, Malcolm his brother and leader crossed the room to him. "As an Alpha you don't need my blessing, but you have it."

Releasing Tashi he pulled his brother into a hug. When they parted he said, "Watch out for Octavia for me."

"I think I already have that part covered," Antoine chimed in from the door as he and Octavia entered the room.

Moving in quick strides across the carpet, noting the glassy look in her amber eyes, he pulled her into a hug. "You're not going to cry are you?"

"Yes," she mumbled holding him tighter.

Chuckling he kissed her forehead and released her. "I promise to always keep my phone on and with me. Will that make it easier?"

Stepping back beside her mate, Octavia said, "Nothing will make this easier. But, I understand you must be where your mate is." She smiled at Tashi.

Glancing behind him, he reached for Tashi. She moved next to him without hesitation. His heart swelled, he and his wolf had finally found what they'd been looking for, unity. "I thought I needed to get away to find myself. I didn't realize that the Great Spirit had my wolf on a royal pursuit."

Oliver glance at the mountains surrounding him, then allowed his eyes to lower to the soil between his toes. African soil. He may not know his past, but he couldn't deny the chills of excitement running along his arms at the knowledge that he now stood in the original place of his ancestors. Gazing at the beautiful woman beside him, he felt grateful for the Great Spirit bringing her into his life.

"What is thy beloved more than another beloved, O though fairest among women?" Oliver quoted as he undressed on the river bank along side his wife. They had been married in a traditional Ethiopian wedding among their people, then left for their honeymoon in the Eitrean Mountains.

Tashi dropped her last article of clothing on the ground. "His mouth is most sweet: yea, he is altogether lovely. This is my beloved, and this is my friend…" Tashi words trailed off as she took his hand and led him deeper into Lake Tana.

"I never dreamed I would have mountains and a mate," he confessed to her.

Pressing her body to his, she wrapped her arms around his shoulders. "Well, since your dreams have been fulfilled lets start on mine."

"I thought I was your dream."

"You and babies. Give me children, Oliver."

"My princess, I bow to your bidding. Yätäwädädä"

"Yes, I am your beloved," she responded, joy evident on her face as he practiced with his new language. "Always."

He began making love to his wife as the waning Hunter's Moon crescent shape smiled upon them with its celestial light.

The End

The Wolf That Wasn't

By

Natalie Dunbar

This book is dedicated to my husband Chet, who always goes the extra mile and has kept the magic going for more years than I care to own up to. Special thanks to Sandra Beard and Jackie Hamilton for helping to make this a better book.

Biography

Award winning author Natalie Dunbar was first published by Genesis Press in 2000 and has gone on to write for BET Books, Silhouette Bombshell, Kimani Press, Silhouette Romantic Suspense, and Parker Publishing. Her stories feature strong heroines and heroes to die for.

Chapter One

Circulating among the convention crowd in the light filled San Francisco Moscone Center, Claire Temple laughed and joked with her cousin Izzy Barker. Beneath the buzz of conversation, the upbeat mood of the crowd made the event seem more like a party than a convention.

People sat at ruffle-skirted tables in the partitioned areas and booths the exhibitors had purchased, sampling food and beverages, taking orders, and simply chatting. Others perused the tables loaded with goodies and added free samples to their conference bags.

Although she had meetings scheduled, she felt ridiculously free and light-hearted after months of planning and work associated with her brother Malcolm's installation as the new head of the Temple Werewolf clan. Now her only worry was the coming pressure from Esther to select a mate. She didn't dwell on it, but she had never been lucky in love. In fact, she'd all but given up on finding the right man. Then there was the reality that her close knit family would have to like any prospective mate.

Izzy's sultry giggle drew Claire's attention back to the present. Izzy was blasting her considerable charm on the tall, sable-skinned representative for Masterson's Fine Culinary Products. Claire focused her gaze on the handsome rep's nametag and read, Tony Jackson. She recognized him as someone Izzy spent time with last year. Stopping alongside her cousin, Claire accepted a sample of marinated beef tartar. It was sublimely sweet and tangy, but then she already counted Masterson as one of the top venders for the French Quarter.

Tony's boss, Randall, recognized Claire and came forward to give her a warm hug. "Good to see you Claire!" His lips brushed her cheek. "And how are you doing?"

"Fine, and I'm glad to be here in San Francisco for some downtime."

Randall eyed her sharply and gently took her hand. "I hope you plan on attending the reception and party we're giving for our best customers."

Claire flashed him a smile and gave his hand a squeeze. "Wouldn't miss it for the world. You guys know how to have a good time."

He retrieved an envelope from the table and withdrew a bunch of tickets. "You shouldn't need these, but if me and Tony aren't around when you arrive…." His voice trailed off. "How many do you want?"

Claire tilted her head. She was in a mood for company and right now she didn't care that it wouldn't be a potential mate. "Give me four. If we don't use the extra tickets, I'll bring them back."

Randall's smile warmed. Claire knew he had a thing for her, but she'd never seen him as anything but a good friend. "I'll look for you tonight then," he said, releasing her hand. "We've got some new marinades and sauces I want you to try."

Stepping into the area reserved by Masterson Fine Culinary Products, Claire took a seat and spent the next fifteen minutes sampling and taking notes on the foods and sauces Randall presented. Then she ordered the ones she thought her chefs and customers would like.

Afterward, she stood, licking the last bit of a scrumptious sauce off her lips as she surveyed the surrounding tables and booths. She felt as if she were being watched. Scanning the large hall, her gaze stopped when it encountered an incredible pair of midnight blue eyes, the deep color of the horizon just above the ocean and filled with mystery and intelligence. Capturing her, they held her until interest and something inside her started to burn.

Claire blinked, breaking the contact. She returned her gaze to the dark haired man with the incredible blue eyes. He had olive skin, a straight nose that didn't dominate his face and a full, sensual mouth. Black, wing-like brows and glossy curls topped his striking face. With a Temple past shaped in slavery long ago, she didn't often view Caucasians as potential mates, but something about this man made all her preconceived notions and ideas meaningless. She couldn't have felt more pull if he had a fishing pole and was reeling her in. On instinct alone she began the walk to his booth.

Halfway to the booth, strong waves of doubts and negativity slowed her steps. What was she doing? She didn't even know the man. He could be a crazy or someone out to harm her or her family.

She arrived, slightly breathless and aware that she'd been holding her breath the entire time.

Mr. Blue Eyes offered a large, well-manicured hand. "Dante De Luca. Can I help you?" he said in a provocative tenor that caressed her ears.

A woody, oriental scent mixed with that of clean, virile male filled her nostrils. Not werewolf, but not entirely human. She accepted his hand, even shook it in a professional manner, but the entire time she felt an intense energy pulsing and flowing between them. Aware that a lot rode on her next few statements, she flashed a brilliant smile. "I ... saw you watching me from across the room," she began, wishing she'd come up with something more original.

His gaze dipped down to her conference badge then locked on to hers. "You're a beautiful woman, Claire. I've been staring ever since you walked into the exhibit hall."

Eyes widening, Claire found herself laughing. Dante's words flattered and intrigued her. "Do you like what you see?"

Dante grinned. "I'm still enjoying the view."

"Well now," she said flirting, "Were you planning to stop at just looking?"

His tone turned husky as his gaze covered her expensive sandals to her white fitted slacks and black Robert Rodriguez cross seam jacket that she'd paired with a tiny animal print camisole. "Well, we have made it all the way to conversation, haven't we?" His lips curved upward and his warm fingers massaged her hand. "I would like to get to know you and give you all of the time and attention you deserve..."

Claire tilted her head, enjoying the sound of his voice and the way his fingers tightened on hers. She wanted more.

His voice dipped lower. "Are you staying at the conference hotel?"

Claire nodded. "Of course. And you?"

"The company has a condo on the bay."

"What do you do for the company?" Claire asked, glancing up at the sign that read, Baxter Food, Beverages, and Exotics for the first time.

Dante was silent for several moments, leaving her to wonder if he'd heard the question or whether he was hiding a secret. "Is it a secret?" She asked, amused.

"I don't have a job description or title," he began carefully, "but if I had to choose, I would call myself a slave. I've developed several of the beverages and exotics and I fill in as needed since our staff is small."

Claire chuckled. "Don't look so serious. I feel the same way sometimes and I work for my family." She saw him incline his head, his eyes starting to twinkle as he appreciated the sound of her laughter.

His question surprised her. "Who are you, Claire Temple?"

"What you see and more," she began, fingering the gold circlet she wore at her throat with her free hand. "My family owns the French Quarter Hotel and Casino in Las Vegas. I manage the food and beverage concessions in the restaurants and bars."

"That's a big job," he murmured softly, reluctantly releasing her hand.

"Yes, but I do manage to have a life too," she countered. "So you've heard of the French Quarter?"

"Yes, it's a beautiful, well run place, and I've heard of the Temple Clan."

So he knew she belonged to a pack of werewolves. Claire swallowed. By law, most humans had been vaccinated against the Lupine virus so being with her wouldn't make him a werewolf. He didn't seemed fazed, but many humans still harbored prejudices against werewolves. And many of the wolves looked on the humans as lesser beings. Straightening, Claire narrowed her eyes and gazed deeper into his. She kept her tone light. "Is that going to be a problem?"

Dante smiled. "No, in fact it only adds to the energy and excitement of being with you."

She scanned his handsome features, and took in the designer suit that enhanced the strength and vitality practically pouring off him. Was she attracted to him for his looks or was it something deeper? She sensed the latter. He was something all right, but he wasn't a werewolf and definitely wouldn't meet her family's expectations. "You're not clan, so what are you?"

He shook his head. "I'm what you see and more too. Is that going to be a problem?"

Not werewolf and not human and yet his skin was like that of the masters that the Temple Clan had escaped long ago. She really was stepping into uncharted territory. He wasn't a vampire either. Deep inside, she knew what he was, but couldn't quite close on the thought. "What you are is not a problem, but I like to know what I'm dealing with."

Staring at her, Dante was silent but she sensed that he was trying to tell her something. Thinking hard, she remembered the things he'd said about himself, about developing some of the beverages and exotics for Baxter. "You're a Mage," she guessed.

"Yes." He turned his hands palm up as if to show that he was harmless.

As a Mage, she knew that he was far from harmless. The energy she felt at his touch, the sheer magnetic attraction that enveloped much more than the physical told her that he was powerful. Maybe, just maybe there was more going on here than she thought. Claire's temper flared hot. "Did you spell me from across the room? Did you--? "

A flash of anger and disappointment sparked his eyes and then closed his expression as he cut off her tirade. "No. That's not my MO. You're free to walk away. Go." Brandishing an upturned hand with a flourish, he turned his back on her and busied himself with the company's display bottles.

How dare he dismiss her? Claire glared at him for several moments, torn between wanting to stay and proving that she could go. Pride won out. She turned and walked away with her head high and a little extra zing in her walk. Threading her way through the aisles of booths and people, she felt no physical pull, but wanted to go back and talk to him anyway. Her pulse was still racing from just talking to him and she wanted to feel the energy that flowed through her when they touched.

She forced herself to check out some other booths. Pushing herself, she even tasted more samples and collected business cards. Feeling the weight of Dante's gaze the entire time, Claire ordered a couple of cases of new champagne. Then she made a realization. For a man at the conference to sell his company's products, Dante had said surprisingly little about them.

Without conscious effort or thought, Claire found herself standing at Dante's booth once more. He glanced up from a notebook he was writing in, curiosity lighting his wonderful eyes.

"I want to apologize," she began. "I'm usually pretty traditional in the people I'm attracted to. Humans are about as risky as I get. I've… never met anyone like you and I don't know what to think or how to act."

114

His expression brightened. He set the notebook aside and came closer till they were almost touching. "Why don't you act like Claire?

Her skin tingled, just from having him stand so close. Reacting to his comment, Claire managed to chuckle and cough at the same time. "Claire has a temper, especially when she's being protective or thinks she's being duped."

"I won't dupe you, Claire, and I won't hurt you either. But you should know that I have a hot temper too."

"Interesting," she said, trying to imagine him interacting with her brothers. Her first boyfriend had been arrogant and ridiculously unsuitable, but did Malcom and Marcus have to beat the crap out of him? And what about the date who'd been all but shaking in his boots when she'd returned from retrieving her evening bag?

Claire reached into her designer bag and drew out one of the tickets she'd gotten from Randall. "I'm going to be at this party tonight. Why don't you come along as my date?"

He accepted the ticket, letting his fingers cover hers for several seconds longer than necessary. "I'm there. What time should I show up?"

"Ten-thirty?" She didn't want to arrive too early.

"I'm there," he repeated. "What about now? Are you free? I'd love to take you to lunch."

Claire glanced down at her watch. She had a meeting in five minutes and the rest of the day was filled with sessions and meetings, including dinner. She told Dante.

He drew a card from his suit pocket and gave it to her. "This is my cell number. If something shakes loose on your schedule before ten-thirty, call me."

"I will," Claire said, preparing to tear herself away. She saw Izzy coming up the aisle and beckoning to her. She glanced back at him and caught a flash of white teeth. "That's my cousin. I've got to go now."

"See you later then."

Claire turned and took the aisle at a fast clip. It would take most of the next five minutes to get to the meeting room. At the hall entrance she glanced back quickly to find Dante De Luca's mesmerizing blue eyes still focused on her. She'd wanted companionship, but she already knew that Dante was a man she wouldn't easily walk away from. Was she making a mistake? Claire followed Izzy out of the hall entrance.

Chapter Two

Dante watched Claire leave the hall and noticed that the room seemed a little darker for it. His life had become so dark and sordid lately that he needed a bit of light. And Claire Temple, with her curvaceous figure and exotic beauty was it. She fascinated and intrigued him with her amber eyes and skin the color of cinnamon spiced chocolate. She would make him laugh and give him a reason to keep on fighting the horror that had become his life.

Despite the fact that the conference day had four more hours to go, Dante began to pack up his display cases. He had today and tomorrow before his life became a living hell once more. Although he'd never run away from anything, now he longed for the luxury of escape. As it was, except for the brief respite with Claire, he'd been spending every free, unmonitored moment searching through his books and ordering ancient tomes in the hopes of finding a way out of his bargain.

He didn't plan to tell her about the mess he'd gotten himself into, the mess that made him a dangerous person to be around. For now he was almost as safe as anyone else in the convention center. In fact, by the time Andrais returned, Claire would be safe in Las Vegas.

Dante idly touched the gold collar hidden beneath his suit. He would tell her that it was a family heirloom that he wore at all times. The crowd was thinning in the hall. Glad that people passed his booth without stopping to sample the wares that Andrais had altered in order to obtain more victims, he finished packing up. Andrais would be looking for new victims when he got back, but today, Dante didn't have the heart or the stomach for it. He wanted to be free like everyone else.

Claire emerged from her round of meetings with her stomach full, her head buzzing, and her body dragging. The thought of seeing Dante and getting to know him kept her going, but falling asleep in the limo on the way back to the hotel confirmed the fact that she needed to rest first.

Hours later, Izzy shook Claire awake. "If you still want to make the party you've got to hit the shower and get dressed, Claire," she kept repeating in an annoyingly high-pitched voice.

Claire opened her eyes and sat up, realizing that she had been dreaming. She pushed her wavy hair out of her face. A full day of meetings and she'd still been dreaming of Dante De Luca. This wasn't like her, but it felt good. She didn't know where this thing with Dante was going, but she couldn't remember being so excited about anyone.

The hot, stimulating shower drove away the last bits of sleep. Claire took care of her skin and added make-up to clarify the shape and color of her eyes. Then she donned underwear and massaged a daily moisturizer into her wavy hair and styled it in a way she hoped he'd appreciate. Smoothing on a shimmering shade of lipstick, she stepped into a short gold slip dress and a matching pair of sandals.

Claire got out of the taxi clutching her gold bag. She knew she looked good, but had she overdone it?

Behind her, Izzy climbed out of the taxi in rhinestone-studded evening shorts and a matching tank. "Looks like a hot party," Izzy remarked.

Drawing a few bills from her bag, Claire paid the driver. In answer to Izzy's comment she scanned the area in front of the Skyline Club and saw several people standing outside, waiting to get in.

Glad she'd gotten the tickets in advance, she fished them out of her bag and offered two to her cousin. "Are you hanging with Tony tonight?" she asked, recalling that they hadn't discussed this in the taxi. She'd been in no mood for conversation.

Izzy only took one of the tickets. "You know we were in those stupid meetings most of the day," she quipped. "I didn't have time to find a date."

"I found a date," Claire put in smugly. She was no slouch, but Izzy was out there on the edge when it came to finding companionship. Izzy was usually the smug one.

Izzy giggled. "You found a date because you were out their strutting your stuff at the Moscone Center while I talked to Tony." She slid the ticket into her bag and put a hand on her hip. "Besides, what's wrong with Tony?"

Shrugging, Claire lifted her brows. "I wouldn't know. I'm not the one who slept with the man the last time we were here."

"Touché. Let's see who's inside." Izzy turned and sauntered towards the entrance.

Claire glanced at her watch, wondering about Dante and if he were inside. It was nearly eleven. As she followed Izzy down the sidewalk, the black sports car that had been parked halfway down the block pulled up to the valet and Dante DeLuca got out. The sight of him sent her thoughts clamoring to the toned body beneath the designer suit. Leaving his keys with the valet, he stuffed his receipt in a suit jacket pocket. He glanced up to smile at Claire. "I've been waiting down the street. Looks like the time got away from you."

Claire couldn't help returning his smile. "Yes, I was exhausted and decided to nap. Sorry I overslept."

He stopped to take in her appearance with a long, thorough look. "It was worth the wait. You are beautiful."

The heat and longing in his stare melted Claire's insides. Thanking him, she accepting the hand he offered. "Come meet my cousin."

Claire made the introductions, noting Izzy's barely disguised incredulity at Claire's choice of date that was spiked with a bit of attitude. As an adult, she didn't need Izzy's approval on the men she dated, but she demanded respect and good manners. Narrowing her eyes, Claire shot her a warning look.

Claire couldn't recall being the center of so much attention. Was it because she and Izzy wore sexy outfits? Or was it because they were with Dante DeLuca? Several of the people standing outside the club watched them approach the doorman and hand over their tickets.

The club door opened and the sound of a primal, pounding beat reached their ears. They stepped forward, listening to the doorman explain the club's different areas and trying to decide where to go first.

As her eyes grew accustomed to the light, Claire recognized Randall and Tony at the bar in a room decorated with cool, contemporary furniture and colors. A large, rectangular dance floor dominated the room. In front of a silhouette of the San Francisco skyline, several couples writhed, shook, and undulated to the beat beneath a ceiling full of twinkling stars and a flashing techno light. White and wheat colored couches and matching coffee tables dotted the room. Along the walls and in some of the corners, large, circular booths with high backed leather seats afforded more privacy.

Spotting them at last, Randall and Tony came forward to greet them. Tony hugged Izzy and drew her towards the bar. Randall stayed for an introduction to Dante.

Something in Randall's tight-lipped expression made Claire uneasy. She'd brought dates to Randall's conference parties in the past, and although he hadn't been thrilled at the prospect, whatever she was reading in his expression had been absent. She tried to define it. Was it fear?

Dante put an arm around her shoulders, the stimulating contact effectively bringing her attention back to him. "Where would you like to sit?" he asked.

"I reserved one of the private booths for you," Randall put in quickly, "and I already ordered your favorite drink."

Claire grinned, and leaned forward to brush Randall's cheek with her lips. "Thanks, Randall. You really know how take care of your friends. Which booth is it?"

"I'll show you." Turning, he led the way to a booth in a corner of the room that wasn't far from the dance floor. Claire and Dante climbed into the comfortable leather booth and scooted around the gilded glass table, impressed with the appearance and location. A waiter had followed them and was busy pouring Cristal champagne into flutes.

Randall glanced towards the entrance. More guests had entered the club. "I'll come back later to visit with you," he murmured, bustling off.

Dante and Claire lifted their glasses. Blue eyes glittering with something that made Claire's pulse accelerate, Dante made a toast. "To us and our time together. May it be everything we want and need."

Claire sipped her drink, enjoying the sweet taste of the champagne and the fizz on her tongue.

Dante glanced back towards the door, where Randall was chatting with guests. "That man has feelings for you."

She returned Dante's gaze calmly. "He's just a friend. Does it

119

bother you?"

Dante reached for her hand. "Only if you regret bringing me here."

Claire shook her head. "No, but I need to know more about you."

Dante moved across the seat until he was sitting next to her with their legs and shoulders touching. "What do you need to know?"

Claire placed her glass on the table. "Are you married? Where do you come from? And what about your family?"

Dante massaged her palm with his fingers. "I wouldn't be here with you if I were married, but I used to be. My wife died in an accident several years ago. We were very young."

Taking in the touch of sadness in his expression, Claire placed her free hand on his. "Sorry. Do you have children?"

"No." Dante's hand massage extended to her fingers. "My great grandparents came here from Italy and my family has been here since then. My mother died in childbirth. My father is Roberto DeLuca. Have you heard of him?"

Claire shook her head.

"He's well known for his skill and power. I have a brother, Anthony."

Coming from a big family, Claire was glad that Dante wasn't an only child. "Are you two close?" she asked.

Dante nodded. "We were, but I haven't seen him in a while. He tends to go off by himself to get deep in his projects. What about you, Claire?"

Claire shrugged. "I've never been married, if that's what you want to know."

"Why not?" Dante's fingers trailed down the side of her face.

"My family is big and it's well-known in Vegas," she began. "I-I guess I've never been interested in anyone alpha enough to allow him to become a part of my family or wrest me away from them. I'm pretty attached to them and they to me. I'm not attracted to Beta or submissive men."

Dante eyed her sharply. "Does the alpha have to be werewolf?"

Claire's lips turned up at the corners. "No, but I've spent a lot of time going out with them."

His eyes darkened. "It's time for a change."

Claire chuckled. "Have you ever been with a werewolf?"

Dante's teeth flashed. "All women are special, each with their own unique beauty, skills, and abilities. I don't limit myself." Releasing her hands, he threaded his fingers into her wavy hair and leaned closer. Then his hot mouth was on hers in a teasing, tasting, caressing kiss.

Lips tingling, body aching, Claire trembled beneath the sensual onslaught. She was highly sensual by nature and it had been too long since she'd been with anyone. She wanted more, much more, but it was too soon. "Let's dance," she said, determined to distract herself from spending the evening making out in the booth or worse.

Dante's voice was low and a little hoarse. "Here?"

Looking at him, still feeling the aftereffects of his kiss she guessed that he was thinking of something more intimate. "Yes here." She panted in the direction of the other dancers. "They do have a dance floor."

Blinking, he focused his gaze on the dance floor. The current song was ending as he stood, offering her his hand. By the time they reached the dance floor, the DJ had exchanged the pounding beat for a slow love song.

Dante drew Claire into his arms. She relaxed against him, one hand in his and the other resting on his shoulder. He moved them around the dance floor with smooth, easy steps, singing to her in a low baritone that made her feel as though they were the only people on the dance floor.

He's good at this she realized as he spun her around and dipped her low, their lips almost touching.

"We don't have time to be careful and cautious and follow the rules," he whispered close to her ear. "I want to be with you, Claire, in any and every way you'll let me. I don't know when we'll get a chance to be together again."

"Why?" she asked, when she was standing again. He turned her body from side to side. "Are you going somewhere?"

"No, but you're probably going home the day after tomorrow," he reminded her.

"I can always come back to visit, or you can come to Vegas," Claire huffed.

Dante spun her once more. "That would be dangerous."

"For whom?" she asked, wondering where this sudden turn of conversation came from.

"For you," he said in a low tone. "I have today and tomorrow before my life goes back to being a living hell."

The music stopped. Instead of heading back to their booth, Claire stood staring at him. "What do you mean? Can I help?"

He took both her hands in his. "No, I won't risk you."

"I'm not yours to risk. Besides, I'm stronger than I look," she assured him.

"Claire, no." He dropped one of her hands and made as if to lead her back to the table.

"I want to dance some more." Claire stopped, refusing to follow.

Another slow dance began and Dante drew her into his arms once more. "You weren't going to tell me there's no future, were you?" she asked, unable to hide the surprise in her voice.

"No." Dante stared down at her, his expression unreadable.

"I'm enjoying myself, but I don't do one night stands," she declared, meeting his gaze.

His warm hand curved around her waist. "Neither do I, but if you asked me, I don't think I could turn you down."

Claire laughed out loud. "Dante, you're safe with me," she declared. "I won't ask."

The look he gave her said that he knew better. Claire tossed him a look of her own. Once she made up her mind she stuck with it. Dante was extremely attractive, but she couldn't see herself changing her standards of behavior. "You still didn't explain why it'll be dangerous for me to be around you in a couple of days," she said, eying him expectantly.

"Death and danger follow me," he answered cryptically.

Claire raised an eyebrow. "Hmmmmh, I've heard that when you magic users have serious problems, it's usually one thing. You didn't sell your soul to the devil, did you?"

Dante's muscles tensed beneath her fingers. His answer came out short and explosive. "No!"

Claire parted her lips, aware that she touched on a deeply emotional issue. Teasing him, she'd somehow made an insensitive comment. Lifting her hand from his shoulder, Claire used her fingers on the frown between his brows. "Forget I asked, okay?"

Dante nodded, dropping her other hand. The music had ended once more. "Shall we go back to the table?"

Claire grinned. "By now, you've probably figured out that I love to dance."

He went back to massaging her hand. "It had crossed my mind. And, I want to kiss you again."

She glanced up at him, laughing, flirting. "So kiss me."

His eyes darkened. Dante's head dipped and his mouth was on hers, scorching, scintillating, and ravenous. Heat strummed through her, melting her insides and making her moan against his mouth. Claire's knees turned to jelly.

The music started again, this time, a driving, down and dirty beat. Claire felt it in her blood and the way she wanted to move her body against Dante's.

Dante ended the kiss, his eyes burning with heat. Claire realized that he was holding her up with one hand at her waist and the other beneath her elbow. He leaned forward to place his mouth close to her ear. "Still want to dance?"

The heat his breath on her ear felt wonderfully erotic. Claire blinked, abruptly aware that she was in a sensual haze. Right now, all she wanted to do was follow Dante DeLuca to the nearest bed. She swallowed. That didn't mean she would allow herself to do it. Forcing her legs to work, she moved away from Dante to stand on her own two feet. Then she began to shake her hips and wiggle to the beat of the music.

Surprise glinted in his eyes. Then he was moving around her, dancing close and well enough to pull her back under his spell. Claire grinned. All fluid, athletic grace, Dante DeLuca could really dance. He fascinated her.

Three dances later, Claire headed for the ladies room feeling sweaty and overheated. Randall intercepted her when she passed near the bar. "What are you doing with him?" he asked. "Do you know what he is?"

"A mage?" she asked, noting that he was taken aback at the fact that she knew. "Olive skinned male?"

Randall's lips tightened. "People around him often sicken and die or disappear."

"Are you saying that he kills people?" she asked, scanning Randall's face.

"I'm saying that he's a dangerous man to be around."

Claire swallowed hard. "So are cops, soldiers, and FBI agents. Do you have anything more specific?" Claire pushed a damp length of hair out of her face.

Randall's hand closed in a fist. "I know people who know people it happened to. Shouldn't you be thinking of walking away?"

Claire reached out to catch hold that fist. "I did think about it, but I've never felt this for anyone. He's worth the risk."

Randall shot her a look filled with anguish as she released his fist and edged past him to the bathroom.

She was in the ladies room, freshening up when Izzy came in. Her cousin watched her silently for several moments. Then she said, "You and the Italian guy are certainly burning up the dance floor."

Caught in the act of blotting the moisture on her neck beneath her hair with a paper towel, Claire laughed. "Yeah, he's a wonderful dancer. I'm having a good time!"

"I can see that." Izzy moved closer. "Claire, I'm worried about you. I've never seen you so swooped over anyone. Are you sure he didn't put something in your drink?"

Claire nodded. "Relax girl. All I've had to drink is the champagne Randall sent over. And exactly what have I done that is so out of the ordinary? I always dance."

Tilting her head, Izzy shot her a withering look. "You don't know this guy. You two were kissing out there in the middle of the dance floor in front of everyone and it was passionate enough to give the entire club a thrill. I thought he was gonna lay you down and have you right there."

Claire lowered her lashes, remembering the feel of Dante's mouth on hers. Something about him made her want to experience him to the fullest and hold on, whatever it meant. "You know how I feel about one night stands and public sex," she said, fishing in her bag for her makeup.

Izzy folded her arms in front of her. "Yeah, I do, but if anybody's gonna change your mind, this guy is it. What's wrong with you Claire? You're not the reckless one, I am. You can't bring this guy home to Vegas."

Claire used her brush to apply a mineral-based powder. "Why not?"

Izzy shook her head. "Uncle Julius and Aunt Esther rescued all of you from slavery. You've heard the stories of the way they were treated. Do your really think they'll just let you bring this guy into the family?"

"That was a long, long, time ago and Dante wasn't the one doing the things to my family," Claire countered. "And lighten up, will you? Things haven't gone that far."

Izzy's gaze met Claire's in the mirror. "Yes they have. I know you, Claire. I'm worried about you."

"What if I told you that Dante's going to be completely out of bounds for me in a couple of days? Would that make you feel better?"

Izzy inclined her head. "Yeah, it would."

Claire straightened her shoulders. "Then feel better."

"Why is he going to be out of bounds?" Izzy asked, watching Claire reapply lipstick.

"Go on back out there and have fun with Tony," Claire ordered. The warnings were unsettling, but being with Dante was exciting and she needed to explore it to the fullest.

After a few moments Izzy left the ladies room.

Raking a comb through her wavy locks, Claire stared at her reflection in the mirror, aware that her feelings and emotions were conflicted. She was still getting to know Dante, but the thought of not seeing him again struck a note of growing discord within her.

Claire returned to her table to find Dante reclining against the leather seat, sipping champagne. She scooted in beside him. "That took longer than I thought it would, sorry."

Nodding, Dante glanced at the dance floor and back to Claire with a glint of humor in his eyes. "Do you want to dance some more?"

She liked his good-natured willingness to continue doing what she wanted to do. Claire studied the people grooving and rocking beneath the flashing lights and decided that for once, she'd had enough. She told him.

Dante's woody oriental scent filled her nostrils as he leaned forward to brush her cheek with a kiss. "Then why don't we go somewhere else?"

Acute awareness of him sent thrills oozing down her spine. The kiss reminded Claire just how susceptible she was to Dante DeLuca. "Where, somewhere else?" she asked, keeping her tone light and easy.

He touched his forehead to hers. "We could go for coffee or walk the waterfront," he said. Her lips were only inches from his. "You could show me your room or I could take you to the company condo or the Ritz."

Claire tilted her chin so that her mouth touched Dante's. Soft, mobile lips melded with hers in passion-laced expertise that made her pulse race. Claire moaned softly. Dante DeLuca was hunting her and she wanted to let him catch her.

In her head she knew that if she had any sense she'd go home, but something about him spoke to her heart and the things she felt just by being with him were too strong. "Let's go for coffee," she said, opting for a place where they could talk but would not be alone.

Dante shifted across the seat and stood, offering his hand to help

125

Claire up. Claire accepted, grabbing her bag from the table as they headed for the entrance. She stopped at the bar to tell Izzy where she was going and to give her one of Dante's business cards.

"If you two want company, Tony and I could come along," Izzy offered uncharacteristically.

Biting her tongue, Claire stared at her cousin. Izzy was the one who was usually trying to get away from her.

Dante put a casual arm around Claire's shoulders. "I think we can manage on our own."

Tony growled, barely audible, but threatening just the same. Claire focused on him, surprised. She wondered, was he challenging Dante?

Dante stepped forward, a deep, threatening growl coming from his throat. His blue eyes gloweded dark and dangerous. Strong power energized the air, ready to be focused.

Tony took a step forward, confronting Dante and ready to back up his challenge.

Muscles tensing, Dante growled again, this time stronger and filled with eminent threat.

Tony's eyes widened, as if he saw more than the olive-skinned man facing him. Abruptly Tony's head dipped, acknowledging Dante as the more powerful alpha. Claire and Izzy were speechless.

Dante waited several beats and then turned and ushered Claire out of the club.

"Where you learn to do that?" she asked as they waited for the valet to get Dante's car.

His expression was edgy and intriguing. "I wasn't born werewolf, but doesn't mean I can't become one. You want an alpha? I'm it."

Claire moved closer, enjoying the lure of the power still streaming off of him. "I'm impressed. Can you pull that off with strong alphas, like my brothers?"

"For you, anything." He slid his fingers down her cheek.

The valet returned with his car.

Claire settled in the seat beside him, aware that she'd only begun to scratch the surface of Dante DeLuca. "I like you Dante. I like you a lot," she began. "I've never seen anyone do that but someone from one of werewolf clans."

"Maybe you've led a sheltered life," he offered closing her door and going round to the driver's side. He climbed in and started the car.

"Maybe you're being too mysterious," she countered.

Dante shot her a incredulous glance. "I told you what I am. Power runs strong in my family."

"Yes, but you knew how to challenge Tony, how to get him to back down respectfully," she persisted, remembering how he'd sounded and how she'd felt.

For a while he simply drove in silence. Finally he turned to her and said, "My godparents were werewolves so I grew up with a bunch of them."

If you aren't born werewolf, the next best thing is to be raised among them. Claire nodded. "Which clan?"

He took the freeway exit. "Thierry."

She recognized the name. Large and well known in California, the Thierry clan often attended council meetings that included the Temple clan. Dante's revelation explained a lot.

Claire studied his olive features in the dim light of the car. "So why does death and destruction follow you?"

He halted the car at a stop sign. "You come from a powerful family. Power breeds power and attracts those who want to possess it. I had to learn how to use mine and I've made my share of mistakes and enemies. Understand, Claire, I'm in an extremely hard place right now and I'm working to find my way out. When I'm free I'll look for you."

"That sounds like such a line," Claire laughed. "If you're that tied up with your dangerous life, how are you free to be with me now?"

Frustration leaked into his expression. "Is trust one of your issues?"

Claire shrugged. "It can be." The funny thing was that in her heart she knew he spoke the truth. Her head wouldn't even let her consider taking anything on faith. It required some sort of proof. "You've got to give on something."

"I told you about my growing up around werewolves," he reminded her.

Claire sighed. "Yes, you did, but I need more. Why don't we go to your place for coffee?" she challenged.

Dante pulled over and stopped the car. "That would be too dangerous."

"I thought you said you were safe for today and tomorrow?" she said, inclining her head.

Ignoring her question and eyeing her steadily, Dante said, "You think I'm hiding a wife at my place?"

"No." She breathed a sigh of relief when the stiffness in his shoulders eased. "But some males would and I don't know what to think about this death and destruction stuff."

He cupped his fingers around her chin and tilted her face until she fully faced him. "Don't think—just believe. I can't take you to my home unless you promise that you will not come back on your own until I tell you it is safe."

Claire placed her hand on his. "I promise."

With a nod, Dante turned the car around and headed back for the freeway. Beside him on the seat, anticipation made butterflies in Claire's stomach. She didn't think he was hiding a wife at his home, but she did hope to find some sort of clue to the sort of trouble he was in. Sensing that they were well suited to each other, she wanted to help him. Hopefully he was right about being safe for the next couple of days. And if he wasn't? Claire suppressed a shiver. Izzy had all the information she needed on Dante and would bring help if rescue became necessary.

Chapter Three

Taking the hill, Dante turned right, stopping at the large, ornate set of gates. He pushed a button on his dashboard and the automatic gates swung open. Accelerating, he turned onto the winding drive of the estate that had been in his family for two generations. Decorative lamps accented the tree lined drive and lights were on in the Italian Renaissance styled mansion, but he knew that no one was there. His family was scattered to the different ends of the planet and he'd laid off and or retired the staff. In the past six months he and the one who tormented him and made his life a living hell had been the only ones to enter its doors.

Dante glanced at Claire, studying the mansion and grounds with admiration. "It's beautiful," she breathed.

Other than Marielle, who had been his wife, he'd never brought another woman here. What was it about Claire Temple that caused him to override his innate caution to bring her here?

At Claire's urging, Dante told her how his grandparents had done well as merchants and purchased the estate. The basic mansion had been built in 1927 and upgraded and remodeled several times since.

Dante drove into a parking spot near his apartment in the east wing. Exiting the car, he went to open Claire's door.

"Is anybody home?" she asked, accepting his hand and maneuvering off the low-slung seat.

129

He got an up close view of her sexy legs as she tried to maintain some modesty in her short dress. They were long, smooth, and shapely, and from what he could see, Claire's entire body consisted of the kind of curves most men dream about.

He wanted her, but he also desired something that spanned much more than the short time they had.

"There's no one here but us," he answered, shutting the car door behind her and leading her to his private entrance. "I'm the only one who likes to come here on a regular basis. My father wants to sell it, but there is just too much family history here."

"I couldn't sell this place if it had been in my family for generations either," she confided as he fitted his key into the lock.

Dante pushed open the door. The lights came on automatically, illuminating the foyer and great room, and the passage to the kitchen.

"I like your place," Claire said, studying the Italian contemporary modern furnishings. She stepped past a collection of low, metal-accented ottomans, sofas, and chairs. Inhaling briefly, she smiled. "Other than the faint scent of cleaners, this place has your scent too, kind of woody and oriental and male."

He moved closer, placing his hands on her arms and shoulders. Turning, she enfolded him in an impulsive hug. Closing his eyes, he nuzzled his cheek against the chocolate cream softness of hers and closed his hands on her tiny waist, just above the swell of her buttocks.

She turned to brush her lips against his. "You are so hard to resist," she murmured softly, pulling away.

"Do you have to?" He let her go reluctantly.

"For now I do." Her tone turned husky with regret. "Where's the kitchen?"

Dante led her to it, taking an odd sort of pleasure in watching her search the cabinets for what they needed.

Claire Temple knew her way around a kitchen. In minutes she had the coffee percolating in his high tech machine and had opened tins of gourmet cookies and nuts and placed them on a tray.

They sat at the table in the window overlooking the bay to nibble the food, drink coffee and talk. Dante took off his jacket, loosened his tie, and got comfortable.

After a while, they moved to the soft pillows lining the seat inside the big bay window. Claire kicked off her shoes and curled her feet beneath her. Then she told him a little about her parents and each of her sisters and brothers.

Dante knew that the Weres usually lived in tight, close-knit groups, so he wasn't surprised when Claire tried to get a sense of his family and their relationships. If he and Claire became mates, he knew he would be expected to join the Temple clan or bring Claire into his.

Finally, he broke down and told her how disjointed and competitive his family was. His parents were estranged because his mother had bested his father in a magic competition and his brother was apprenticing with a mage rumored to possess legendary skill and power.

Claire opened her arms to hug him impulsively. She rubbed her soft cheek against his, filling his nostrils with her subtle, earthy scent of vanilla and jasmine. "I'm sorry about your family," she said softly. "Maybe you'll all come back together in the future."

"I wasn't whining," he assured her, aware that she was comforting him and he liked it.

"I know," she laughed, pressing a quick kiss to his lips. "I thought you looked like you needed a hug."

The funny thing was that he had. Dante closed his eyes, enjoying the feeling of Claire's arms around him, her scent, the closeness of her body. He needed this, had been needing this for along time.

She nibbled at his lips, laving the fullness of his bottom lip with her tongue and gently sucking it into her mouth.

His stomach clenched. Searing heat flashed through him, filling him with a more erotic need. Dante's body hardened. Still, he kept his hands at her waist, waiting for a definite sign that she had made a decision to sleep with him.

Her mouth covered his in a warm, wet, exciting blend of want and need.

Opening his eyes he locked gazes with her, infinitely more honored and excited by what he saw there. She was giving herself to him and he sensed that neither of them would ever be the same again.

The heat of her body seemed to burn through his clothes. Holding her gently, Dante eased down full length on the cushions. His hands slid to knead and shape the ripe fullness of her butt.

Working the buttons of his shirt and spreading it open, she stopped, moaning softly as he continued his exploration and extended it to the length of her legs and soft thighs. He cupped her sex, smoothing the soft fabric of her tiny lace throng and removing it to slip his fingers into her moist, silky center.

Laving his chest with her tongue, she wiggled against him and panted. Her mouth closed on his nipples and he almost lost it as she came. Slick moisture coated his fingers.

Briefly, they separated as he shucked off the rest of his clothes and he watched her pull the dress over her head. Almost nude, she was beautiful, everything he'd imagined as they'd danced. Dante removed her tiny lace bra and thought of chocolate cream as he feasted on her breasts and moved lower to kiss her intimately. Her breathy sighs egged him on.

Unwilling to wait any longer, he arranged her on the pillows. Once she'd slipped on the condom, he spread her thighs, and pushed into her. Drawing him closer, Claire locked her legs around his waist. Finally they rocked together, slow and easy, building tempo and speed to collapse in a wild, trembling tangle of moist satiated flesh.

"That was wonderful," Claire whispered as Dante carried her to his bed and placed her between the silk sheets. Joining her on the bed, he drew her into an embrace.

"This is beautiful," she said, fingering the ornate gold collar that had been hidden beneath his shirt. "It looks very old."

Dante stiffened as she fingered the writing and symbols scrawled across the front. Grasping her hand and moving it away he tasted her soft lips.

Claire smiled up at him. "What do the writing and the symbols mean?"

Dante nuzzled her cheek, hiding his expression and searching for an explanation that would not be a lie. "It's Latin. Some would say it confirms my status as a slave," he began, "especially since I got it when I started with the company."

Claire chuckled, but her eyes grew serious. "You've got to stop kidding like that. My family has roots in slavery and they wouldn't understand."

Treading on the edge of a bunch of tricky questions, Dante risked letting her see his face. "Who says I'm kidding?"

She stared at the collar, frowning. "Come to think of it, it does look like something a slave might wear, except for that fact it is gold. I don't think I like it. Can you take it off?"

"No." Dante trailed an open mouthed kiss on the soft skin from her neck to her navel. "Can we make love again?"

Sighing with pleasure, Claire curled into him. "Yes, oh yes."

They threw themselves into the intimate exploration of each other's bodies and the art of giving and receiving pleasure. This time it was slow and easy and infinitely more thorough and fulfilling. Exhausted, Claire dozed against the pillows, looking like a sensual Nubian goddess with her thick wavy hair splayed across his pillow and her rich brown curves a deep contrast against his white sheets.

Curling his body around hers, he cuddled, touching her wonderingly and enjoying every minute as if it could be his last.

Unwilling to sleep away precious time, Dante watched her sleep and tried not to think about the time when she would be returning to Vegas.

Dante filled the bathing pool with soothing scented salts and awakened Claire as the sun came up. They bathed together, washing each other and nestling together beneath the swirling jets before making love again.

By the time they got out of the bath, both were hungry. In bathrobes, they padded to the kitchen and prepared breakfast. Dante sat close to her at the table, needing the contact and warmth of her personality as they ate.

"What time do you leave for Vegas?" he asked as they finished breakfast and Claire insisted on cleaning the mess.

Claire stared down into the sink. "Seven-thirty."

"I'll take you to the airport," he offered, determined to spend as much time as possible with her.

She threw him a sharp glance. "Are you trying to spend every possible moment with me or making sure I leave?"

"Both," he answered honestly.

She dried her hands on a dishtowel. "I can leave now."

Dante came to stand behind her and lock his arms around her waist. Hunching over, he kissed her temple. "Don't. Please. I need this time with you and I don't want you to go away mad."

Claire covered his hands with hers. "I'm not mad. You told me how this had to be up front. The thing is I don't understand what's going on Dante, and my imagination is going wild."

He was silent for several moments. "I can't explain."

"Why not?"

He shifted his feet, knowing that his explanation would not satisfy Claire. "It's dangerous."

"For who?"

"Both of us." He moved away from her to stand in the window and look out over the bay.

He heard her footsteps closing in on him. "Has anyone actually died?" she asked.

"Yes." Dante turned to face her, knowing that guilt shone in his eyes. He blamed himself for not being able to save those who died and for not freeing himself from a living hell. "I couldn't save them. I'm still trying to save myself."

Claire touched his cheek with her fingertips. "Maybe I know someone who could help you."

"No. I won't willingly bring anyone else into this and that's not negotiable."

Studying him silently for several moments, she sighed and shook her head. "Fifty points for your integrity and fifty demerits for being a pig-headed male who may have signed his own death warrant."

"I have to be able to live with myself." Dante drew her into his arms, locking them around her waist. "What do you want to do today?"

Claire rattled off a list of tourist attractions.

"Get dressed. You're on."

They spent the day in and around the San Francisco tourist attractions. As it got closer to the time she would have to leave, Dante asked her to wait in the car while he ran an errand back at the convention hall. Claire waited twenty minutes then decided to go in to help him finish his errand.

At the Baxter Food, Beverages, and Exotics booth, Dante was packing up.

"Why didn't you ask me to help?" Claire asked, entering the booth to confront him.

Dante shook his head. "I didn't want to make you work."

"Well I didn't want to be by myself and I do want to help," Claire said, putting her face close to his.

He grinned. "I guess you can put some of those bottles into the boxes beneath the table."

Claire dragged one of the boxes out and began to pack it.

"Don't tell me you've been hanging here all day."

Izzy's voice startled Claire. She didn't need to look up to know that her cousin was still in a funky mood and she'd have to assert herself. "Izzy, grow up," she said, not bothering to slow down her pace of packing.

"Did you sample the goods?" Izzy eyed Dante and fiddling with some of the beautiful crystal bottles on the table.

"What do you think?" Claire shot back. She was beginning to think she would have to get ugly to force Izzy to behave or go away.

Dante's voice cut into their interchange. "Please be careful with that."

"If I break it, I'll pay for it," Izzy snapped, fingering the fancy gold label attached to the neck of the bottle.

"The danger is not that you will break the bottle," Dante added, extending a hand for the bottle.

"I want to read the label," Izzy insisted, moving away from him.

Giving Izzy another annoyed glance, Claire turned to Dante. He seemed...tense. More than the situation warranted. She scanned the area around them to see if there was something she was missing.

"It says that this drink makes a person irresistible." Izzy put the bottle down.

Dante promptly grabbed it and put it in his pocket. Claire let herself breathe.

Izzy moved down to talk to Claire. "I brought all our stuff from the hotel and left it with Tony."

"Thanks." Still on the floor packing samples, Claire glanced up at her cousin, noting the secretive set of her lips and something false behind the innocence in her eyes. What was Izzy up to now?

Dante went to get a cart. Claire stared at her cousin, hoping she was done acting like a spoiled brat. Izzy chattered on while Claire finished the packing, sometimes bringing her an item or helping to tape a box. Checking the tables and behind the curtains to make sure they hadn't missed anything, she caught Izzy rummaging through one of the boxes. "Girl, what is your problem?" she snapped. "I've never seen you act like this."

Ignoring her, Izzy drew a crystal bottle from the box and checked the label. Quickly pulling out the stopper, she giggled. "I thought there'd be more than one of these. I think I could learn to like being irresistible."

Claire's stomach knotted. There was something bad about the stuff in the bottle and she didn't want her cousin taking it. "Izzy..."

Izzy lifted the bottle to her nose. "Interesting smell."

"Don't drink it," Claire warned, covering the distance between them as fast as she could without alarming Izzy.

With lightning quick reflexes Izzy lifted the bottle and drank.

Watching her, helpless, Claire felt sick. Izzy froze. Claire gasped, reaching her too late.

Suddenly Dante was back with the cart, his blue eyes narrowing angrily as his thick brows furrowed together. "You shouldn't have done that." He took the bottle from Izzy's hand and checked the label.

"I-I couldn't stop her," Claire stammered. "What does it really do? And why is she standing there like that?"

Something dark in his expression made Claire afraid for her childish cousin. Dante flicked his fingers in the air.

Claire saw Izzy moving again. Izzy's fingers closed on empty air. "Dante, talk to me," Claire insisted.

"Whew." Bending over the table to hold on, Izzy gasped, shaking her head and blinking. "That stuff packs a wallop."

"It wasn't meant for her," Dante said, bending down to rummage through some of the boxes beneath the table in a determined way.

"Who was it meant for?" Claire persisted, putting an arm around Izzy.

Dante didn't answer.

Izzy straightened. "I'm all right." She grinned at Claire. "Is it working?"

Could the stuff work that fast? Claire studied her cousin, not knowing what to look for. Izzy did look more beautiful than usual. Her brown eyes sparkled and her honey-colored skin positively glowed. Somehow she filled out that hoochie dress she was wearing much better than before and managed to look more graceful.

Izzy dug in her purse and came out with a $50 bill. "This should cover the cost of your product."

Still searching through one of the boxes, Dante shook his head. "I won't take your money for this."

A man passing behind them stopped and stared at Izzy. As the stranger began to talk to her, Dante pressed a small brown bottle into Claire's hand. "I can't undo what she has done, but this will help. She must drink it on the night of the next full moon. All of it," he said urgently, "And whatever you do, don't bring her back to this city."

Claire caught his hand. "There's something bad about the elixir she drank, isn't there? What is it? Tell me."

He shook his head. "I can't, but know that I want you and your cousin to be safe." He checked his watch. "We should head to the airport."

Claire glanced at her cousin who was now at the center of a group of enthusiastic admirers. "She's not herself." Izzy didn't seem hurt, but Dante was upset. This fed her fear. She examined the bottle in her hand and swallowed hard. "What if it doesn't work?"

"I warned her. I tried to keep her away from the elixir." Dante put his hands on Claire's shoulders, his eyes sparking with frustration. "I've done everything I can to help. I can't do anything more until I come for you."

"You're scaring me," Claire said, staring into those blue eyes with her thoughts circling frantically. "How long do I have to wait? What if you don't come?"

"Then I'm dead." Dante grabbed her and hugged her tight. "I should have stayed away from you."

"No, I'm glad we had our time together." Blinking away tears, Claire held onto him. She was worried about him and worried about Izzy and yet there was nothing she could do. Her thoughts cycled uselessly while the need to do something grew.

Releasing her, Dante began loading the cart. Seeing that Izzy was in no immediate danger, Claire helped. By the time they finished, a transport company representative had arrived. With that task out of the way they pried Izzy away from her admirers and headed for the airport.

Claire watched Dante most of the way, her thoughts troubled. Would Izzy be all right? And if she wasn't how would Claire get help if she couldn't come to Dante?

Chapter Four

Vegas was the same as Claire had left it, but her thoughts stayed with San Francisco and Dante DeLuca.

At a popular club, Claire watched her cousin out on the floor dancing with three guys. Izzy was enjoying herself, but Claire could see that something was not quite right. Izzy seemed less energetic. Claire remembered that the last two times the pack had gone for runs, Izzy declined. It wasn't like her.

Claire had given Izzy the brown bottle and Dante's instructions and tonight was the night of the full moon. Claire spotted the brown bottle in Izzy's purse when Izzy paid for a round of drinks. The uneasiness that started when Izzy drank from the bottle of elixir in San Francisco grew.

When it was time to leave, Claire opted to walk the Las Vegas Strip back to the French Quarter.

Outside, the colorful lights and signs on the strip illuminated the buildings and surroundings and commanded attention. Feeling the pull of the moon, Clair looked up. The full moon shone down on her, tightening her skin as her body threatened to shift. She could control the change, could even change when the moon wasn't full, but tonight the pull of the moon was hard to resist.

Beside her, Izzy was also looking up, but her face was a study in anxiety.

"What's wrong?" Claire asked. The niggling worry that had essentially hidden in the background of her thoughts burst forth.

"I feel…sorta strange," Izzy admitted. "I haven't shifted since we got back from the conference. I want to. I'm not sure I can."

"Did you try?" Claire asked, clenching one of her fists.

Izzy nodded slowly. "But it felt weird, almost as if I lost my connection with whatever makes me shift.

Claire unconsciously quickened her steps. "We'll go out to the ranch and you can take the antidote. I'll help you."

"And if it doesn't work?" Izzy asked, her eyes troubled.

"It will," Claire promised. She'd make it work.

"I'm not sure I want to try any more of his products," Izzy said flatly, "All the attention is nice, but I'll go crazy if I can't change."

Feeling more than a little guilty for causing Izzy to be anywhere near those products Claire said, "He told you not to do it, Izzy."

Izzy blew out a breath that came close to a sob. Her eyes were shiny with tears. "Yeah, but what's he doing selling products that could something like this to me?"

Claire shook her head. "I don't know. I'm not even sure that the stuff you took was for sale, or even if it's responsible for your problem. Dante had secrets he wouldn't let me in on, but can you blame him? We hadn't known each other very long."

"Well if we can't fix this you're just going to have to hunt him down and make him help," Izzy snapped, blinking back tears.

Claire looped an arm around her cousin's shoulders. "It's going to be all right. The stuff in the bottle is supposed to make you better."

As they continued up the strip Claire tried to ease the growing apprehension creeping over her. She could fix this couldn't she? After all Dante's warnings she didn't want to think about failing and having to go back to San Francisco.

Later Claire and Izzy were behind the main house at the ranch. The others were out on a hunt. Crouching close to the warm ground, Izzy stared up at the moon, her face a stark study in hard planes and angles. She'd placed the brown bottle on the ground beside her.

"Drink it now," Claire urged.

Izzy lifted the bottle and twisted the cap off. With a quick flip of the bottle she drank it all.

"I feel kind of strange." Izzy slid to the ground in a fluid movement.

"Don't scare me like this!" Claire rushed to her cousin's side. "Girl sit up. Is it working?"

"Can't keep my eyes open," Izzy mumbled. Her eyes were closed.

Using her werewolf strength Claire knelt and lifted her cousin from the ground. Then she carried her into the house and put her on the couch in the den.

Claire studied her cousin. She didn't know what to do. What if Izzy never woke up? What if she slipped into a coma? She tried to reassure herself with the fact that Izzy's heartbeat was steady.

Claire shivered as she killed all thoughts of calling her family for help. They were a dynamic bunch and would charge to the rescue the way they always did. This time Claire wanted to charge to the rescue and she wasn't willing to risk more of her family getting hurt.

When she'd taken the sharpest edge off her hysteria, Claire called cousin Garen's former Preternatural Police partner, Ashalon Fouqua. It took surprisingly little to wheedle the number out Garen's boss but a lot more talking to make him promise not to tell Garen.

Ash sounded calm and self-assured. It took a while to explain what had happened to Izzy.

"You shouldn't fool with things you don't understand," Ash scolded, but he finally agreed to help.

Ash was a thin man of average height dressed in black slacks and shirt. Piercing, leaf green eyes seemed to see clear through to her soul and his blade of a nose stood out in an olive skinned face that seemed oddly pale. He introduced himself then asked, "Where is she?"

Claire showed him to the den and watched him examine Izzy. He lifted her eyelids and peered inside. Then he passed his hands through the air above the length of her several times. Finally, he studied her silently for several minutes.

Anxious to get Izzy awake and well before anyone returned to the ranch, Claire moved closer.

Ash turned to face her, startling her. He asked for the bottle Dante had given her.

Drawing the bottle from her pocket, she gave it to him.

He scanned the label. "This is powerful stuff," he murmured. "I can wake her, but she will still have the problem with shifting to wolf. There is an element in the magic that I don't recognize. Where did she get the elixir?"

"Dante DeLuca, but she took it against his advice. Do you know him?"

"I know that power runs strong in the DeLucas, but what has been done is not something I would expect of them."

"What are you trying to say?" In her head, Claire could still hear Dante's warnings.

Ash turned his penetrating gaze on Claire. "Tell me about Dante DeLuca. Did he do or say anything strange or unusual?"

Claire scrubbed the back of one hand over her eyes. "He told me not to bring Izzy back to San Francisco, no matter what happened. He told me not to come back either."

Ash frowned. "Anything else?"

"He knew about wolves and the politics involved. Sometimes he acted like one. He... said death and destruction followed him when he warned me to stay away, but I didn't think—"

"Did you see markings on his body, tattoos, or anything unusual?"

An image of Dante's naked body formed in Claire's thoughts and her face heated. She'd spent a lot of time looking at it, touching it. There'd been no scars, markings, or tattoos. She told Ash about the gold collar with Latin words engraved on it.

Ash's green eyes lit up. Bending, he unzipped his case and removed a black book. The pages of the book shone as he flipped through them and stopped a third of the way through. "Is this what you saw?"

Claire caught her breath as she stared at the illustration, aware that it's appearance in Ash's book meant something bad. "That's it. What does it do?"

"It makes its wearer a slave to someone else," Ash said flatly.

"He said he was a slave, but I thought he meant his job," Claire confessed. "What does this have to do with what's happened to Izzy?"

Ash lifted a brow. "Enslaved people are forced to do things they don't want to, things they wouldn't normally do. We need to find the one behind the collar and the components of the elixir keeping your cousin from shifting."

Claire nodded and made a conscious realization of what she'd known all along. "I have to go back to San Francisco."

"I'll go along and do what I can to protect you."

She sighed with relief. "Thank you." Claire met his gaze. "If I have to go back, it should be as soon as possible. Can you wake Izzy while I arrange for the tickets?"

Ash scanned Izzy's prone figure once more, said, "She's better off sleeping until we get back."

At a loss, Claire's gaze went from Izzy to Ash. "What will I tell the family?"

"Why tell them anything?"

"Uh—I guess you're right." She picked up the phone and began dialing.

An hour later Claire and Ash left for the airport. Claire planned to call Esther in the morning to make arrangements for Izzy if she and Ash did not get the cure tonight.

Excitement charged Claire's thoughts as she sat in the window seat on the flight out, staring into the darkness outside the plane and trying to imagine what she would do and say when she saw Dante. Izzy's problem and the stubborn part of Claire's brain that kept repeating Dante's warnings sharpened her sense of impending trouble. She hoped that Ash was strong enough to handle whatever trouble Dante had gotten into.

In San Francisco, Claire eased the rented Toyota Corolla up the hill towards Dante's home. She didn't know what she was going to do when she got to the ornate gates that helped guard the DeLuca estate from the public.

Ash had rented a vehicle of his own. For a few miles he'd been right behind her, but she'd lost sight of him as she got closer to the Dante's home.

At the top of the hill the gates were open. Instead of feeling relieved, Claire tensed up. She'd promised not to come back unless Dante came for her. Was he expecting her after all?

Darkness coated the area as the car nosed down the tree-lined lane. Peering around, wishing she could see better, Claire imagined she saw something moving behind the trees, parallel to her car.

Pulling into a spot next to Dante's sports car Claire switched off the engine. What was she going to say? What if the big bad, whatever he'd been warning her about was real and inescapable?

Swallowing her fear, Claire opened the car door and got out. The wolf inside her bristled, threatening to force the shift. Holding onto the car door, she spent several precious moments struggling with her wolf and forcing herself to relative calm.

Moving again at last, she cringed at each noisy slap of her shoes on the paved stone drive. Finally she bent down and took them off.

Her wolf senses told her that someone moved close to her in the quiet of the night. She hoped it was Ash, but she hadn't seen or heard from him in more than twenty minutes. The light breeze blew against her, taking her scent away and preventing her from getting a fix on her night companion.

As Claire approached the entrance to Dante's apartment, it swung open. Dante stood there, his eyes wide as he shook his head from side to side. "You shouldn't be here," he said in a low voice.

She smelled fear and something else, something kin to death and decay. That smell had not been present when she last visited Dante.

Claire lifted her hands in a helpless gesture. "I didn't have a choice. Something's wrong with Izzy."

"At least she won't die from it," he answered glancing over his shoulder. "You have to go now. I can't protect you."

Claire grabbed his hand, heartened that she still felt a familiar jolt of electricity at the contact. "But what about Izzy? Can't you give me something to reverse the elixir?"

"I did everything I could when I gave you the other bottle. Until this is over, it can't be reversed." Turning his head once more he stiffened. "Too late," he whispered. "Don't—,"

A man's voice rang out. "Dante, who's at the door?"

Apparently frozen in place, Dante didn't answer. Claire realized that he couldn't and it had something to do with the person who approached.

Torn between shifting into her wolf and running for the car, Claire did neither. A horrible dread filled her as a pale, mahogany haired man with piercing gray eyes moved into her line of sight.

Something odd about his eyes drew Claire and held her captive. There were two rings around his ice gray pupils, the first a charcoal gray that deepened as she stared, and the second a dirty gray that shone as if there was a light behind it.

Blinking, Claire tried to look away, to think of something besides those compelling eyes.

As if he were aware of her efforts, the man laughed. "Come in wolf," he ordered in a commanding tone. "Come see what you've gotten yourself into."

To Claire's horror, her body ignored her urgent pleas and stepped forward to stand beside the man like an obedient puppy.

The door closed behind her.

Lifting claw like fingers with thick black nails, he gripped her chin. "Dante is my obedient slave while I am around, but when I have to leave he does everything he can to escape. You will find, as he has, that escape is impossible. Somehow he brought you here and you are mine now."

"No!" The word stuck in Claire's throat.

Releasing her chin, he placed his hand on Dante's head and used the other to widen the opening of Dante's shirt. The gold collar gleamed in the light. "Did he show you his collar?"

"Yes." Despite her determined efforts, Claire's body answered clearly.

"Let me show you how it works." The hand gripped Dante's head till it seemed that the black tips of those fingers would enter his head. The man's other hand touched the gold collar. It glowed. The glow intensified until the collar shone with a bright light that threatened to blind Claire.

She could not shut her eyes. Worse, she saw that Dante's olive skin was turning a pasty gray. His body shook.

A realization hit Claire with a staggering impact. The man was feeding off of Dante, taking his life force, his soul, and killing him. Claire's scream echoed in her head. Warm moisture slid down her face and onto the floor. She was crying.

Insidious sounds of pleasure came from the man as he fed off of Dante. Claire teetered on the edge of consciousness. One word echoed in her mind. Vampire. The man was some sort of vampire.

The collar's glow dimmed. Dante's body crumpled to the floor with heart wrenching finality. Was he dead? Unable to make a sound she gasped inwardly. Claire stared, desperately looking for signs of life. When she had almost given up she saw one of Dante's fingers move. Dear God, where was Ash?

Positively glowing with renewed vitality, the vampire circled Claire. "I don't need a collar to bend you to my will or take your life force," he said with a little laugh. "And your ability to shift into a wolf will renew your body over and over again. I couldn't have asked for a better present. I'll have to thank Dante when he's feeling more himself." Laughing again, he told Claire to sit down.

Claire sat in one of the upholstered chairs, trying to think of way to escape. The vampire hadn't hurt her yet, but she was on the menu. Anger with herself for walking into a trap despite Dante's warnings fueled her will.

"You can call me Andrais." The vampire took a seat on the couch facing her. "What is your name?"

Claire told him.

"I'm a frequent visitor here so I welcome you to his home. It was rude of me to eat without offering you something. Would you like something to eat?"

Bile roiled in Claire's stomach. "No."

Andrais stretched his arms out along the back of the couch. "Good. Then we can talk. I'm sure Dante warned you about coming here. What was so important that you risked walking into danger?" he asked pleasantly.

Claire bit down hard on her tongue. The gesture didn't stop it from giving him the details of what had happened to Izzy.

Andrais smiled. "Another wolf to fill my needs! Maybe I should allow Dante more freedom. I left because I had business to attend, but this was also a test. I knew he would try to release himself. Now I have Dante, you, and all who drank the elixirs."

He peered at her as if he saw something in her expression. "He didn't tell you about the elixirs?"

"No." Claire barely recognized the emotionless sound of her voice.

Andrais crossed a foot over his knee. "Then let me tell you. The elixirs are his, potions that he developed over the years, but the secret ingredient is mine. All mine, and it makes all who drink them willing contributors to my sustenance."

Claire swallowed painfully against the dry desert of her mouth and throat. With her sensitive ears she heard stealthy movements in the room. Dante? Ash? She could only hope.

Startling, Andrais glanced over his shoulder, threads of suspicion tightening his expression. Abruptly the vampire stood, hauling Claire to her feet. "Magic. I sense the use of magic in this room." He shook Claire like a rag doll. "What do you know about this?"

Again Claire bit down on her tongue. This time the maneuver worked.

The vampire's clawed fingers closed on her throat as he dragged her to the spot where he'd left Dante on the floor. Dante had disappeared.

Straining her ears, Claire scanned the room, looking for Dante and Ash, trying to determine the best way to help them.

Andrais jerked Claire in front of him. "If anything happens, you'll be first to die."

Claire felt her body temperature plummet. She suddenly felt...weak. Stunned, she realized that the vampire was pulling energy from her. Going limp in a simulated faint she became deadweight in his grip.

Going from room to room searching the house, the vampire dragged her along, ordering Dante to come forward. He threatened to kill Claire if Dante did not appear. His grip eased...

Drawing on a natural skill she's honed through the years, Claire's skin tightened over her expanding bones, stretching and reshaping itself as she fell to her knees. Feet became paws, nails became claws, and gloriously soft fur covered everything. She's fast shifted into her wolf. Claire leapt for his throat.

Andrais's arm shot up to protect his neck.

The wolf's powerful jaws snapped on the vampire's arm, crushing the bones together. Bitter blood dripped from its jaws, splattering the carpet, painting it red.

Uttering a cry of pain mixed with rage, Andrais smashed the wolf into a metal table.

Sharp pain exploded in Claire's head as the table edges bruised the wolf's fur covered skin and broke bones. The wolf held onto the vampire's arm. Where were Ash and Dante?

Andrais lifted his arm to smash the wolf into the table once more.

In a twisting motion the wolf's jaws snapped off the end of the vampire's arm. Blood sprayed everywhere as it dropped the severed limb on the floor. The wolf backed up as Andrais brought his remaining arm up.

Seeing the vampire's fingers curve and aim at the wolf, Claire stared death in the face. The injured wolf could not move fast enough to dodge a lightning bolt.

Suddenly a bright stream of pulsing blue light hit the vampire's heart. Staggering, Andrais lowered his curved fingers.

The vampire and the wolf turned to the source of the light. Dante stood in the doorway, raised hand in front of him. The gold collar was still around his neck.

"Energy!" Andrais roared, extending his hand towards Dante. The collar began to glow.

"No!" Dante hit the vampire with another burst of pulsing blue light.

Claire noticed that as the gold collar glowed brighter, Dante's blue light started to dim.

The air heated as a stream of pulsing red light from the other side of the room hit Andrais in the center of his forehead. Staggering, he threw up his hand, countering with a beam of light that was sometimes blue, sometimes a silvery color.

Claire saw Ash in the entryway on the other side of the room, aiming the red light. He made a forceful flinging motion with his other hand.

The vampire's silvery beam went wild as he went airborne, crashing backwards to land against a set of wooden bookcases.

The air around Dante shimmered a soft blue, drawing Claire's attention away from the fight. His hands moved in distinct patterns, as though he was drawing pictures on the air. The air vibrated as he chanted in singsong voice.

Out of the corner of one eye, Claire saw Ash airborne. Instead of going wild as Andrais had done, Ash's red beam of light sliced into Andrais' throat.

Screaming, the vampire tried to cover it, as it aimed another silvery blue beam at Ash.

Claire turned back to Dante. The gold collar was slowly losing its shine and turning black. Several moments later she watched, fascinated and overjoyed as it fell off his neck. Dante was free.

Ash and Andrais were still fighting. The cracked and shattered walls shook and smashed furniture littered the floor. Still the two of them continued to fight. Claire noticed that once Dante's collar hit the floor, the lethal beam Andrais threw turned pure silver-gray. She wondered, Was that because he could no longer draw energy from Dante?

Directing an intense stream of blue light at the vampire's heart, Dante joined the battle. This time the vampire staggered and fell.

As Dante and Ash stood over Andrais, preparing to finish him off, he cried out, "No, wait! I can show you the secret of the black jewel and I know where to find the Monocan Wizards."

Dante shook his head. "That's what got me into this mess. Besides, you could have killed Claire. That's more than enough reason to end your life." Dante locked glances with the wolf as if to assure himself that Claire was all right. He turned to Ash. "Are his secrets worth you saving his life?"

"No." Ash shot Andrais a condemning look. "We can never bring back all the people he has hurt and killed."

Ash reached into his jacket and drew out what looked like a thin ceremonial axe made out of a black, obsidian-like material. Etched gold symbols ran the length of the handle.

Andrais struggled, trying to push himself up from the floor. Dante motioned an open palm in the air above the vampire's form, stopping all movement. Then he raised the axe and brought it down hard on the already healing spot where Ash had sliced open the vampire's neck.

The room echoed with the force of the blow. Something rolled across the floor. Claire bent down and found the vampire's head against the woodwork on the other side of the room.

Murmuring something in a low tone, Ash threw a sparkly powder on the vampire's torso. It burst into bright yellow flames.

Grabbing the ripped and torn remains of her clothes, Claire slipped outside the room to shift. By the time she'd slipped on her skirt, Dante was there, drawing her into his arms with the familiar pulse of energy in his touch. "I'm sorry I put you in danger," he said, wiping Andrais blood off her face and rubbing his face against hers.

Claire leaned back and stared into his midnight blue eyes. "You didn't put me in danger. You warned me, but I had to come for Izzy. I-"

"I thought I was going to lose you."

"And do you have me now?" she asked, unable to resist teasing him.

"You're here, aren't you?" Dante's warm lips covered hers in a deep, emotion-filled kiss that reestablished his claim. "I am yours, if you want me, for however long that may be," he said.

Claire held him tight. "When you crumpled to the ground I thought he'd killed you," she admitted. "It sounds silly, but I thought my heart would stop beating."

"It's not silly." Dante's lips brushed her temple as he slid his fingers along her spine.

Claire winced.

Turning her to face the wall, Dante lifted her top to examine her back. "It's starting to heal," he said, lightly touching the area, "but you have dark bruises and maybe even crushed and broken bones. I could take you to the hospital or find a healer..."

"We have healers of our own," Claire told him. "If you could take away the pain, it would be enough for now."

Claire felt the air beneath Dante's fingers heat as he murmured something in another language and motioned along the length and breadth of her hips and back.

Ash cleared his throat from the open doorway. "Anywhere I can get cleaned up?"

Dante moved away from Claire. "Sure. I'll show you to one of the guest bedrooms. There's plenty of my brother's clothes you could borrow. He's about your size and most of them are brand new."

Once Ash was settled in the guest bedroom, Dante turned to Claire. "My mother's clothes will fit you." His gaze slid down her body to linger on her hips. "The pants may be a little tight in the hips." he added.

Claire giggled. "Is that a good thing?"

Dante shot her a heated look. "Oh yeah." Taking her hand, he led her to his private suite.

They spent the next twenty minutes lovingly washing each other's bodies beneath the hot shower spray. Then Dante led Claire to the bathing pool and lowered her into the water.

"We can't linger here with Ash waiting and Izzy in trouble," Claire reminded him as he slipped into the water to join her.

"What makes you think I want to linger?" Dante asked, His hot mouth blazed a trail from the insides of her soft thighs to the hard, chocolate colored tips of her breasts. Then he was sliding her across the masculine terrain of his olive-skinned body until she was positioned on top of him. His fingers curved around the fullness of her hips and butt. "I've got three years of living to make up for."

Rocking his hips forward he pushed into Claire's willing heat. She wrapped her legs around his waist, holding onto one of his shoulders and the side of the pool, riding his satiny steel length.

Dante grunted, going deeper as he rocked faster until they collapsed together in a warm, wet, trembling tangle of flesh.

Basking in the afterglow, Claire lay against Dante's damp shoulder. The warm water in the pool still circled around them. This man was hers and she wanted him, but at what cost? Could these feelings weather the violence or banishment that could come if her family did not accept him?

"I know it's too soon to say this, but you're the one," Dante whispered close to her ear. "That's why I couldn't send you away when we met at the Moscone Center."

"What are you saying?" Claire asked, very much afraid of what she already knew.

Dante's voice was strong with conviction. "I'm saying that I love you and if you don't love me already, I'm going to do whatever it takes to make you love me back."

Claire's heart lifted. She pressed a kiss on his shoulder. "I love you, but I don't know how much. I don't know if it can stand up to--to ..."

"A lot of static from your family?" he guessed astutely.

"Yes." Claire bent her head, hiding her eyes. She'd been a grown woman for several years, so what her family thought shouldn't matter, but it did.

Dante lifted her chin with his fingers. "I'm standing by you, whatever it takes. I'll make them like me."

Locking gazes with him Claire saw a heady combination of love, conviction, and determination. "I believe you will," she said.

By the time they'd dressed and prepared for the trip back to Vegas, it was very early in the morning. Dante commandeered the company plane and arranged the trip.

Claire spent the time on the plane holding Dante's hand and preparing herself for the inevitable round of questions and comments from her parents, brothers, and sisters. She worried about Izzy too, but Dante assured her over and over again that with Andrais dead, he could wake Izzy with all of the abilities intact that she'd had before drinking the elixir.

Ash and Dante filled in some of the time talking about magic and some of the things they'd experienced.

Claire called ahead and had the hotel limousine waiting at the airport. Once they'd settled in the vehicle, the thirty-minute ride was anticlimactic.

Glad there were no other vehicles at the ranch, Claire virtually ran into the ranch house. Izzy was still asleep on the couch, looking fresh and relaxed.

Dante drew a small bottle from his pocket and screwed off the cap. Lifting Izzy's head, he poured a small amount into her slightly open mouth, tilting her head until she swallowed. Then he made patterns in the air, chanting slowly.

Izzy's eyes opened. Sitting up, she stared at all of them in wonder. "What happened?"

Ash gave Dante an approving nod. "Good work."

Claire took a seat beside her cousin on the couch. "What do you remember?"

Izzy scratched her head. "I dreamed that I drank a potion to make me irresistible. "

"That's what happened," Claire and Dante assured her in unison.

Izzy stared at Dante. "I remember you. Sorry I was such a brat. I think I was a little envious of what was going on between you and Claire."

As Izzy's gaze moved to Ash, Claire made introductions. "This is Ashalon Fouqua. He works with Garen."

The two made polite introductory conversation, distinct interest sparking between them.

The telephone rang. Claire answered out of habit. It was Esther. "Morning Claire, is Izzy awake?"

"Yes," Claire answered, glad that the night's work was resolved and over with. "Do you want to speak with her?"

Esther laughed. " No, I actually wanted to invite the two of you and your guests to breakfast in my suite."

Claire glanced around the room. How did Esther know she had guests? "Someone told you that we got picked up at the airport," Claire guessed.

"No, but I was awake when James left for the airport," Esther replied, "Don't you have someone you want me to meet?"

"Yes." Claire locked gazes with Dante. It was time he met the rest of her family.

"Well hang up the phone girl and get over here before breakfast gets cold," Esther said in a light, teasing tone.

Claire, Dante, Izzy, and Ash climbed back into the limousine for the short ride to the family hotel. Coming in through the private entrance, they made their way to Esther's private suite. Claire stifled a gasp as they entered. A large table, covered with food had been set up to run the length of Esther's living room and kitchen. Seated all around were her parents, brothers, and sisters, and several cousins, uncles, and aunts.

Since Ash was a family friend, he and Izzy were ushered to special seats close to Garren.

"The word is out that we're getting a new member in our family." Julius stood to address Claire and Dante.

Claire felt like she was two years old, but she found her voice and stepped forward with Dante. "Daddy, Mom, everybody, this is Dante DeLuca. I met him at the conference in San Francisco and I-I love him."

Julius and Esther came forward to shake hands. "Welcome to our home, Dante. We've been looking forward to meeting you."

The other family members came forward too, shaking hands, and introducing themselves. A couple of the women even hugged Dante. As expected, one of her brothers actually growled at Dante. The entire room fell silent.

Tensing and preparing to fight, Dante growled back, low, dangerous, and all alpha male.

Then Claire's brother extended his hand in friendship. Marcus, with his new mate at his side came forward and slapped Dante on the back. "This guy is all right," he told Claire.

Kellie came and hugged them both. "I can take care of those bruises and whatever else you've got after breakfast," she assured Claire.

Claire thanked her.

"I don't believe this,' Claire whispered as they sat down to eat. "What have you done to my family?"

"I did a spell on them before we left San Francisco," Dante said in a matter of fact voice.

"You didn't!" Claire gasped, glancing around the room.

"Nah, I didn't," Dante said laughing. "But I did call to speak to Julius and Esther when you took so long to get ready to go."

"You did?" Claire stared at him, trying to reassure herself that he was telling the truth this time.

"Yes, I did. You have a great family and they want you to be happy."

Claire pulled him close for a hug. "I am happy. I've never been this happy in my life."

"Me either," he replied.

With all the family seated everyone began to eat, enjoying their time together.

The End

The Nature of the Beast

By

J. M. Jeffries

Miriam Pace and Jacqueline Hamilton comprise the award winning writing team of J.M. Jeffries. They have been writing together for ten years and still going strong. Miriam and Jackie live in Southern California where the margaritas are tart and salty and the pool boys are lusty and fine.

Dedication

To Parker, without you none of this would have ever happened. We will miss you always, Love Miriam

Acknowledgements

Miriam: To Jackie, you rock.

Thank you to

Jeff Pace and Erin Stephenson-Pace (We miss you too, dad.),
Kym Reed,
Miriam, Peter, Kathryn, and Frederik Stein (We love you dad),
Jax Cassidy,
And
Sherrie Fletcher.

James Parker Pace
January 26, 1947 - November 22, 2007

Chapter One

The decision to find another home for the three werewolf boys still sat poorly with Marisol Santiago. She sat in the stretch limo with all of her children around her, staring out the tinted windows at the strangeness that was Las Vegas. The boys craned their necks trying to see everything at once. Even though Rio de Janiero was the cultural icon of Brazil it seemed strangely sedate when compared to Las Vegas.

As the limo traveled down the highway, huge signs advertized entertainers Marisol had never heard of. One hotel was shaped like a pyramid and a little further down another one shaped like a castle made the city feel like a fairy tale. Even though she had read up on Las Vegas, she was still surprised at the brightness, the traffic, and people who surged down the sidewalks despite the heat and sun.

"I want to go home," Carlos said angrily. "I don't like this place."

He looked ready to bolt. Marisol tried to soothe him, but she felt awkward and out of place, as well. But she couldn't go back. Not now. Not when safety for the boys was so close.

She had rescued the three Were children from an arms dealer and tried to integrate them in to her rag tag pack of Were strays, but they fought her at every turn. Maybe if they had been younger, or hadn't been abused at the hands of their captors she would have had a chance, but they were too much for her to handle. There was no doubt in her mind that one of their squabbles would turn into a death match between her and them. If she won, she would have to kill the brothers. If they won, her other orphans would end up with a violent wolf as their alpha or dead.

If she didn't have seven other Were children who needed her as desperately as they did, she could have given them the time they needed to heal.

Carlos, the oldest of the boys, glared at her with dark condemning eyes. His long black dreadlocks framed a teak brown face and he had the distinct smell of an alpha about him. With his tall muscular body he was easily confused for a grown man even though he was only fourteen.

Unlike cats, wolves tended to be more patriarchal. Not that female wolves weren't strong. They could run a pack as well as any male, but cats especially jaguars tended to be matriarchal.

So Marisol made the choice to find them a wolf pack. A strong pack that could help heal them. A pack as far away from the violent Martinez and Del Torro packs, which warred for control of Rio de Janeiro, as she could get them.

The trip to Nevada had been hard with all her children in tow, but things were too volatile in Rio to leave anyone behind, or trust that the boys would arrive safely in Las Vegas if left to their own devices. The Temples had agreed to let the boys in on a trial basis. Esther Temple had sent the family's private jet to get them and two limos had been waiting at the airport to greet them. Marisol had taken the lead limo with the Carlos, Juan and Pablo and put the other children in the second one with Alberto Chavez to look after them. They would be behave without her there to remind them of their manners.

Esther and her husband were leaving the Temple's Las Vegas home for Alaska. There they would teach the boys to be the wolves they needed to be.

Pablo, the middle boy, snarled as the car stopped in front of the hotel. His dark skin was flushed with rage. The scent of wolf and other worldies was everywhere. In a strange way the scent was comforting.

"Pablo, do not start." Marisol drummed her fingers on her thigh trying to keep her anger in check. The last thing she needed was for them to show disrespect before they'd even unpacked their luggage.

"You should have left us in Rio." Carlos whined.

She narrowed her gaze at Carlos. "Tell me, Carlos, how would you protect your brothers?"

He thumped his broad chest. "I'm alpha, I protect what's mine."

Unlike the United States with its tradition of equal rights even for the non-human kind like her, Brazil was not so open-minded. Unless a person could buy protection from the local and national governments, they were a target. Weres, vampires, demon kind, and magic users alike sold their services to the highest bidder to keep themselves safe. Or they stayed under the radar and hoped for the best. In her world survival of the fittest was the only law. They may be stronger than the humans, but their numbers paled in comparison. And the humans could always find other worldies ready to fight battles with their own kind. "The police would have you rounded up in a week or shot and left for dead in some gutter like the human street children."

"Bitch," Carlos said quietly.

Juan, the youngest of the boys scowled at her. Although as dark as the others, his features were more Indian than his brothers. If he'd been by himself she could have done wonders with him, but like all younger brothers, he idolized his older siblings and had something to prove.

She understood their anger. She'd been mad at her parents for dying on her and leaving her unprotected and vulnerable in a world that would just as soon have her dead. Had it not been for Alberto Chavez finding her just after she'd been bitten, she would have been dead ninety-six years ago after her village had been attacked by a rogue were-jaguar.

The limos turned into a driveway that led to the entrance of a huge casino, the French Quarter emblazoned on the sign over the door. A man and woman stood at the curb while behind them a crowd of people surged in and out of open doors of the casino.

As the limo slowed to a standstill, the woman stepped forward and opened the door and hot, dry heat, so different from the tropical humidity she was used to, flooded the car. The woman was a tall, beautiful black woman with improbably brilliant orange hair. The woman smiled easily at Marison even as her strange scent made Marisol wary. The woman wasn't a Were, nor was she human. Marisol first instinct was to shut the door and order the driver to drive away.

The woman stuck her head into the limo, her orange hair swirling around her. "Hi, you must be Marisol. I'm Ali!"

Ali was so friendly with her open smile and her fun-colored hair, Marisol began to relax. She was a hellhound and Malcolm's wife. Esther had told her Ali 'volunteered' to help with the boys. Marisol bowed her head in respect. "My lady."

Ali giggled. "No need to be so formal. I'm not official yet." She glanced around the limo. "Where are the pups?"

Marisol pointed to the sullen looking boys on the other side of the limo. A look of disappointment crossed Ali's face. "I was expecting babies." She sighed. "Oh well, come along. The family is waiting to meet you."

Pablo flashed his teeth at her. "You don't smell right."

"Pablo!" Marisol couldn't believe he just insulted his new alpha's mate.

Ali grabbed Pablo by his shirt collar, hauled him out of the car and placed him on his feet. "You don't smell good to me either. That makes us even."

Carlos attempted to leap out of the car to his brother's defense, but the man standing next to Ali reached into the limo, gripped him tightly and pulled him out.

"You don't want to mess with her, puppy," the man said in a cool, calm dangerous tone, "she's a hell hound and if she wants, she can eat all of us for breakfast."

Ali smiled and her teeth grew. Her canines were longer and sharper than any Were creature, Marisol had ever seen wolf or cat. Marisol looked at the man dangling Carlos. He was tall with closed black cropped hair. His skin had a coppery undertone like hers and his features suggested that he might have a touch of Native American. Marisol's blood was mixed. Her grandmother had been a freed slave who had been found by and married one of the Amazon River people.

Marisol held out her hand. "Please don't hurt them. They are young."

The man lifted Carlos higher. "Where would the sport be in that?" A smile spread on the man's beautiful mouth.

Marisol stepped out of the limo and smiled at the man. He had high cheek bones that could cut steel. A mouth so full and lush, it made her remember she'd been without a lover for a long time and hazel eyes that saw straight into her soul. He smelled musky and fresh like the Amazon forest after a gentle rain. Her heart began to race and she heard herself purr as a lanquid heat spread through her.

The man put Carlos back on the ground.

"Thank you," Marisol said fighting to keep her emotions under control. She lowered her gaze politely even though she wanted to stare at him like a tourista.

159

The man put his arm around Carlos' neck and pulled him close. Carlos glared at him, but didn't struggle. "No problem." He held out his hand to her. "Troy Benton."

"Senior Benton. Thank you for meeting us." She shook hands with him and found her much smaller hand engulfed in his. His skin burned into her and she resisted the urge to pull her hand away.

"My pleasure." He lifted his eyebrow with a knowing look in his eyes. "And call me Troy."

Marisol suspected he knew what her reaction to him had been. "Please call me Marisol." She pointed to the boy still in a headlock. "That is Carlos." She hitched a thumb over her shoulder. "That is Pablo, and Juan has decided to stay in the car."

Troy flashed her another smile. "Want me to help him come to the right decision?"

She shook her head. Once he took control of Carlos the other boys would fall into line. "He will come out on his own."

Troy took his arm from around Carlos's neck and the boy stood there sullen, but silent. He understood he'd met his match in the tall muscular man.

The other limo parked behind Marisol's, the door opened and Alberto stepped out. The old jaguar was followed by the rest of her little family. As the children jumped out, Ali bent down and touched each one of them. None of the children flinched or shied away from the hellhound, but then there was something about the hell beast that put everyone at ease also. Pablo slinked over to his older brother and Marisol could smell a hint of fear on his skin. She didn't know if that should make her happy or bother her. All she knew was that their fear kept them in check around the obviously more power creatures. Juan chose that moment to venture out of the car and he stood next to his brothers. Of his brothers, he was the most timid, with Carlos the most violent and Juan caught in between.

Troy raised his hand and five male wolves walked out the door. Carlos puffed out his chest. One of the men nodded in approval. He bent to say something to Carlos and Carlos listened, nodded his head once and when the men herded the boys into the hotel, Carlos went willingly despite one last lingering, almost fearful look at Marisol who tried to project confidence into her smile. This was for the best, though she felt another prickle of tears in her eyes. She had to stop this crying. Alpha females did not cry.

"They'll be safe?" Marisol asked.

Troy shrugged. "As long as they behave, we won't have any trouble."

Marisol forced herself not to cry. She'd failed Carlos, Pablo and Juan and for that she would never forgive herself.

"Ola'! Meu nome é Ali," Ali said in Portuguese.

The children all said hello in Portuguese to Ali. Although they could speak English because Marisol insisted they learn, they preferred their native language. She was glad Ali could talk to them to.

Troy stood next to her studying the children. "They don't all smell jaguar."

Marisol pointed to the tall black boy and girl. "Only Dulce and Luis are jaguar, they are my oldest and have been with me for the longest time. The one with the blonde hair is Ramiro, he is a puma." She pointed to the small black boy. "That is Victor, he is a Spectacled Bear."

Troy tilted his head and studied Victor. He leaned close to her and spoke. "What's wrong with his eyes?"

"He was blinded by silver acid." It still pained her to look at his scarred face. At such a young age he'd endured so much already. "His pack was going to kill him, but I bought him."

"Jesus, who would do that to a cub."

"His alpha's mate. She hated Victor's mother and wanted to strike at her through the child. With him blind, his mother rejected him and I took him." Marisol felt a wave of rage roll over him and she knew he would never hurt her children.

His jaw clenched. "Tell me where to find these miserable Weres."

"No one knows what happened to any of them." Marisol lifted her chin at her sort of confession defying him to judge her. "They just disappeared one day. The bodies have never been found."

He nodded. "To bad. So sad. Does he need any special help?"

She liked that he looked impressed and wanted to help Victor. "No, he will be fine. His sense of smell is impeccable and his hearing is excellent. Victor wouldn't accept help from you. He rarely lets me or the other children help him either."

"Who are the rest?" Admiration gleamed in his eyes.

She pointed to Emilio, her only Indian child. "Emilio is an Andean Fox." Then she pointed to the two bi-racial twin girls. "And the sisters Bibianna and Sarita are Ocelots."

He laughed. "You got the United Nations of Weres goin' on, don't you?"

She had never intended to be a mother, the children just fell into her lap and she couldn't leave them to their fates. "They had no one else."

Marisol watched as the luggage was unloaded from the trunks. "How did you end up with the knuckle head wolves?" Troy asked curiously as a bellman started packing the luggage onto a wheeled cart.

"I rescued them from a Columbian arms dealer." If she hadn't they would have become assassins for one of the most vicious criminals in South America or they would be dead.

Troy eyed her appraisingly. "How did a beautiful woman like you get mixed up with a South American arms dealer."

Because she did what she had to do to survive and selling arms to drug cartels was easy money despite the danger. She'd done a lot of things to keep her family together and not everything was legal, nor was she ashamed of her past. She would worry about karma later. "It was an easy way to make a living without being gone from my children for a long time."

"Oh." His eyebrows rose. He gave her another searching look.

She could tell he wasn't used to being surprised. "Now you think badly of me," she said. Not that it mattered, he wasn't going to be a part of her life except for the next few days. Let him judge her, she didn't care. Or did she?

Troy shrugged. "That's not my place."

"Esther has been generous and I no longer have to bend the law to survive, or to keep my children safe." But if that were her only choice she'd happily still be doing it. Being a gun runner paid well, almost as well as being a government assassin.

Troy stuck his hands in his pockets and rocked back on his heels. "She's cool like that."

Marisol took a long breath. "I owe her my life." And she would never be able to repay that debt.

All the children were nopw out of the cars and their things being loaded on to the bellman's carts. "Let me show you to your suites. Now the big brouhaha is over I'm putting you in the Delta Queen."

She turned to see Ali talking to the children about making plans for activities talking in flawless Portuguese. As she talked her hair changed color from orange to red and then to purple with green streaks. The children stared at her. Sarita reached out and touched a tendril of the purple hair and the tendril snaked around her wrist and Sarita pulled back, anxiety on her face.

"Ali is very good with children," Marisol said.

"That would be because she's a big kid herself."

"I envy that." Marisol couldn't remember what it had been like to be a child and carefree. Alberto had been demanding, but then he had to teach her how to be a jaguar in a world that was harsh and unforgiving. At least she was able to give her pack a childhood and safety.

Troy laughed with affection. "Ali can wear out the wind. She is a force of nature."

She wanted to ask how a hellhound had become a part of the pack, but was afraid she'd be rude. Finally she said carefully, "I have never met a hellhound before."

"Neither did we until a few months ago. All I can say is that life has never been the same here since she and Malcolm became a pair."

She sensed there was a lot of story here, but Troy wasn't about to say anything. And like all cats, curiosity always seemed to get the best of her. So she asked even when she knew she shouldn't. "Was there trouble?" She didn't want to leave her boys in a place where trouble would make things even more difficult for them to adjust.

The bellman had finished piling the luggage on the cart. A second cart had also been loaded. Alberto had his arm around Bibianna who looked at Ali shyly. Ali's hair changed color again to white and black streaks. Bibianna laughed suddenly and pulled away from Alberto to touch Ali's hair.

Ali…sees things differently then we do. A couple of minor problems, but nothing we couldn't handle," Troy said as he led her into the hotel, Alberto and the children following. He would say that. Weres never liked to show weakness.

Ali laughed and clapped her hands and her hair changed color again as they walked past the reception desk to a bank of elevators. People turned and stared at Ali. Marisol saw that many of them were human, but at Ali's energy and laughter everyone smiled and then went on their way.

"When will I see Lady Esther?" Marisol asked as Alberto and Ali took the children into one elevator while Marisol and Troy took a second because there wasn't enough room for all of them and the luggage.

"She wanted you to get settled in first."

Esther would do that. Kindness had always been her strong point. "I appreciate that. And what about Carlos, Juan and Pablo?"

"Don't worry about them. I'll be helping them assimilate into the pack."

The pained expression on his handsome face almost made her laugh, but she didn't. "Where did you put them?"

"In my suite. I want them to start bonding with me and the other males in the pack as soon as possible."

Dare she ask what the bonding process would consist of? She opened mouth, but thought better. The door closed and the elevator ascended to the upper floors. "I feel as if I'm betraying them."

"Listen. I know where those kids are coming from. I was a knuckle head boy. If Esther could tame me, I'm sure I can handle those three. They're not evil, just angry with a little stupid mixed in."

Marisol forced herself not to cry. "Thank you."

"Don't thank me yet." He reached up and touched her cheek. "It ain't gonna be easy."

Marisol went on instant alert. All of her senses shifted into overdrive. His scent surrounded her, invading her to her innermost core. This man could crawl beneath the walls she'd erected to protect herself, if she let him. She missed a man's touch, but when she took on her brood she knew they needed her more than any man needed her. She couldn't remember when she'd craved a man's touch as much as Troy Benton's. "Please help them."

He smiled and dropped his hand. "I will."

The elevator door opened and she hurried through the open door and down the hall where she could hear the children's voices intermixed with Alberto and Ali's. At the door she stopped and turned around to see where Troy had gone. He stood in the elevator, one hand on the door to keep it from closing. He smiled at her and for a moment she simply gazed at him trying to hide her longing.

Marisol stepped into the hotel suite and closed the door. She leaned against the hard surface, trying to control the racing of her heart. For the first time since she'd made her choice she didn't feel quite so guilty. And in the back of her head, she knew she could trust Troy not only with her boys' futures, but with her heart. And that scared her to no end.

Chapter Two

The elevator doors closed inches from his face. Troy ran a hand over his face unable to believe he'd touched the jaguar woman. But he had to. He wanted to know if her toffee colored skin was as soft as it looked and it was. Troy needed to find out if the lush berry red lips were as kissable as their fullness suggested. He'd never been attracted to another Were species before, preferring to stay inside the wolf packs. But he couldn't seem to help himself. Her ebony hair begged to be freed from the old-fashioned bun at the nape of her neck. She looked so vulnerable and small he just wanted to protect her almost as much as he wanted to make love to her voluptuous petite body for the next three weeks.

Stop that train right now, son.

No way was he going to get involved. Not after Talia. Hell no, him and woman troubles were going to stay as a far apart as possible. Sure he was all for a knocking his boots and running with a warm willing playmate, but this woman had baggage--ten pieces to be precise in assorted ages and genders. Which in his head was ten pieces too many. Actually only seven now.

He was going to get those boys up to snuff, integrated into the pack and then he was going to do some traveling. He hadn't been out of Vegas since he'd returned from Vietnam over thirty-five years, and it was time to go see the world again. He wanted a little adventure.

Maybe he'd go back into the Army so he could be all he could be. Living rough with nothing but his wits to protect him. Now that was living. And no cute butt and beautiful smile was going to stop him. The elevator doors opened into the pack's living quarters. He could smell the tension in the air as he stepped into the hallway.

As he passed Iva's room, he wished his pack sister were here. She had a good touch with kids, but she was still AWOL in a snit over having a hell hound as the new alpha female. He opened his door and he saw Marcus, Guy, and Dexter sitting casually on chairs while the three boys huddled in the corner. He didn't even need to take a breath to smell the hate coming out of those three. It was rushing his skin and the room was heavy with emotion. Time to put the fear of God into these boys. "How is the new meat?"

His brothers all laughed.

From the corner Carlos, the one with the dreads leaped for Dexter. "I won't let you hurt my brothers." Even though he tried to look tough, fear lurked in Carlos' eyes.

He jumped Dexter knocking him and he started hitting on him. Troy forced himself not to intervene, that would have sent the wrong message to Carlos and embarrass Dexter. Although more wiry than muscular, Dex could handle himself. He gave the kid a few seconds to pound on him then he used his body weight and flipped him over and pinned him to the floor. The two younger ones leaped up to join the fray but Marcus and Guy stopped them. There was something not right about what set off the kid. Something that needed to be explored. "All right Dex, let him up."

Dex raised his head showing his canines. "Dang it, was just getting fun."

Troy smiled, reminding Dex gently, "He's just a boy."

Dex got off of Carlos and then held his hand out for the boy. Carlos declined the offer and stood on his own. "Why don't you leave me and Carlos alone and you all go get something to eat. Carlos and I are gonna have some man talk."

It took a few minutes but Troy was finally left alone with the oldest boy. Carlos sat hunched in a chair at the kitchen island while Tony made a couple sandwiches.

For a long while, he concentrated on the sandwiches and then he set a plate down in front of Carlos and sat opposite him. He ate his sandwich slowly and was rewarded with Carlos taking a tentative bite of his own. Feed them first, Esther had said. Soothe the stomach, soothe the beast.

When Troy finished his sandwich, he continued to sit quietly, waiting. He didn't talk but put the stare on Carlos. A minute passed then a couple more and boy eyed him defiantly as he finished his sandwich. He wasn't going to break. But then neither did Troy.

After five minutes Troy sensed the boy weakening. Finally after about seven and half minutes Carlos lost his composure. He didn't quite crumple, he looked away. If he had been in his wolf form he would have rolled on his back and exposed his neck. Troy was impressed. At fourteen even with all he'd gone through Troy hadn't been this tough.

"Not bad," Troy said.

Carlos tried not to show it but there was an inkling of pride and self-satisfaction in his gaze.

"So what's your story?" Troy asked conversationally.

Warily, Carlos said, "What do you mean?"

Troy crossed his arms over his chest. "You got a sweet deal with Marisol, why you trying to mess it up?"

Carlos's lip curled in a sneer. "I'm not going to be told what to do by a woman."

Just to mess with him, Troy poked him in the chest. "Kid, you're a dumbass." Bossy women were the best kind.

Carlos growled.

Troy knew Carlos wanted attack, but was smart enough to know not to. Okay, the kid had some brains. He could work with that. "Anytime you feel like you're ready for your shot you step up."

Carlos bunched his fists. "She's throwing us away." Pain threaded his voice.

That wasn't what Troy had expected. After only ten minutes in Marisol's company he knew how torn up she was about giving this kid and his brothers over to the Temple pack. "You don't understand pack. You gave her no choice." Let him chew on that.

"What?" Carlos' eyes widened in confusion.

He could see that Carlos and his brothers didn't understand the politics of extended packs. Rules were a bit different in the nuclear family. Actions were less rigid and more informal. He needed more information and would have to ask Marisol. Which meant he got to be around her some more. He could live with that.

"You and you're brothers," Troy said, "were the newbies. Do you think she's going to risk the ones who have been with her for the longest for you? Especially if you were nothing but a hard ass? In my pack your ass would have been dead a long time ago. From what I understand, you all didn't get with her program."

Carlos rolled his eyes looking like the ill-tempered brat he was. "All she has is rules."

"Rules keep you alive. If you had a brain cell in your head you'd know that." Troy shook his head. "You don't think this is killing her?"

"I don't care." Carlos shrugged trying to seem uncaring. Again that sense of abandonment filled his eyes.

Troy stood and hauled Carlos to his feet. "She brought you to us. That tells me all I need to know about the kind of woman she is. She could have kicked you to the curb and gone on with her life, but no she hauled you and your sorry ass brothers to us, because she knew we could protect you, teach you, and keep you safe."

Carlos hit his chest with his fist. "I don't need you to protect me or my brothers. I don't need you to teach me anything."

"Yeah, you do."

Carlos pushed against Troy's chest. "Fu--"

Troy didn't budge. "When you can kick my ass you can tell me what to do. From now on you will show me respect and I won't show you pain." Troy smiled. "You get me?"

Carlos said nothing.

Troy grabbed him by his shirt and hauled him to his chest. "Did you just whisper, sweetheart, because I didn't hear your answer."

Carlos's mouth twitched. A second or two passed. "I understand."

Troy smiled. "Good, you still hungry?"

Carlos broke eye contact. "Not really."

"Okay then you can watch me. I have chocolate chip mint ice cream for desert." Troy let go of Carlos' shirt and opened the freezer. He wasn't sure, but he thought he'd made some progress. Carlos was in pain and feeling insecure. This was not going to be an easy job, but he was going to succeed. Not just for the sake of the boys, but for Marisol. He wanted her to be able to go home, without the weight of guilt pulling at her making her feel that she hadn't tried hard enough to help Carlos and his brothers. That at least he could give to her.

Marisol sat at the café table in the private courtyard of the casino sipping ice tea and nibbling at a lunch salad. Esther sat across from her looking very regal in a pale cream pants suit and a bright colored scarf about her neck.

Several days had passed and Marisol hadn't seen much of the boys except at dinner with the pack. And last night's dinner had been a disaster. She still burned with embarrassment at Carlos, Juan and Pablo's behavior.

She watched Ali jump into the air holding Victor in his bear cub form. Victor caught a bright blue Frisbee in his teeth. The second Victor bit down on the disc, Ali howled. Somehow Ali was able to teach her blind son to do something that required sight. A thrill moved through Marisol. She could feel Victor's triumph from where she sat. "She is wonderful with the children."

"Ali has such incredible joi de vie." Esther clapped approvingly.

Ali set Victor down. Her hair was a gorgeous red and pink today, blowing wild over her shoulders. She wore matching pink shorts and knit top with purple sneakers on her feet. Marisol had never known anyone so outrageous, yet so easy to like. Everyone liked Ali.

"She needs her own family," Marisol said sadly. At one time she'd wanted her own family, too. A husband, children, along with a quiet little place in the world where no one got hurt or murdered or blinded. Instead, her life had taken a very different turn and each full moon reminded her of what she'd gained and what she'd lost.

"Personally," Esther said, "I am surprised she's not pregnant yet, the way her and my son go at it. They're like bunnies."

Marisol watched as Ali helped Victor throw the Frisbee to Sarita. Sarita giggled as she jumped up to catch it. "Do you think that they will be able to have children, with her being a hellhound?"

Esther sighed. "They will if her parents are to be believed."

"That is quite a coup for your son to be married to the daughter of the Lord of Hell."

"We shall see." Esther shaded her eyes. "Well, it looks as if our young pups are finished sweeping my parking lot."

Carlos, Juan and Pablo entered the courtyard, a dejected air about them. She bit her bottom lip. She wanted to rush to them and tell them how sorry she was, but this was for the best. "I'm sorry about their lack of good table manners."

Esther burst out laughing, her eyes alive with mischief. "Your boys just got their first lesson in being a member of the Temple Pack."

Marisol eyes were riveted to Troy as he walked alongside the boys, his stride long and confident. Behind him, Carlos, Pablo and Juan trotted to keep up with his quick pace. Even from this distance she could tell the boys were tired. "What is that?"

"He who slurps soup at Esther's table gets to sweep the entire parking lot." Again, Esther chuckled.

Marisol cringed as she remembered their ill mannered display of the night before. They were still testing the waters with the new pack, but every turn the challenge was met by wolves who were stronger, smarter, and meaner then they could ever be. "I'm sure they were overjoyed."

Esther rolled her eyes. "Those three could chew nails about now." Esther stood. "Well dear, I have things to do, I'll see you and the children at dinner."

"You do not have to have us for every meal. I'm sure you have other guests to entertain."

Esther waved her hand. "Nonsense, I love being around the little ones. I'm practicing for grandmotherhood."

Marisol jumped up and grabbed Esther's hand overcome with gratitude. "Thank you. Thank you for everything. I'm in your debt."

Esther bent over and kissed Marisol on the cheek. "I'm sure you'll find a way to pay me back." Then she walked off.

Troy sauntered over to her and sat in Esther's vacated chair. "You look pretty today."

Marisol felt herself blush. One would think with the harsh realities of her life that a compliment from a man wouldn't turn her inside out, but he made her feel like a young girl in the midst of her first crush. "Thank you."

The boys began to pull the chairs out. They all looked frazzled, but Carlos' face had a tranquility to it Marisol had never seen before.

"Oh no fellas, did I say you were done?" Although Troy's face remained smiling, she could hear the undertone of command in his voice.

Pablo shot Troy a nasty look. Carlos opened his mouth to say something but a look from Troy stopped him. Juan simply stared down at the ground.

Troy lifted an arm and a seven foot tall man ambled over. He was heavily muscled with hands the size of basketballs. His long blond hair waved in the breeze. He smelled like bear. "What kind of bear is he?" Marisol asked curiously.

170

"Zeke is a polar bear. And he's going to take over for a bit. The boys need to the scrub out the dumpsters."

The boys said nothing, though Carlos blanched. Stunned Marisol could only stare at Troy, she could barely get them to pick up their rooms without a knock-down, drag-out fight.

Zeke raised an eyebrow and the boys scuffled along in continued silence. No howls of outrage, no whining, no threats. They fell into step behind Zeke. Marisol wanted to protest, but suddenly Juan slid his hand into Zeke's and held on tight. Juan never let anyone touch him.

Marisol watched them disappear around a corner. "What is the purpose of having them work as maintenance men around the casino?"

Troy leaned back in his chair. "Number one: they learn the lay of their territory. Number two: they learn to care for their territory. Number three: they interact with all kinds of different people and number four and most importantly it gives me a cheap thrill to boss them around."

Marisol bit her lip so she wouldn't laugh. "Isn't that a bit cruel?"

Shrugging, he crossed his feet. "They have a lot of anger to burn off." A waiter brought him some iced tea and he thanked the woman in a gracious tone.

Marisol sighed. That they did. "I know."

"What happened to them while they were in captivity?"

She never really knew and they never talked about it to her. "When I found them they'd been starved and tortured. And I think they were forced to fight, but other than guessing I don't know. They never talk about it."

"We have a vampire from Caracas who works the night shift; he gave me a heads up about life down in your neck of the woods. Says life in Rio can be brutal. Which got me to wondering why did you save the boys?"

Ali and the children had given up Frisbee and the children were now grouped around her demanding she change the color and length of her hair. Long light blue locks wrapped around Luis, who was laughing. A tendril of bright yellow headed for Bibianna. "I couldn't walk away. Just like with my other children." Someone had to care because no one else did. Weres were considered lower than low in Brazil. Even the homeless street children were higher on the ladder than Weres.

He took a long breath. "Sometimes you have to."

Marisol sensed he knew exactly what she was talking about. "I have walked away, and I still regret each time I do. I only have so much in the way of resources and I know I can't save them all, but I save the ones I can."

He took a long breath. "We've all had to walk away at one time or another. Don't let it eat you up."

On that she disagreed with him. "You are a wolf. Wolves don't walk away."

"I wasn't always a wolf."

For a second there was glimmer of sadness and regret in his hazel eyes. "Tell me."

A pained look crossed his handsome face. "When Esther and Julius decided to escape the plantation, they took as many of the kids with them as they could. But we had to leave people behind."

He'd left someone behind, someone he loved. "Who did you leave behind?" Her words came out as barely a whisper.

"My grandmother."

Marisol forced herself not to reach out and touch his hand. Part of her was sad for him to have such sad memories of his grandmother when she didn't even remember her parents. "I'm sorry."

He smiled as he poured himself a glass of iced tea. "Don't be. She knew she was too old to make it and loved me enough to let me go. She knew I would have escaped eventually. It's not like I hadn't tried before."

"How old were you when you ran?"

"The first time about eleven. The second time thirteen."

He was still a child and he yearned for freedom so young. She couldn't even imagine that. "So young." Younger than Carlos.

Suddenly, she knew she didn't want to go back to Brazil, back to the uncertainty of their existence. She wanted to stay here in the safe cocoon the Temples had woven about her. She didn't want to go back to the run down house they lived in, crammed into three bedrooms because fixing the house would alert people to the fact that she had money. She didn't want to go back to running guns or drugs, or doing things that made her skin crawl. She didn't want to go back to homeless children without hope. She wanted to stay here with Troy, with this man who sat so close to her and made her remember she was a woman with a woman's needs and desires.

Marisol bit her bottom lip as he picked up his glass in his large hand and swirled the ice around. He had the most beautiful hands for a man.

"Slave children weren't young for long," he said, his voice distant with the strength of his memories. "As soon as you learned to walk you started to work."

He talked about it as if he were talking about the weather. This man was resilient. Like her. He did what he had to do to survive and keep those around him alive. As far as she was concerned that was the most noble of traits. "Did you ever see your grandmother again?"

He shook his head. "After the Civil war, I went back to look for her, but she'd passed about three weeks after we left. Matter of fact, she passed the same night I was given the gift." He eyes went unfocused as he looked inward. Then he shook his head and pulled himself out of the melancholy of his memories.

Marisol took a sip of iced tea. The sweet raspberry flavor rolled over her tongue. This was ambrosia. "She knew you were safe, she could leave this world in peace."

He looked her straight in the eyes. "I'm going to do everything I can to make sure you can leave here in peace."

Marisol heart beat faster, he had no idea how she needed to hear those words. Maybe she would get over her guilt. In her head, she knew she'd made the right choice, but her heart continued to rebel. She should have been able to make this work. They were only children. "Then you will truly be a miracle worker."

"I'll do my best." Troy reached over and covered her hand with his.

His fingers were warm and callused. He did not shy away from hard work or was that left over from his slave days. And she yearned to let him take all her burdens from her. But she knew she couldn't and she pulled her hand away and flicked a strand of hair behind her ear. "Are the boys going to be allowed to eat with the pack again?"

Troy rubbed his hands together and a sly smile curved his mouth. "Actually we're taking them out for their first pack hunt. We have some nasty cape buffalo roaming around the ranch."

Her breath caught. She wasn't sure if they were ready for this. "I don't think they've ever been on a hunt before."

"Have you?"

Her body went tense. More times than she cared to admit. "I've hunted before."

"For food?"

She thought for a second about answering. She knew he'd know if

173

she was lying. And what she'd done was for survival was not considered well in polite society. But then again she had nothing to be ashamed of. "For many reasons."

"Exactly what does that mean?" Troy leaned forward putting his elbow on the table.

"For awhile I was a solution to my government's political problems."

"Wet work as well as gunrunning?"

Her world was brutal and she had to be brutal to live in it. "If you work for the government, they will leave you alone." And they won't ask questions.

Troy let her words run around in his head. What did a person say to that? "Interesting." He understood about killing. God knows he had an impressive body count to his record, but he'd never killed for money. He protected himself, his pack, his country, and to eat. But there was something so cold about killing solely for cash. Not that he had a right to judge her. This was a woman who was on intimate terms with surviving. She was like a wary kitten, afraid to come in out of the dark, but afraid of the light as well.

"Thank you," she said.

He didn't understand. "For what?"

She looked at the children running around the courtyard. Ali's hair was gold and green and fuzzy. "For not judging me."

Hell, he had no right to judge anyone. "I'm a wolf, killing comes as easy as breathing."

She swung her gaze in his direction. "You've never killed for money."

"How do you know?"

"I would smell it on you." Her head lifted and she inhaled. "You're a hunter, not an assassin."

"You sound envious."

Her eyes narrowed as she studied him. "Perhaps, a little bit."

She had no idea about his years as a soldier. He'd killed at the drop of a hat, for God and country, and didn't even feel bad. The jungle was a harsh mistress who didn't look kindly on failure. "Don't be. We all do what we have to."

"I will do my best to follow your advice." Her mouth turned down in a frown.

He was trying to be nice and failed. Damn he had to fix it. He didn't want her to think she'd shocked him. "Do you want to join the hunt?"

She laughed. "Is that the wolf's way of asking me for a dinner date?"

Troy couldn't help it, he laughed realizing what he'd just done. There was no shame in his game. "You know, I never thought about it that way."

"I think that would not be a good idea."

"Why not?" She sounded as if she didn't want to hang out with him and that kind of hurt his feelings, but then again maybe it was her natural cat uppityness. He'd met plenty of cats in his day and they all seemed to have this natural standoffish thing going on. He guessed it was a breed thing.

"I've never hunted with wolves. And I'm sure most of your pack has never hunted with a jaguar." Her graceful hands moved in the air in a helpless gesture. "I don't think our methods are compatible?"

This he had to hear. "What we're not up to your speed? I won't let my pack embarrass themselves in front of you. I promise."

"No. With the exception of lions, cats are solitary hunters. Wolves are not."

Okay good, it wasn't personal. It was a breed thing. That he could understand and work with. "Are you telling me you're sneaky?"

"Sneaky sounds so underhanded."

Her smile told him she took it as a joke and not as an insult. "I'm impressed with a cat's method, buts ours is more efficient."

Her brown eyes sparkled with humor. "I think most of the time your prey panics and dies of a heart attack or you run it to exhaustion."

Troy couldn't see anything wrong with that. "Works for us."

"And once in Panama it nearly did me in."

What had put the fear of God in her? "Who would want to hurt you?"

Her eyebrow rose. "Besides Carlos, Pablo, and Juan?"

He liked that she could find humor in that situation. "Okay, there is that." Troy took another sip of his iced tea.

Her face took on a pensive look. "Manuel Noriega controlled one of the most powerful packs in Latin America. I did some work for your government that hastened his downfall."

He'd been asked to join that operation but declined. At the time he'd been all wrapped up in Talia and kinda lost track of his life. Maybe if he had accepted the assignment, he would have met Marisol earlier. "That was you?"

"You were in Panama?"

How would things have shaken out if he'd met her then, instead of wasting his time on a bitch like Talia. They'd have lit Latin America on fire. "No, but a buddy from my old army days wanted me to come down and do some work for him. But I couldn't."

"I was hired by your government." She lifted her glass and swirled her ice around. "They pay very well."

"I know."

She took a sip. "And they don't always kill you if you fail."

That was true, but she hadn't failed. Troy had read the reports afterward. She'd eliminated a very tough pack and the United States was able to catch a very nasty bad guy. "There is that."

"Are you mated?"

Stunned, he said nothing for a couple of seconds. *She's coming on to me, and I'm going to let her.* It thrilled him that she was interested. "That is a strange turn in the conversation."

Her elegant shoulders shrugged. "What is it they say a woman's prerogative?"

Was she throwing signals at him? If she was, he was catching. "That's to change your mind not the topic of a conversation."

"My English is not so good." Her accent got heavy and a bit slower.

He grinned. He loved the lilt in her voice and the way she talked. He liked that she wasn't shy about making the first move. "There is nothing bad about you from where I'm sitting."

"You are flirting."

What could he say? He liked her. He wanted her. And he intended to have her, he just hadn't worked it out in his mind how he was going to go about it. But he would, he always did. "It's the dawg in me."

"So you are not mated?" she asked

"I was almost caught."

One eyebrow lifted. "That doesn't sound so good."

Talia had used him to get the alpha of her pack to pay attention to her by flirting with him. And that nearly got him killed. Had he been alone when he was attacked, he had no doubt he'd be dead. From that moment on he'd played it safe with women. Marisol made him want to live dangerously. And part of him didn't think that was such a bad thing. "It wasn't. I learned my lesson the hard way."

"That is too bad, you are a very good man."

"Not so good." At least he liked to think of himself as bad but only in the fun way. He hadn't needed to be bad in any other way for a long time. "Tell me, kitty cat, why aren't you mated?"

"Very few jaguars would accept cubs from another jaguar, much less my assortment of children."

What kind of dumb ass cats did they have in South America? If she could love children others had thrown away, he could imagine what a great mother she'd be to her blood cubs. That was the kind of mate a man wanted when he was ready to mate. "Some cats aren't so bright."

"I agree." She checked her watch. "If you will excuse me. Some of the children have lessons to attend to."

Troy got the impression this was a tactical retreat and he forced himself not to jump up make her stay with him. "I understand."

Marisol finished her iced tea and stood. She called the children and they stopped what they were doing and came to her quickly.

Although they looked disappointed, they didn't argue. He liked that. These kids were all well behaved and so unlike Carlos and his brothers. But then they were wolves and wolves tended to have harder heads. Getting ideas through needed more knocking. How hard was that to get a bunch of rambunctious Were kids to toe the line. That was another thing that spoke volumes about the kind of woman Marisol was.

Ali pouted at the interruption of playtime. But Marisol had been adamant that the children would continue their lessons. Ali ran over and hugged the children good bye and made Marisol promise that they could play again tomorrow. She agreed and kissed Ali on the cheek and thanked her for watching her children. Then the little group walked off. Ali's shoulders slumped as they headed for their suite.

Troy didn't want Marisol to go either. She fascinated him. Even though he hadn't been looking for a relationship, he was drawn to her. He liked the air of quietness about her. Wolves were always moving, but she seemed so still and centered. It was comforting and calming. The type of calm he seemed to crave, even though he didn't understand why.

Chapter Three

Troy watched Carlos prance in front of the male cape buffalo cutting him off from the rest of the herd. The target had been chosen. It was an ambitious choice. This male was powerful and in his prime. A smart wolf would have picked an easier meal. This kid had something to prove and Troy was going to let him prove it. Pack politics was never subtle.

Troy signaled his pack mates to stand back. It fought against their instincts, but he had to know if this kid could back his shit up. Juan and Pablo, their fur on end, nipped at the buffalo's haunches. Like their brother, they had something to prove and Troy watched them wanting to see how they worked as a team. Troy loped after them and watched the three young wolves bring the buffalo down. It took them nearly half an hour, but they made a kill. The boys howled in triumph.

Two new scents crossed his path. One he knew was Ali. The other was cat. Marisol had come to watch. If he wasn't in his wolf form he'd smile. Malcolm lifted his head and howled. Ali returned his with a bone chilling howl. He would never get used to Ali in her hellhound form. She was bigger than all of them and meaner than all of them. He'd seen her in action once, deadlier than all of them if a person got on her bad side.

He had to give her props; she never used her hellhound status to intimidate them. If she wasn't a member of their pack, he'd be having a heart attack right now. Ali trotted by him to her mate. He watched Malcolm nuzzle her and a sharp pang of envy ran through Troy. He'd never been jealous before when his pack mates started to pair up. Hell, he was happy for them. But after Talia, he figured forever wasn't in the cards for him. Not that he was lonely, he had plenty of company, just not on a permanent basis. But something gnawed at him. He felt at loose ends and he didn't like it.

He swung his head toward Marisol and watched her elegant black on black jaguar body turn toward the ranch house. Gentleman that Esther raised him to be, he headed toward Marisol. Can't let a lady be alone in a strange land. He trotted until he caught up to her and she stopped. She was all sinuous grace and black shadows. As he moved next to her, he rubbed his body against hers. She didn't move away and her long tail swished over his back. He figured that was cat speak for hey yeah, let's get it on.

Her body vibrated with her soft purring. Now that was a good sign. He licked his canines. He could almost taste her soft musky scent on his tongue. He just wanted to drown in her smell.

Out of the corner of his eye he watched her walk. Her front paws crossed in front of each other with every step. Like most cats she gave the illusion of a leisurely pace. Wolves always bristled with energy that was ready to pop at any time except when they were sleeping, cats just seemed to roll along as if the world was waiting for them to get where they needed to go. God knows he altered his normal pace to accommodate her. And to be honest it didn't seem to bother him one bit. Not that he'd ever share that fact with her or anyone.

When they reached the veranda she leaped up over the railing and sprinted in the house through the open door. Startled he stood stock still for a second. But the urge to move traveled down to his paws, she was inside the house and he heard a door slam. He ran through the house following her scent and found her bedroom. He nearly crashed into her bedroom door.

Troy's mouth fell open. He'd just been dissed, cat style. For a second he thought about breaking the door down, but stopped himself. He wanted to howl his frustration, but didn't. The last thing he needed his pack mates to know was that a cat had gotten the better of him.

Behind the door he heard her moving around and some strange cat noise. He wasn't sure but he thought she was laughing at him. No one laughed at him, unless he was busting a joke. Especially not a woman. And certainly not some overgrown tabby cat.

Marisol disconnected her cell phone and stared at it. Alberto had called her to let her know that Lady Esther was camping with the children in her penthouse suite. They'd built tents using the furniture and were making something called s'mores. They were excited about sleeping on the floor in sleeping bags. Americans were so strange sometimes. She had spent many nights sleeping on the floor and wished for a bed. Now her children were eschewing perfectly good beds for a hard floor.

Marisol hadn't expected all the wolves to take to her children since they were all different. In her country the Weres stayed with their own kind. She was the only one she knew of who had different species in her pack. This was just one more confusing thing to add to her list about tonight.

A heating flush crept up her neck as she recalled her blatant mating invitation to Troy Benton tonight. Thank God he wasn't a cat and didn't understand any of the signals she'd sent him. She couldn't help herself from rubbing against his body or purring.

Something about him called to her. Watching him with the boys, she sensed his patience and gentleness. None of which detracted from his wolf. Very few men, especially Weres let their gentleness show. To be seen as anything but a ruthless killer was a weakness. Troy was who he was and wasn't ashamed of it. That just made her like him more. She couldn't afford to get mixed up with any man in anything but the most casual circumstances.

As she finished dressing, the scent of salmon tickled her nose. And like most cats, she loved fish almost as much as she loved caiman meat. Why he was cooking was beyond her. She slipped her cell phone in her jeans pocket. Then she remembered he hadn't taken part in the hunt or the meal afterwards.

Thinking about the hunt, she was stunned by how Juan, Carlos and Pablo had taken down the Cape buffalo. They had worked as a team, running the animal to ground and then finishing it off. Even as the buffalo rallied to survive the boys had not given up. She didn't know whether to be happy or sad. This was one more example of why they needed to be with their own kind. Troy and his pack members could teach them things she never could. Deep in her heart she knew she made the right choice, it just didn't feel right. Her failure saddened her.

Shaking off the pity, she had to go and face Troy and stop hiding. Her stomach grumbled. The savory taste of salmon was driving her crazy. She had to eat.

Ruled by her nose and the hunger in her belly she left her room and followed her nose to the kitchen and stopped. Troy's back was bare and the first thing she noticed was the old scar slashing up and down his back. The raised scar stood out stark against his brown skin. Marisol bit her bottom lip. She couldn't seem to tear her eyes away from his damaged skin. Then she'd remembered he'd been a slave. A slave who'd run away twice. Her interactions with humans was so minimal, sometimes she forgot they could be as cruel as her kind.

It didn't bother him that she was staring. In fact he liked that she took such an avid interest in him. He could feel the heat warming his skin. "They don't hurt anymore."

"Forgive me, I'm not normally so rude."

"Nothing to be sorry about." He flipped the salmon one more time and lowered the heat, then turned around to face her. "If I could stare at them I would."

Marisol took another step into the kitchen. "You were whipped for trying to run away?"

"That and a few other things."

"Does it hurt to talk about it?"

He shrugged his shoulders. "I'm over it. It happened a long time ago."

She tilted her head studying him as if she were trying to find a flaw in his statement. "Do you really get over that kind of abuse?"

"I don't know if getting over it is the right word. But time and distance can change a person's perspective." The overseer who did whipped him was long dead and in Troy's book that meant he'd won the war. Of course it didn't hurt that the man had killed himself.

"How old are you?"

"One hundred and sixty."

Her eyebrows rose. "That old?"

"How old are you?"

"Almost a century."

So cats aged like wolves, she barely looked a day over twenty. "How old were you when you were turned?"

"I was three when I was attacked."

Attacked and survived. That said a lot about how strong she was. His pack sister, Solange was the youngest of their pack to be turned and she had barely made it through her first change. She was nearly ten before Esther would let her be given the gift. "How did you survive?"

"Alberto said I had a cat's natural disdain for being told what to do, even before I became one."

He laughed. That he had no problem understanding. "It's one of your more interesting traits."

She walked further into the kitchen and leaned against the counter. "I have never shown you my stubborn side."

Honey, he thought, that's as plain as the nose on your face. "You don't need to."

When she crossed her arms over her chest, it plumped up her full breasts. "I'm not sure if I should be insulted or not."

"Don't be." Troy almost went cros-eyed at her cleavage. "I like it." He had to force himself not to lick his lips at the sight.

"Do you know what I like about wolves?"

"I'm dying to know." There was a lot of things he wanted to show her about wolves. Number one being his stamina.

"There is no mystery to you."

That surprised him. "You think so?" Maybe being mysterious was something he needed to work on. If that's what she liked. He just never saw the point. He saw something he liked, he went after it. Until he got what he wanted. It was a simple philosophy and it had worked well for him over the years.

"Yes, I do. If you don't want to be bothered, you show it in your body language immediately. Or you growl, move away, or you attack. You never hide behind a wall of indifference."

"What do cats do?"

She took a deep breath and he hoped she would just pop out of her shirt. But she didn't. Not that it affected the heat spreading though him. "We think about things and study them for awhile, and then get comfortable. We might even purr and if we don't want you near us, we attack or leave, we rarely give anyone any indication what we're going to do from one moment to the next."

That's why he never liked to fight cats. They had no regard for the rules of engagement, but it did make for a lot of fun. They didn't fight unless they were willing to get bloody. "That is why your kind is always underestimated, by your enemies."

"You make that sound as if being a cat is a good thing."

"Good isn't quite the right word," he said and thought for a moment.

"More like exciting."

"You're toying with me." She smiled. "You must crave excitement."

He walked up to her and stopped only an inch away. "What I crave is a kiss."

Pushing herself to sit up on the counter, Marisol moved a bit closer. "Now that you've confirmed your next movement, what if I decide to run?"

Her words were low and they caressed his ears. "I'll chase."

"What if I let you get close and then attack?"

Her canines grew slightly and slipped over her bottom lip. "I like to tussle with pretty girls."

"Remember Wolf, guile is not your strong suit. You are all about showing your prowess."

He trailed a finger down her cheek. Her skin was as soft as spun silk. "It's worked for centuries with my kind."

"Your arrogance knows no bounds," she said with a half grin.

"Is that bad?"

"Sometimes."

She leaned into him. His body was on fire. He was so hard he thought he was going to burst through his pants. "You never know how far you can go unless you push."

She pressed herself against him. "So let's see how far you can get."

As her soft body pressed into his, Troy smiled and grabbed her around the waist, and lowered his mouth to hers.

Chapter Four

Without breaking the kiss, Troy picked her up and hurried to her bedroom. Marisol clamped her legs around his waist and enjoyed the ride.

After what seemed like the world's longest minute, she felt herself falling until she hit the soft mattress. She sat up, took off her shirt and tossed it. "Get undressed."

"You're a bossy kitty cat."

She purred, "Does that displease you?"

Troy whipped off his sweat pants. "Hell no."

Marisol licked her bottom lip. Staring at his muscled body the heat of desire flooded her. Her eyes traveled down his muscular chest to his hard cock. He was a like a statue covered in dark chocolate. "Good." Then she toed off her shoes and wiggled out of her pants.

Troy smiled. "Like what you see?"

"Of course. I hope you do, too."

He put his knee on the bed and crawled to her until he was on top of her. "Yeah." He bent over and took one hard nipple in his mouth.

Marisol gave herself to the deep sensation of pleasure as it spread through her. He worked his mouth over her skin sending trails of heat up and down her body. She gave herself over to the sensation of his touch, feeling the wetness pooling between her thighs. She couldn't remember ever wanting a man so much. Troy had bewitched her.

He moved his mouth along her skin until he reached her other breast. "You taste so sweet."

She arched her body. Her nipple rubbed against his mouth and he licked the hard peak as she struggled to get closer to him.

His hand slid between her legs and buried a finger inside her wet core.

Her internal muscles tightened around him as he stroked inside her. Pressure built and her body vibrated. It wasn't enough, she had to have more. "More."

"We have time."

No, she didn't. There was no way she could have more than this moment. And they had been dancing around this issue for days. "I'm getting cold."

Ab eyebrow raised as he pushed her down until her shoulders were flat on the mattress. "Far be it from me to make you wait, Kitty Cat." He shoved himself inside of her and began pumping hard.

Marisol relished his unleashed passion as he filled her completely.

The sound of skin slapping on skin filled the room, and they warred with each other for control. He wasn't giving up and she wasn't going to be happy until she got what she wanted. She cried out, her voice sounding strange to her own ears.

Her entire body tightened up and she knew she was going to come. Sweat covered her as he kissed each breast. A low growl her mouth and her back arched.

Troy slammed into her one more time, his whole body went stiff, and his howl filled the room.

Marisol lost control. Her muscles clenched and her orgasm built until her muscles convulsed and the pleasure/pain at her center spiraled out and she gasped, groaned and spasmed until she went limp. A second later Troy followed her into ecstasy. Covered by his hot hard body Marisol knew that her life would never be the same.

Troy stroked Marisol cheek. They'd been lovers for the last three days. And he had yet to figure out how he was going to let her walk away from him. She hadn't set a date to return home, but he knew it would be soon. The boys were doing well and adjusting to life as the newest members of the Temple pack. Carlos had lost most of his sullen anger while Juan had started to ask questions in a tentative voice. Pablo was the one lone holdout. Someone had mentioned school and Pablo had already announced he wasn't going. Troy was convinced even Pablo would come around.

Marisol's skin was warm and velvety. God, it took everything he had not to mark her as his. He knew that she was thinking about going home. He knew it was painful for her to watch the boys making the transition from her care to the Temple pack. She was in no emotional condition to make any choice about her future. The man in him understood this. The wolf didn't give a flying fuck. He saw. He wanted. He took. His wolf was screaming for her, demanding to be satisfied. Didn't matter the outcome, the circumstance, or the cost, his wolf had to possess her. The wolf was greedy, selfish and demanding and he barely was able to rein his beast in. It was the beast's nature. And nature was a bitch when it didn't get what it wanted and it wanted Marisol.

She shifted on the bed and rolled to her feet. Her body was compact and toned and he knew every inch of it intimately.

"Stay." There was an edge of demand in his voice that bothered him. His wolf was doing his talking and it was in complete agreement with his dick. And as any Were knew, that was a lethal combination.

Naked, she walked across the room and picked her jeans off of the floor. "I can't. I have to be back in the suite when the children wake up. They get upset if I'm not there."

Turning his eyes away from her delectable ass to the clock on his night table he squinted at the LED readout. "It's six in the morning."

"That means I'm late." She slipped on her jeans over her naked butt. Her red bra was hanging off the door knob near the chair and she put it on.

Watching her dress was almost as sexy as watching her strip. And he spent the last three nights witnessing that fine display. And every morning he had to see her throw her clothes on and sneak out of his room like they were having some hole in the wall affair. The thought began to grate on him.

Troy wanted to lie in the bed with her until noon, he wanted to announce his ownership of her, to tell the world she was his, but she had a strange notion about her kids not knowing they were bumping uglies. He knew she wasn't ashamed of him, but damn this could hurt a brother's ego.

Then she stuck her hand in her pocket and pulled out a hair band

and secured her long locks in a pony tail.

Scratching his head, he couldn't remember when the last time was he wanted a woman to stay. Usually he was the one pushing her out of his bed. That made him uncomfortable. "You don't have to go."

Taking her black t-shirt off the chair arm, she slipped it on. "Why is it that I think you mean Las Vegas and not just your bed?"

He wasn't going to be coy. He wanted her stay with him longer. "Because that's what I mean."

Turning and facing him she sighed. "I have a home to get back to. A life."

The tension knotted in his stomach. "What's wrong with staying a few more days?"

A shoe lay next to the night table and she bent over and grabbed it. "Because in a few more days, I'll want a few more days and then more days after that."

"So?" Troy was willing to negotiate for more time with her.

She bit her bottom lip. "If I didn't have the children maybe, but our life is in Rio."

Crossing his arms over his chest he felt himself getting angry. "And it's a crappy life."

Marisol scowled at him. "We have each other."

That was the wrong thing to say and he did something he rarely did, but he thought she was worth the effort. He backtracked ... at least a bit. "Maybe I want to be part of that life."

"You're a wolf." Marisol put her hands on her hips. "I'm a cat. We can't be part of your pack and you can't be a part of mine."

What the hell was she talking about? "Like all your kids are jaguars."

She rolled her eyes. "It's different."

He knew it was, but he was just being a hard ass, because he wasn't getting his way. Damn he hated that. "Different? How?"

Marisol rubbed her forehead. "I knew what I was getting into. And I didn't ask anyone to accept my choices. You're asking your entire pack to accept us."

No one would question his choice. At least not anyone who was important to him. "So what?" After all, they'd accepted Ali when half of them were frightened to death of her.

"Maybe everyone in your pack isn't so open-minded?" She drummed her fingers on her hips. "I can't risk my children's safety on a maybe. They are the most important thing to me. And they have been through too much already. I can't risk uprooting their lives no matter what I might want."

So she did want to stay at least that's what the subtext sounded like. "My alpha's mate is in love with your kids. Trust me, no one going to get on the hellhound's bad side."

"Do you want to mate with me?" Marisol tapped her chest. "A cat?"

That stopped him short. Put into words, he hesitated. He hadn't really thought about the long haul until this moment. "What's wrong with what we have now?"

"It's fine for us at the moment, but I have to think about the future. I have people who depend on me."

Troy held up both his hands. "Relax and take it easy. We can work this out."

"I don't think so." She grabbed her purse and walked out of the room without another word.

He'd handled that well.

Troy got out of the bed and gathered up his clothes. In the bathroom he tossed his things in the hamper and turned on the shower setting it to cold. He yowled as the cold water pelted his skin.

Yeah he wanted her. He didn't know why but the cat had gotten under his skin. And in that second he figured it out, he wanted to mate her, he just didn't know how to tell her. Hell, he loved her baggage and didn't care if they weren't wolves. Damn it. He knew he had to let her go so she could get used to the idea her and her damn cat attitude. He'd give her couple of hours but she belonged to him and he wasn't giving her up.

Chapter Five

Marisol was frantic. She'd returned to their suite to find everyone in an uproar.

Bibianna was missing. Sarita told Marisol her sister had snuck out a few hours ago to be with some Were hyenas she'd met at the pool earlier. If only she hadn't been with Troy she would have stopped her daughter from sneaking out of the hotel suite. She should have known, Bibianna had been testing Marisol's limits for the last few months. But she'd been so wrapped up in Carlos, Pablo and Juan she had ignored her daughter's small steps toward independence. Normally, a quite tractable child, she thought Bibianna would never overtly disobey her. Well she'd been wrong.

Marisol stood in the middle of the casino, closing her ears to the massive noise of slot machines and yelling and clapping trying to isolate Bibianna's scent. Over the mixture of humans, Weres, vamps and demons, her nose was in overdrive. The smoke, food and cleaning products didn't make her job any easier. Clearing her mind, she began to eliminate all the smells but Were. Ocelots were the rarest of Were-kin and tended to be shy. They seldom created a pack, tending to be isolated and independent. Sarita and Bibianna were more than likely the only ones of their kind in the hotel.

"Stay calm," she whispered to herself.

She closed her eyes and stood still and began to eliminate every strange smell, every half familiar smell, the loud noises, the tiny noises, the jingle of coins in the slots.

A familiar scent drifted past her.

"Marisol," Carlos said.

Carlos stood in front of her with a small broom and dust pan. "Carlos, have you seen Bibianna?"

He shrugged his shoulders. "No."

She wanted to grab him and shake him. "She was with some young hyenas."

Carlos hitched a thumb over his shoulder. "The only ones I ran into were near the bar."

"Thank you." Maybe they'd know where to find their kind.

He stopped her by grabbing her arm. "Do you want me come with you?"

Now that surprised her. Her eyes widened. "You would help?"

He suddenly looked shy and tentative. "I've been doing a lot of thinking and…"

She heard a cat scream. Bibianna. She heard the panic in the tone. "Get Troy!" She took off running toward the scream.

She zigzagged through the crowds of people until she found a closed door leading to a small bar off to the side of one of the cafés. She rattled the knob and noticed the signed said closed for renovations. Bibianna's scent was strong and laced with fear. She could smell the musk of the hyenas.

Marisol threw her shoulder into the door. The wood splintered. She did it again and cracked pieces of wood went flying. A sharp pain stabbed through her arm, but she didn't stop, as she yanked a large piece of wood stuck out of her arm. Blood welled and dripped down her hand. She followed her nose and raced around the large wooden bar.

Two young hyenas stepped into her path. One was tall with long dark hair and the other was short with dirty red hair. She began to rip off her shirt so she could shift, but her body refused to cooperate.

The smaller one took a step forward. "I smell fresh pussy…cat."

The tall one laughed. "Now we don't have to wait our turn with the other one." He smiled showing his canines.

Marisol grabbed the small one and yanked him toward her head butting him. Her head rang, but her rage kept her focused. She pushed him toward the bar and heard bone shatter as he crashed into the marble counter top. She landed a hard kick into the solar plexus

190

of the other one and watched him fall to his knees. As she elbowed him in the back of neck, she saw three blurs hurry passed her--Carlos, Pablo and Juan. A loud howl rent the air.

She hurried behind them and into the large store room, to find the boys fighting another six hyenas. Bibianna was on top of one them beating his head into the concrete floor, her blouse was torn, but she seemed untouched.

Marisol grabbed one of the hyenas that had leaped on Juan's back and threw him against a wall. Although outnumbered by size and strength her children were winning the battle. As she fought the hyena she felt a sharp stab just under her ribs.

She let go of the hyena and sank to her knees. Carlos leaped over her. She looked down and found a silver dagger protruding from her side. She tried to grab the hilt but it burned her palm. She could feel the leech of silver poisoning coursing through her body. She was going to die. Pablo caught her before she hit the ground. She tried to breathe as her eyes shifted to his panicked face. Lifting her hand she touched his cheek. "Everybody?"

"Fine."

"Thank you."

Carlos brushed her hair off her face. He looked so young and vulnerable. He would be a fine man some day. "Don't talk, mamacita." Panic made his voice tremble.

"Take care of the babies." She looked up and saw Troy. "Sorry."

Troy took her from Pablo. "We have to get her outside so she can shift."

As she tried to keep breathing she felt her body moving fast. So this was death. She sensed rather than felt her body shutting down. She had only a few more minutes to live. Dear God let my children be taken care of. "Troy."

"It's okay, baby, I have you. You need to shift."

She licked dry lips. "Can't."

"We're outside you can do it here."

"Can't." Marisol commanded her body to change, but it refused to cooperate with her.

"Do it for your kids."

Marisol tried to force her body to shift, but her cat was weak. "Can't."

"I'm not losing you."

Her eyes fluttered and her gaze was blurry. "What?"

Troy's bottom lip quivered. "I love you."

Did she hear him right? Had he just said he loved her. "Help me."

Before he answered, Troy bent over and took her lips. Somewhere in his kiss her cat roared to life. And her body began to shift. Her bones broke and reformed. And her skin shimmer as the black fur covered her body. Flexing her hand, her claws formed and the beast sprang to the surface begging to be freed. Her canines broke through the roof of her mouth and she heard a fierce roar and knew it was her beast finally relishing being released. She took a deep breath and passed out.

Troy watched Marisol sleep. Her chest rose and fell slowly, but steadily. Her skin was an unhealthy gray. She looked so tiny in his big bed. He wanted to crawl under the blankets and hold her and force her to live, but the all the kids sat on the bed or on the floor next to the bed refusing to leave her. They touched her, patted her hand, Dulce crooned a faint song that seemed to have no words and no melody. Juan lay curled up next to her sobbing. Troy gently patted the boy. He knew how it felt to lose something so incredibly precious. And he didn't want it to happen to him again.

Marisol hadn't been able to hold her cat for long. He hoped it was long enough to reverse the silver poison. He looked up and saw Carlos wiping away a tear. So he'd gotten it through his thick skull Marisol cared for him and his brothers.

"I thought I could handle it myself," Carlos said.

Troy put his hand on the boy's shoulder. This was not the time to give him attitude. "You took care of your pack. I'm proud of you."

"There was no time to get you." The kid looked guilty as if he'd done something wrong.

"If you three hadn't gone right away, she would be dead and so would Bibianna." He squeezed his shoulder.

Carlos lowered his head, his long dreads covering most of his face. "We failed. If we had been more--"

Bibianna choked on a sob. "It's all my fault."

Troy let go of Carlos and walked over to the girl. "Learn your lesson. Don't let it happen again." It's not as though Troy and his pack brothers hadn't done some stupid life threatening things in their day. He'd had this same conversation with Julius and Esther more times than he cared to count, but never before had a life been at stake.

Emilio stroked Marisol's cheek, tears tracking down his face. "Is she going to die?"

Troy heard the terror in the young boy's voice. "Not if I can help it." He sounded fierce and relentless.

Troy didn't like the fact that all of the children were all in the room, but Esther said that it would help Marisol heal if she knew her pack was around her. Looking in the corner Ali and Esther had their heads together. He didn't have to hear what they were saying but his new alpha's mate had just issued her first dictate. If Marisol didn't make it the children were going to be taken in by the Temple pack.

He was cool with that.

Malcolm wasn't here but he assumed Ali would let him know how things were going down. At the moment Malcolm was having a meeting with the local hyena alpha. And from what he saw in Ali's eye, blood would be spilled to pay the debt and Troy was going to make sure he got first kill on what was left of the fucking bastards who had hurt his woman.

Esther came to the bed. She touched Marisol cheek and checked her pulse. "No fever. I think we can safely let her rest." She started getting the children on their feet and easing them off the bed. "Come on, children. I promise later on we'll all come to visit again."

Each of the children kissed her cheek or her hand. Even Carlos, Pablo and Juan--the little bastards finally figured out what being in a pack meant.

Victor slipped his hand in Troy's and looked up with a pleading look in his eyes. "Please tell her not to die."

Troy tightened his grip around the boy's little hand. "I promise Yogi."

Victor smiled and eased his hand out of Troy's. He let Dulce lead him out of the room.

The door closed with a click. He heard the vibrating of a cell phone. It's was Ali's and he listened while she talked. The conversation was short. She disconnected and look at Troy. "When you are ready, we hunt hyena."

Amazingly enough he found he really liked her. She was fun and she turned out to be more wolf than he'd thought. "Hail the new queen."

She snickered and walked out of the room leaving him alone with Marisol.

Troy slipped out of his shoes and carefully lay down on the bed next to Marisol. He slid his arms around her and held on tight, refusing to give up the fight. For all he knew this was his last moments with her and he wouldn't waste them. He swallowed the lump in his throat. "I love you, Marisol."

Her body felt so right in his arms. He nuzzled her ear. He never thought he would fall in love again...ever. Not after Talia and the way she'd used him. Now that he had the woman he needed and wanted, she was a few breaths away from death. "Damn you woman, if you can't live for me, live for your kids." He could hear the pleading in his voice.

Still nothing.

"Do you want a hellhound raising them? Shit they'll spend all day chasing their tails, rolling in the grass, and catching frisbees. 'Cause I don't think Ali's growing up anytime soon. And those are her favorite things to do in her down time."

He buried his nose in Marisol's hair, loving the scent of jungle flowers and musk. No matter what, he would always remember her smell.

He wanted to cry. He wanted to scream. He wanted to tear the room apart. He wanted blood.

"I like catching frisbees," Marisol said in a faint, trembling voice. Her eyes opened briefly and then closed again.

Troy raised his head. "You're awake?"

"Hard not to be with all the noise." She sounded faint and breathless. Her color had improved and when she opened her chocolate brown eyes again, he could see they were clear.

"Were you awake the entire time?"

Her smile was shaky, but genuine. "No, but I did hear you say you loved me. And you're not getting out of that."

"Caught," he said with such relief, he rained a shower of kisses on her face. "Do you think now that you're going to be okay I'm going to back out?"

She opened her mouth.

"Hell no," he said with ferocity his entire body quaked, "you're mine. I don't care if you want to find yourself some Were armadillo kids and take them in, I'm keeping you and them. We're going to be one crazy mixed up Were family. You understand me."

Marisol took a deep breath and whimpered slightly. "I'm a cat. I don't like to be told what to do."

Troy kissed her again. He couldn't stop kissing her. "Woman, tell me you don't love me."

She remained silent, but her eyes narrowed into slits, her lips pressed together tightly as though the words would never be said.

"You love me." He smiled knowingly at her. "Your kids love me. Even your knuckle head wolf boys love me."

Her eyes widened as if she remembered why she was in bed. "Is everyone all right?"

Troy remembered the scene as he'd found it. The boys standing over their prey, body parts pretty much everywhere. "They took care of business," he said feeling pride in the boys. "There were only two hyenas left by the time I got there. And when I'm ready there won't be any."

"You're going to hunt them down?"

He shook his head. "No, their alpha gave them up. Given the fact that the Temple pack has allies the hyenas don't ever want to meet, it was easier to give up a couple of rogues then to fight a war they would lose." And war no one wanted to fight. The eyes of the whole world watched the Temple clan and the transfer of power waiting to see if they lived up to their savagery or could make the transition peacefully.

Her fingers curled into a fist. "They are mine. No one harms my children."

Troy lifted an eyebrow and corrected her. "You mean our children."

Her chin went up. "I don't believe I've agreed to anything yet."

He loved when she went all stubborn on him. He kissed her—a long lingering passionate kiss with the promise of more to come. He put all his love into winning her heart. "Tell me you don't love me." His voice held a challenge.

"I love you, but—"

"No buts." Troy held up a finger. "There is nothing we can't work out. And if we can't work it out here, we can work it out in Rio. I've always loved the tropics. I don't care where I am as long as you and the kids are with me."

Marisol smiled and she put her hand on his cheek. "I don't want to go back to Brazil, I want to stay here and so do the children. They like having a big family—especially you and Ali."

His heart raced. This was more than he'd ever hoped for, ever dreamed of having. "Damn, I'm gonna be daddy."

"I'm going to be a wife."

He didn't think better words could be spoken. He looked into her dark eyes and saw love shining there. "A mate. That's a hell of lot better." A mate lasted from now until the final breath.

She touched his face. "I love you."

Troy smiled. He'd found his next great adventure and this one would last him a lifetime. He couldn't ask for anymore than that.

Epilogue

Later that night as Troy made his way down the hall to the children's room. He wanted to share with them that Marisol was going to be all right. As he passed Iva's room, he stopped wanting to share his news, wanting his little sister to come home. He needed her to come home.

He laid his hand against the door. He knew she had some shit to work out. But as his hand slid down the door and he turned to leave, the song I'm A Bitch started playing. That was Iva's ringtone. Was she back? He knocked. No answer.

"Iva," he called. Still no answer. He pounded on the door. An odd dread slid through him. Something wasn't right.

He fumbled in his pocket for the master key card that opened all the doors. Everyone in the Temple family had one.

Panic raced through him. He slid the master through the digital reader and opened the door.

Inside, Iva's suite usually neat and tidy was a mess. The phone was still ringing and he followed the sound to her bathroom where the phone lay on the counter attached to its charger. The call finally went to voice mail and flipping open her phone he saw that the message box was full. She left her cell phone behind! Iva couldn't take a breath without her phone.

He walked out into the living room and looked around at the mess. Now that his panic had receded slightly he sniffed to sort out the scents in the room. Iva, Malcolm, Esther and two strange scents.

Something had happened here. Something that told Troy, Iva hadn't taken a leave of absence to sort out her thoughts.

He reached for the phone on the table next to the sofa and dialed Esther's phone number. When she answered, Troy said, "Iva's gone and I don't think she went willingly. I think she's been kidnapped."

The End

Watch for Iva's story in From Vegas With Love by J.M. Jeffries coming out in late 2009 from Parker Publishing.

Books By J. M. Jeffries
A Dangerous Love
A Dangerous Deception
A Dangerous Woman
A Dangerous Obsession
Code Name: Diva
Blood Lust
Blood Seduction
Virgin Seductress
Creepin'
Suite Seduction
Suite Nothings (coming in December 2008)
Suite Persuasion (2009)
Lotus Blossom Chronicles 2 (November 2008)
Vegas Bites
Vegas Bites Back
Vegas Bites: Three of a Kind
Soldier Boys